SKIN DIVERS

ESMEE OTTER

COVER HAND-PAINTED BY

MAARTEN VET (VETART)

Content warnings: This book contains frequent use of strong language, violence, references to drugs and alcohol abuse, depression, and murder (graphic).

SKIN DIVERS

ISBN: 9789083484174

I want to thank Maarten Vet, my dear friend and an incredibly talented artist,

for creating the cover design. I envisioned something unconventional, bringing the concept of a 'skin diver' to life.

You have turned that vision into something truly remarkable.

Chapter 1

Our mom killed a 4-year-old girl. It was an accident. That's what everybody says at least. But they didn't see what I saw. A skin diver, that's what I call it. A little dog, with eyes like a bee, creeping towards the neighbor's daughter as she played with her ball by the street. It took her, fast. But all everybody saw, was the back bumper of our Ford Escort colliding with her limp body.

It was a beautiful summer morning in The Keystones State, like any other, pretty much. The sun was shining bright and the street was quiet. That was normal, back in 1992. There were some sprinklers spraying, casting moisture into the air. Ruth, an elderly lady, hummed as she strolled the sidewalk. David, our neighbor across the street, mowed his lawn.

And then there was Ashley, wearing a little blue dress with white flowers, playing with her yellow ball. She was *always* playing with her ball. I knew. My mom knew. Everybody knew. And everybody was mindful of that. Always.

I'd often watched my mom drive off, back in the day. I don't really know why, maybe it was my love for cars. So, on that faithful day, I stood in the driveway and watched my mom leave.

She walked up to the car and waved me goodbye. She said she'd be back within the hour—the supermarket wasn't far, only a fifteen-minute drive or so—and got into the blue Ford Escort, which I had thoroughly washed the day before. My younger brother, Andrew, was already sitting in the back seat.

My mom slowly backed out of the driveway, thoroughly checking her mirrors. She saw Ashley, who was now near the curb. I know she did, because she always smiled when she looked at her. She had always wanted a daughter, you see, but her total hysterectomy had destroyed that wish of hers and left her with just us three boys. My older brother, Michael, who was 16 at the time. Andrew, who was only 6. And my 10-year-old self.

Like usual, I paid attention to my mom's heartbreaking smile and I paid attention to Ashley, the reason for that smile. I also noticed a dog—a small Jack Russell—that was creeping closer and closer to her. I remember finding it strange because Ashley was really afraid of dogs and she'd would surely scream if she saw it. I don't think she ever did. I don't know if anybody did.

I mean, they screamed. That, they did for sure. But did anybody see the dog as it sped toward her, with its eyes morphing to those of a giant bee? Did anybody see it leap into her, diving into her skin, like it was his to take? And did they see how Ashley's body went limp, yet propelled onto the street, as if she got hurled like the ball she'd been playing with?

David didn't see it happen because the car was blocking his view. Old lady Ruth had very bad eyesight, so, even though she was close, she only saw what had happened after the fact. And my mom swore—to me, to my father, to Ashley's parents, and to the police—Ashley was still playing with her ball on the sidewalk when she backed out of the driveway. Ashley had just bounced the ball on the ground, when the car accelerated backward to make the usual turn.

There was a loud thump, as if someone pounded on a street light with a sledgehammer. My mom slammed the breaks, her eyes wide, her face pale and horrified.

Ruth looked at the back of the car and screamed.

David shoved the lawnmower away, sprinting toward the car. He got around and screamed in terror—I can still hear his scream bouncing off my bedroom walls on some sleepless nights.

My mom got out of the car and slowly walked around, still with that horrified expression plastered on her face. Her hand touched the roof of the car, as if she was about to fall over and needed the support.

Susan ran out of the house across the street, past the lawn-mower—still with its engine running—and ran toward Ashley. She collapsed to her knees and started screaming at the top of her lungs.

Both David and Susan slumped over their daughter's lifeless body.

My father came running out of the house, with Michael on his heels, and quickly assessed the situation. He grabbed Andrew from the car and brought him inside as Susan started wailing on my mom, shrieking and crying.

My mom kept on apologizing, with tears running down her cheeks, and let herself get hit over and over and over again.

David finally grabbed Susan and pulled her away from my mom, trying to calm her down.

My father didn't come back outside. It was only when the police arrived, whom he had called right away, when he came out of the house. I'm not sure whether he was trying to keep my brothers inside, away from the horror in front of me, or he just didn't want to face the music. Their marriage had been strained for a long time and this incident would prove to be the last straw, as my father often called it.

The first person to check on me—the 10-year-old boy staring at Ashley's corpse with urine-soaked pants—was a police officer by the name of William. He took me by the hand and led me away from the scene as he calmly asked me questions. What was my name? How old was I? Had I seen what happened? And what exactly did I see?

I told him precisely what I had witnessed, including the dog diving into Ashley's skin, right before she smacked onto the bumper of our car. William had looked at me with a puzzled look on his face, scratching his ear.

I was 10, but I didn't understand that I'd just uttered the words of a crazy person—at least in the eyes of others.

My father, who walked over to us mid-conversation, looked at me with anger and disgust. He grabbed me by my arm, hard. "Shut the fuck up with your nonsense, James. This ain't a playground. Now go back inside!"

William sussed him and told me it was going to be okay. I had had a traumatic experience and it was quite common to react *in this way*—and by that he meant *making up stories*.

I felt angry and betrayed because I wasn't lying and I definitely knew what I had seen. But I had to go inside if I wanted to avoid my father's torment, or at least avoid worsening it.

As I walked up to the front door, I glanced over to the car and saw the Jack Russell. It was just sitting there, by the back of the Escort and within reach of Ashley. I wanted to run up to William and point it out, but I was afraid. Afraid of the look my father had given me. I knew I was in trouble and I didn't want to make it any worse.

So, I got inside the house and sat down on the couch, next to Andrew. I watched him play with his firetruck, but my attention kept being pulled toward the window. I looked out and saw the policemen talking, mainly to my father. I found that strange because he never even saw what had happened—he had been in the shed, like usual, and only rushed outside upon hearing Susan's screams.

The incident was soon officially ruled an accident. The police confirmed that the car couldn't have driven so fast as to kill the girl—clearing my mom of murder—but the girl was dead nonetheless.

My statement was ignored, just as much as David and Susan were ignored. The police barely even looked at them. Looking back now, it was a cruel display of racism.

Only two weeks after the incident, my father left my mom. That's when she started drinking. It wasn't too bad at first, but it quickly would be. Michael was still in high school at the time and he did his best to take care of Andrew and me, but he really resented her for it. He had always liked our father better and now that he was gone, the cracks in his relationship with our mom would start to show.

Andrew seemed alright, even though he had been in the car when it struck and killed Ashley.

And me? Well, I'm ashamed to admit it… but I started wetting the bed. I had been potty trained by the age of 2, but I was soaking the mattress every single night.

I also had nightmares. Really bad ones. I had nightmares about the Jack Russell attacking me or one of my brothers. I had nightmares about seeing the dog morph into strange creatures and watching it jump into people's bodies. I had nightmares about the day it happened and I was forced to watch Ashley die over and over and over again. I also had nightmares in which Ashley rang our doorbell in the middle of the night. I would open the door, as I was home alone, and she would stare at me for a long time, not saying a word. Her eyes would widen, darken, and

continue to grow as they took on the shape of a bee's eyes. She would
start to make strange sounds, as if leafs were rustling in her throat. And
then she would jump at me and tear into my stomach—deeper and
deeper, soaking our welcome mat with my blood. I could feel her taking
over my body and me falling into a pitch-black darkness, as I watched my
body move beyond my own volition.

Those nightmares were the worst and I'd usually wake up screaming. It
woke up the entire house. It always did.

Michael tried to comfort me as best as he could. My mom just sort of
yelled at me and Andrew started crying. Michael was everything to me
during that time. He would help me clean my sheets and he took me to
the mall for… I'm just going to say it: diapers.

I felt really ashamed to be wearing diapers at night, but it did save us the
work of having to change the sheets and working the washing machine
every single night. And there was already so much on our plates,
especially on Michael's.

At the time, my mom didn't have a job, as we lived comfortably on just
my father's wages. And after he left, he paid her a reasonable amount of
alimony. It was probably his way of taking care of us, without having to
visit us. We did go over to his new house every other Sunday, but I don't
know if that was just a legal arrangement—I was too young to really
understand what was going on at the time and I guess I never asked
Michael about it after.

Michael would always be the one driving us to our father. It was a good
thing that he got his driver's license before the incident because it would
prove especially useful in the years to come.

My mom did the best she could, under the circumstances. She would
start the day with a glass of wine, clean the house and do the cooking.
But she wouldn't set a foot outside.

My brother had to buy the groceries on his way back from school. He
took the car, since my mom would never drive that thing again, and
made sure that the bills were paid on time, like the mortgage and the
electric bill.

I walked Andrew to school every morning because we went to the same
school and tried to help out as much as I could. I'm not sure whether I

did enough because I also wanted to play with my friends and I was away from home a lot—I'd get on my bike, scour the neighborhood, and sometimes actively look for that damn Jack Russell.
We were getting by.

As the years passed, our situation got bleaker.
Mom just lay on the couch or on a sofa in the backyard, drinking. She switched out the wine for brandy and she switched to vodka later on. The only money we had coming in was the alimony my father paid. She still didn't work and she still couldn't set a foot outside.
Michael did his best to keep the money away from mom, since she had blown it on booze several times—and I mean *all* of it. He kept doing the groceries and cooked the meals we ate, even after his long days at school. I also did my part. I cleaned the toilet and the bathroom on a weekly basis, washed the car Michael drove in, cleaned out the empty bottles. I even cleaned the couch when Mom shat herself. It took me nearly three hours to get the stench out.
Andrew got more and more quiet, but it wasn't too concerning at the time. Looking back, that's when someone should've done something to help him. Put him in therapy or something. In these days, he likely would've gotten the proper help, but back then… I don't know, it just wasn't a *thing*. Therapy was for lunatics. Andrew wasn't a lunatic, as my father once said sternly. He was just… odd.

In 2002, my father remarried. He was 54 at the time and his new wife had just turned 34. He knocked her up within a month and she birthed twins. Two girls: Nancy and Pam.
That's when things took a turn for the worse.
Michael had left for uni, two years prior, to get a lawyer's degree at Boston University School of Law and that meant everything was up to me.
I was now the man of the house, at the age of 20. Paying bills, cleaning, doing the groceries, cooking and taking care of Andrew, who had seriously hit puberty and was hanging out with strange kids. I also worked on the weekends at a local car shop, since my father's alimony

just didn't seem to cut it anymore—I later found out that Mom had been stealing money from my wallet; I guess I wasn't as bright as Michael, in that regard.

I was so overwhelmed at the time that I had to drop out of school in my final year. I never got my degree. But it did give me more free time, which meant I was able to work more. More work meant more money. And man, did I need that money.

I scraped together the money for my driver's license and now I was the one driving the blue Ford Escort. That wouldn't be for long, however, as the model was being discontinued and garages wouldn't take that rusty old shit anymore. They didn't have the parts to repair it and even the shop where I worked wouldn't take a look at the damn thing. So when the rust bucket finally broke down, I had to buy a new car with my own money. My father wasn't going to help me out. He made that very clear and I really resented him for that. He had no idea how difficult it had been for us—especially for me.

By then, we would only see him twice a year. On Andrew's birthday and on my birthday, that's when he took us out for lunch. I don't know about Michael, though, because I saw him on a Christmas card with my dad's new family a few years later.

Michael and I didn't talk much anymore after he got into uni. He was really busy and so was I. I think I was also angry at him for leaving, because he was the only one I had.

Mom had become completely apathetic toward absolutely everything since the birth of our half-sisters. I honestly liked it better when she still yelled at me for pissing the bed. And yeah, in case you were wondering, I still pissed the bed at times. I didn't wear diapers anymore, obviously, but I did have a special sheet on my mattress to absorb the fluid. Try explaining that to a girl when you take her home for some much-needed affection.

The one relationship that I had didn't last long and I spiraled into a depression. I started taking pills, which was a huge mistake. Not so much for what they did to me, but the fact that Andrew got his hands on them. I still feel guilty about that.

Andrew got really messed up. I later found out that Mom made him
wear dresses and even makeup when I wasn't at home. There was
nobody to stick up for him. Nobody to protect him from our spiraling
mother. He ran away from home when he was 16 and I didn't see him
again until four years later.

Maybe I would've foreseen it if I hadn't been so obsessed by the skin
divers. I had never seen another one since the Ashley incident, but I was
still frantically looking for them anywhere I went. Every Jack Russell
sparked my attention, more than Andrew's nightly crying did, before he
ran away from home.

I didn't find the dog, nor any other skin diver.

In 2006, I lost my virginity at the age of 24 to Daisha, a beautiful woman
with braided hair, fair skin and a quirky personality, in the back of my
Honda Civic. She was a few years older than me, much to my delight. I
loved her, but I never took her back home. I was afraid of introducing
her to my mom, who had become a raging alcoholic over the years, and I
couldn't let her see the house. There was a lot of trash lying around and
I had trouble keeping the place clean. My mom didn't lift a finger
anymore, so it all came down to me. And I made damn sure to stay out
as much as possible. I would drive around town, take Daisha to the
movies or out for food and I even started playing the guitar. In that way,
2006 was like a turning point for me.

About two months after that sweet encounter in the back seat—with
many more to follow—I suddenly ran into Andrew. It was a mere
coincidence. I was walking around town during my lunch break and he
was on my mind. I hadn't talked to him in the years prior and I knew his
20th birthday was coming up, so I just wondered how he was doing.

I crossed the street in the searing sun and walked along the pavement, on
my way to the deli. Sweat trickled down my back and made my shirt stick
to my body. I passed the alley next to it and was about to head inside
when I stopped in my tracks. I did a double-take and confirmed that it
was indeed my little brother, sitting on the ground with his back resting
against the wall of the deli. His clothes looked ragged and dirty, his hair

was long and shabby and his face looked like it hadn't seen a washcloth in ages.

He didn't see me at first, but when I approached him, he looked up with a blank stare. Truth be told, even as he looked directly at me, it's as if he still didn't really see me. His arms were marked with puncture wounds and it turned my stomach inside out to see him like that. I helped him up and offered to take him home. The first thing he asked was whether Mom was still there. When I said she was, he immediately refused. I told him he could at least take a shower and that he didn't have to see her, but he kept declining and got increasingly agitated. So, I bought him a sandwich and we sat on a bench in the nearby park, in the shade of a large tree.

He told me little bits and pieces of what had happened to him in the last four years. He was nearly taken by the police—who wanted to bring him home, since he was only 16—and he knew he had to run away even farther. He stole a car, even though he didn't know how to drive, and he planned to drive as far as the gas tank would take him. He didn't make it far; he crashed the car into a lamp post before the tank ran out.

At some point, he was taken in by an elderly lady, and he was doing quite alright. He had thought of calling me a few times, but he never did. He was afraid I'd make him come back home. The lady had a heart-attack about a year later, when her pacemaker gave out, and he had to hit the street once more. He had to steer clear of the cops, since he was still a minor, and that's how he ended up at some shelter for runaway kids. The shelter was run by two men who made the boys earn their place. It started with selling pot. The more he sold, the better they treated him. He then moved on to selling pills—the same kind that I had taken—and even some stronger drugs. But he couldn't keep his hands out of the honey jar and the dudes kicked him out—literally. He broke two ribs, and his stomach, back and arms were black and blue for five weeks.

He crashed on the couch of a guy he met, who was in his 50s, and he seemed to be doing better again, even though he was still addicted to pills. The guy—he wouldn't tell me his name—helped him get the pills, but he also had to do things in return. He didn't specify the favors, but I could tell it wasn't right. Not at all. After a fallout with the guy, on a specific night, he ran away once again.

He was 18 by then and, in theory, he didn't need to avoid the cops anymore. But, he didn't have a place to stay, he didn't have any friends, and he didn't have a job. It was just him and his pill addiction. So, he started stealing other people's hard-earned money, attracted the wrong kind of people and fell down the deep end. That's when he got hooked on heroin.

I still didn't understand what made it so hard for him to come home, especially after suffering through all that. I asked him point-blank and that's when he finally told me about the dresses and the makeup. How my mom locked him up in the shed if he didn't do as she said. The way she kept calling him Andrea.

Suddenly, it clicked in my head. I always figured that she slurred her words because of the booze and just mispronounced his name because of that. I never once thought there was something else going on.

I didn't offer to take him home after hearing his story, obviously, but I did want to help him somehow. I took him to the car shop where I worked and started apologizing to my boss, Robert, for taking a two-hour lunch break. He didn't mind. He gave Andrew a place to sleep for the night and offered to help him get back on track.

As I pictured Andrew sleeping soundly on Robert's sofa, I withdrew a third of my savings from the bank. After, I stuffed it in an envelope and handed it to Andrew the next morning. I wanted to help him get his shit together. Rent a room, buy some proper clothing, eat a decent meal. But I guess I should've expected him to run away once again—triggered by the trauma inflicted upon him by the unnamed man.

Maybe I would've foreseen that he'd pump all my money into his veins if I hadn't been so damn preoccupied with myself. I was so up in my own business that I had even forgotten about the skin divers for a while. I was just thinking about earning enough money to buy my own place and getting laid. I was 24, after all.

Later that year, when the fall season turned cold and particularly dark, I got a call from my older brother, Michael. He told me he had gotten his law degree and that he had met a woman, Stacy, who he planned to marry. He figured I should know about that, since the day might come when I had to show up as his best man. I chuckled out loud when I heard that, since we had barely spoken since he left home six years ago. I still loved him to death and he meant the world to me, but I wasn't sure whether he even liked me anymore, so I was pretty surprised by his request.

When he actually did get married, in 2010, his best friend got the role of best man and I wasn't even invited, but that's beside the point.

After I hung up the phone, not knowing if he'd ever call me again or if he'd even pick up when I tried calling, I needed some air. I was happy for Michael that he'd gotten his degree and was about to propose to his lady, but it also hurt me in a childish way. I was never able to get my degree, since I was the one stuck with the care for mom. And the whole white picket fence idea seemed like a distant dream to me.

I got into my Honda Civic and started driving—without a particular destination in mind. I just needed to be away for a while. I didn't even call Daisha because I wanted to sort out my thoughts and I needed to be alone for that.

I turned onto the highway and put the pedal to the metal. I let the cold wind rush through my car's open windows and drove until my arms froze. By then, I had gotten off the highway, stopped for gas once and was now driving along some dirt road in the middle of nowhere, seemingly. I had no idea where I was. There were no streetlights and the car's headlights were the only source of light to brighten the pitch-black darkness.

After driving for another ten minutes, I eventually saw some houses in the distance. I kept on driving with moderate speed until I reached them. I slowed down and looked at the lit up windows and the people behind them. My eyes lingered on one particular window, of a small house with a large yard. There was a dining table right in front of the window and two people sat on opposite sides of it. One elderly gentleman, he might've been 65 or so, and a woman, who looked like she was in her early 70s. They stared at each other without moving.

I unconsciously slowed down further, until I came to a halt. It might have looked suspicious to anyone in passing—seeing a man in his 20s sitting in his car, staring at an unsuspecting elderly couple inside their home—but I didn't care at that moment. There was something about that scene. Something that called me and made me stop in my tracks. Then I saw it. I saw what had caught my eye subconsciously. It wasn't the old people staring at each other without muttering a word. It was the dog standing dead-still in the archway of the kitchen. Its eyes were as big and oval as those of—yeah, you guessed it—a bee. It wasn't a Jack Russell, though. No, it was a small Cocker Spaniel with black-and-white fur.

I gasped for breath and stared at the dog. It can't be, I thought. But it must be, I figured.

I turned off the engine and got out of the car, keeping my eyes locked onto the Cocker Spaniel. It hadn't moved yet, it just stared at the old people. Or maybe it was staring at me. I couldn't tell with eyes like that. I was about to open the door and get out of the car when the dog suddenly leaped at the man, just like the Jack Russell had done to Ashley. It dove into his back, burying itself in the old man's skin and disappearing completely. The man's body shook for a moment.

I hesitated. I didn't know what the thing was or what it could do. I didn't know if it would take me next and, honestly, I was fucking afraid. I was so afraid that I was about to shit myself. It had been fourteen long years since I first saw a skin diver and I had spent so much time looking for another one, but I had never thought of a plan. What would I do when I actually ran into one? What *could* I do?

Still sitting in the comfort of my car, I watched the old lady. Her mouth moved. Maybe she noticed her husband's body shaking and she was asking him what was wrong. Shit, I thought to myself. What if he lunges at her next? What if that skin diver kills them both? I can't sit idly and watch that happen. Not again.

Carefully, I opened my car door as silently as possible. I didn't want to attract the skin diver's attention. I got out of the car and stood in the cold dark night. How was I going to save the old lady without putting myself in danger? Could I save her if I *didn't* put myself in danger?

Maybe I could throw a rock through the window and lure the thing out.
Maybe I could then run it over with my car. But that would definitely kill
the old man as well—and then it would look like I ran over an old man
with my car, and I'd be the one needing to be cleared of murder.
I walked up to the door, still without a proper plan. I didn't have a gun
and I really wished I had one on me. Then again, if I'd shoot at it, it
would also kill the man. Perhaps the man would be dead either way, but
that tragedy shouldn't end with me sitting behind bars.
I was about to knock on the door when my hand tried the doorknob
instead. To my surprise, the door was unlocked and it swung open with a
light creaking. I shuddered. Please, don't let it hear me, I prayed.
I stepped into the hallway and looked at the door opposite me. I could
see the light from the kitchen creeping underneath. As quietly as
possible, I sneaked across the hallway and got to the door. I placed my
hand on the doorknob, took a deep breath, and opened the door. The
knob slipped from my grasp and the door swung open.
I stared dead into the lady's eyes and she shrieked. I put my hands in the
air and tried to shush her, apologizing while pressing my back to the wall
behind me—the old phone hanging from the wall poked at my shoulder
blade.
She jumped from her chair, despite her bad knees, and started yelling at
her husband to do something. She called me an intruder and shouted
something about a shotgun.
My heart dropped. This wasn't what I meant to happen! I looked over to
the man and saw him still sitting in his chair, like nothing was happening.
He didn't look up at his wife, nor did he turn toward me. He just sat
there, motionless.
In a normal situation I would've guessed that he was deaf, but I knew
what was lurking inside him. And I knew it was going to try and kill him,
one way or another. I didn't know how to get a skin diver out of
somebody's skin—this was only my second encounter, after all. All I
could think of was to try and save the old lady. But it was getting crystal
clear that she wouldn't leave here willingly. I was an intruder, after all,
and I was planning to drag her out of her home, away from her husband.

It was a bad situation, especially if you didn't know what was going on behind the surface.

The lady started crying and a foul stench rose from the pool of piss and shit beneath her feet.

"Please," I begged her. "Please, hear me out. I am not trying to hurt you! I am trying to warn you. Your husband… something has taken him. You have to come with me. Please. I'm trying to save you. Please, listen to me!"

I said *please* so many times and tried to make myself look as harmless as possible, but it was to no avail. The lady was having none of it. She was murmuring about calling the police, but she was sobbing so much that I could hardly understand her.

All the while, her husband sat there with a thousand-yard stare and did nothing, and that probably scared the lady even more.

I wasn't sure what to do next, but I couldn't take my eyes off the man. He could try to do something within a second. It was dangerous to stay here any longer, I felt that in my core. So I did the one thing that I could think of: I walked over to the lady, grabbed her by the wrist, and started dragging her out of the kitchen with an apologetic attitude. She screamed and started hitting me, but I ignored her and kept eyeing the old man.

We were almost out of the kitchen when it happened. The head of the Cocker Spaniel emerged from the husband's back, eyes first. The huge bee-like eyes locked onto me as it crawled out from the man. As soon as it left his body, the man slumped over the kitchen table. It hit me then— the man had already been dead when his body shook, back when I was still sitting safely in my car.

The skin diver sprang at us with terrifying speed. I fell backward and pulled the old lady with me, in an effort to shield her from the monstrous creature.

I failed miserably.

While the lady was still on top of me, smearing the shit sticking to her legs onto my pants, the skin on her back tore open and the Cocker Spaniel buried its head into her, eyes first. I grabbed the legs of the beast and tried to pull it out with all the strength I could muster. But that fucking thing was *in* there! It was stuck like a boot in a concrete block. The lady screamed as I kept on tugging at the legs, making her body shake like a rag-doll. She rolled face-down to the floor and the beast slipped from my fingers. It dove all the way in, emitting a cloud of black ash. Her body shook and I crawled backward, trying to get away from it. It became dead silent.

My heart was throbbing in my throat and I stared at the woman, still lying face-down. I knew I needed to get up and get the fuck away from there, if only my damn legs would move.

A loud fart cut through the silence, and I looked at the lady with a horrified expression on my face. She had completely emptied her bowels. The foul stench was so strong, I gagged. I slapped a hand over my mouth to stop the puke from splattering on the floor.

For a moment, I forgot the danger I was in and realized that I was now at an active crime scene. And if anyone were to investigate, it would likely lead back to me. My footprints were all over the place, as were my fingerprints. I was pretty sure I had shat myself too—I'd never longed for my good old diapers as much as I did then.

I went inside the house, drawn by the skin diver, in an effort to save the elderly couple—or at least one of them. Now both of them were dead and, to anyone but me, it looked like I was the one who killed them. What was I supposed to do in this fucked up situation!?

There was no time for me to think it over because the skin diver emerged once again. The snout of the Cocker Spaniel came out from the back of the lady, and those ugly, giant insect eyes followed, locking onto me like a predator on its prey.

I scrambled to my feet and bolted out the door, slamming it shut behind me, before the skin diver was fully emerged. I ran toward my car, jumped inside and revved the engine. I heard glass shattering as the Cocker Spaniel burst through the kitchen window. It tumbled over and fixated on my car. I put the peddle to the metal and sped away in terror, watching the skin diver disappear in my rearview mirror as it sprinted after me.

My lungs and throat burned, my heart stung, and my stomach churned.
My mind was so chaotic, it felt like a tornado was wreaking havoc in
there.

I kept driving until I was as sure as I could be that the skin diver wasn't
on my tail anymore. I stopped the car on the side of the road, nearly
driving it into a ditch and stumbled out. I puked on the grass and gasped
for air. My eyes trembled in their sockets and my body felt weak and
sluggish. I sat on my knees for what felt like forever, trying to get myself
together.

As my body eased up, my mind started spinning more and more. What in
God's name had I done!? What the hell happened in there!? I fucked up
with a capital F!

I heaved a heavy sigh and looked up at the sky. The cold air took some
of the nausea away, but my anxiety skyrocketed.

Should I go back and tamper with the scene? It can't look like I killed
them because that would destroy my life—it's also not what happened,
but nobody would believe me if I told them what did. I would be behind
bars for God knows how long. Everyone would think I murdered an
elderly couple in their home, and they would judge me and hate me for
it. Daisha, my boss Robert, Mom, Andrew, Michael, my father…

"What do I do?" I asked the sky, begging for an answer. "You saw what
happened. It wasn't me. You know it wasn't me. But everyone will think
it was! Tell me what to do, please… Be quiet anytime you like, but not
now. Please send me a signal of some sort. Show me a sign."

I sat there on my knees, begging and pleading until the break of dawn.
No answer came.

Chapter 2

I got home around 8 a.m. that morning, in my shit-stained pants, with dark circles under my eyes and large sweat stains under my arms. Luckily, I didn't have to walk far to the door, so there was little chance the neighbors would spot me. Plus, we were outcasts, so few paid attention to us anyway, as we continued living in that worn-down house.

That was probably our first mistake after the Ashley incident. If we had moved, maybe Mom would have gone outside. Maybe she wouldn't have fallen off the wagon. Maybe she never would've forced her trauma onto Andrew and it all wouldn't have ended up like this big, stinking mess. David and Susan moved within two weeks after burying their little daughter, and I've never seen them again. I really hope they made a clean start and were able to enjoy their lives, despite the gaping hole in their hearts.

As I got inside, took off my shoes, and entered the living room, I noticed Mom lying on the couch. Her eyes were closed and she was surely out for the count, seeing as there were two empty bottles of vodka on the coffee table. For a moment, I wished she had drank herself to death, so that I could make a clean start as well.

I hurried upstairs to the bathroom and stuffed my shoes in the washer. I took off my clothes and put those inside the washer too. I let the washer do its thing as I stepped inside the shower and turned the water on. The water was as cold as ice, and I shuddered. I clenched my jaw and stood there under the icy stream, filled with feelings of all kinds. Not a single pleasant one, I can tell you that. I noticed that I felt increasingly responsible for the deaths of those people.

It would have been better if I had just kept on driving, instead of trying to interfere. I should never have tried to save any of them. Maybe the skin diver would have left them alone if I hadn't gone inside.

I said all those things to myself, but deep in my heart, I knew I didn't believe those words. I acted on my nature and my intentions were good. It just backfired tremendously—and then some.

As the water warmed up, I sank to the floor and curled up into a fetal position. That's when the tears finally came and it would take a long time for them to stop.

The year that had seemed to be a turning point for me, in which I'd struggled less with my depression and had some things going for me, had taken another turn that night.

In the weeks that followed, I barely slept and I was constantly anxious. I tried to act as normally as I could, trying not to draw suspicion to myself, but my mental state didn't go unnoticed.

Robert, my boss, said I was spacing out a lot and that he was worried— he thought my mind was still on Andrew taking off with my money, ready for another bender.

Daisha was annoyed that I didn't spend much time with her anymore, and when I did, she thought I was too self-absorbed and absent-minded. She broke up with me.

Some colleagues also joked about how ragged I looked, as if I had seen a ghost and couldn't shake it off. If only they knew.

My mom didn't say a word about my strange behavior—which was no surprise, honestly. I'm not sure if she even knew left from right anymore, by that point. The only thing she'd notice was the content of her precious bottles.

For a while I pondered upon the different scenarios.

The cops bursting through the front door with a battering ram of some kind and roughing me up as they finally put their murderer in cuffs.

The cops waiting for me as I got to work and humiliating me in front of the entire town.

The elderly couple not being found until their remains had decayed. Who knows if they even had visitors still—although the mailman would likely come by and someone would definitely notice the broken window.

Me calling Michael, my lawyer brother, to defend me in court.

Me running away and joining Andrew in his gutter lifestyle.

I never did go to the police. There were never any news articles in the papers. Nor any sobbing relatives on the radio. No broadcasts on television. And no flyers hung on around town, begging for information

18

on the unexplained deaths of the elderly couple. I guess that was a relief
for me—not being confronted with their deaths, their faces, every single
day. But it affected me nonetheless. How couldn't it?

I fought to keep my depression at bay without much success, and my
search for the skin divers grew into a full-blown obsession. Every spare
hour, in which I wasn't working, sleeping or eating, I dedicated to my
hunt. I scoured the internet, which was a whole different place back in
2006, hit the streets, drove around, and even started prepping—not for
an oncoming doomsday, but for a probable fight. I decided that if I ever
ran into one of those shitty things again, I would be prepared.

I took some shooting lessons, got my license, bought a gun, got my
hands on a machete, and even trained at a martial arts school, about ten
minutes down the road from the car shop.

I made drawings of what the skin divers looked like, both the first time
around and the second time. The Jack Russell and the Cocker Spaniel
had two things in common: they both looked like dogs and they had
those monstrous bee-like eyes. I drew those eyes in detail and plastered
them on the walls of my bedroom. I even made an eerie painting of that
Jack Russell and it turned out pretty damn well.

I also wrote down every little detail I could think of. The way they
moved, their thousand-yard stares, the fact that their eyes could morph,
and the way they lunged at people and dug into them. I noted that I was
able to physically grab them and, therefore, should be able to harm them
as well.

Those were the only characteristics I had to go on. I didn't know the full
extent of their powers. Like the way they could creep into other people's
bodies, taking their dog-like body with it, and not leave a trace of
themselves. And the way they killed their… *host*.

As the word *host* crept into my mind, I was reminded of so many movies
I had watched with Michael. Invasion of the Body Snatchers. The
Faculty. Shivers. Invaders from Mars. The Hidden. I was probably way
too young to be watching those, as I saw most of them prior to the
Ashley incident, but I enjoyed them nonetheless. They scared the shit out
of me, sure, but I could table my fears, knowing they were just movies. It
wasn't real. Well… fuck me, right?

I tried analyzing the deaths of Ashley and the elderly couple. They were all approached by a skin diver in the form of a dog. I wasn't sure whether the Cocker Spaniel belonged to the couple or if it had sneaked inside. I also wasn't sure whether anyone really saw the dogs, I never got that confirmed.

When the Jack Russell took over Ashley, it flung her body toward the back bumper of our old Ford Escort at an incredible speed—a speed I was sure wasn't humanly possible, especially not for the likes of a 4-year-old girl.

In the case of the old man, his body just shook for a moment and he only slumped over when the skin diver left his body. And the lady… her body shook, and then she let out that incredible fart, along with everything else. Was it some sort of heart attack for the both of them? Did it kill them instantly? Or was it like a poison, spreading through their organs?

I had so many questions and so few answers. And on top of that, I felt like a fugitive.

Three weeks later, the medical examiner who performed the autopsy the day after their deaths officially ruled their deaths accidental. The news came in a small article in the newspaper—that was when I learned their names. It was stated that the old man, William Abbott, had had a heart attack, and his pacemaker sadly malfunctioned. The old lady, Dorothy Abbott, was probably beside herself, having her husband of 36 years dying at the table across from her. In her panic, she must have overlooked the telephone and, instead of dialing 911, she likely attempted to run over to a neighbor's house to ask for help. The shock must have been too much to handle for her weakened heart and she collapsed in the hallway. There didn't seem to be any indication of foul play.

I scratched my ear as I read the article. What about the broken window? And what about my prints? I couldn't recall the night vividly anymore, apart from when the skin diver took the old la—Dorothy, I mean—and I wasn't sure whether or not there had been a trail of shitty footprints, since Dorothy had squirmed all over me while covered in shit, staining my pants at the very least.

I sighed and folded the newspaper. I grabbed a pair of scissors from my desk, cut out the article and hung it on the wall next to my notes on the Cocker Spaniel skin diver.

I looked at the wall and sighed again. I felt sorry for William and Dorothy Abbott, but I was relieved nonetheless. I really dodged a bullet there. Maybe the heavens listened, after all.

In the spring of 2007, roughly half a year after my second run-in with a skin diver, I was particularly fed up with my mom. She was my sole social contact apart from my boss, my colleagues and the cashier at the supermarket, and she was no fun to be around. She started getting more and more forgetful and she became a handful. She hadn't been helpful around the house in years, which really took a toll on me since it all came down to me.

But now, she wouldn't shower or eat either, claiming she already had. She also told nonsensical stories and seemed to live in a world of her own. My role as caregiver had now solidified and I couldn't handle it anymore. For a while, I tried to cope by working relentlessly, smoking pot and drinking beer. I never reached for anything stronger, afraid of ending up like my mom or Andrew. I also tried to stay away from the house by sleeping in my car and hooking up with random girls one town over. But after three separate incidents with my mom, I couldn't let myself do that anymore.

One time, she fell down the stairs and broke her arm. I had to take her to the hospital the next morning and, of course, foot the bill.

Another time, she puked all over my bed—what was she doing in my room, anyway?—and smashed the bathroom mirror with her bare hand. That time, I didn't take her to the doctor, but I spent about two hours getting all the tiny glass shards out of both her fists.

On the third occasion, she went outside and wandered the streets in her pajamas, only to be picked up by the police—can you imagine my heart dropping as they called me? I was still scared that the deaths of William and Dorothy Abbott would come back to haunt me. Apparently, my mom had masturbated in the back seat of the patrol car, and they seriously considered keeping her in jail for the night. I pleaded with them to bring her back home. They did, provided that I'd take her to a doctor to have her checked out and, possibly, put her away in an institution. They didn't really care whether it'd be a mental hospital or a nursing home.

The next evening, I finally mustered up the courage to give Michael a call. I hadn't talked to him since he told me about Stacy, the woman he was planning to marry. He picked up after eight rings and seemed a little taken aback by my sudden phone call. I immediately started blabbing about Mom and all that had happened in the past months. I think I spoke for nearly fifteen minutes before I finally gave him some room to respond. All the while, he listened to me calmly.
"Look man," I said. "I really need your help here. I can't do this anymore."
"Calm down, James," he replied. "Just… give me some time to think. It's a lot to take in, all at once. I wish you would've called me sooner… Why didn't you?"
"I don't know," I said. I thought for a moment. I had been too caught up in my own affairs to think of him—obsessed with the existence of the skin divers. But then I recalled the night after the Ashley incident, when I told Michael about what I saw happen to her. He had looked at me with a blank stare and kind of shrugged his shoulders. He had told me I'd be better off keeping that story to myself. A *story*—that's what he had called it. I couldn't confide in him—as much as I wanted to. It broke me. He was the one person who had always been on my side and even he didn't believe me.
"Well, I'm glad you called now," he continued. "Let me discuss things with Stacy. I'll try to come over and help you and Elizabeth get sorted out."
Elizabeth? I thought to myself. That's what he calls Mom?
"I'll call you back tomorrow," he said and he hung up without so much as a goodbye.

I felt both sad and angry. I wasn't too sure why. But, I was excited as well. I hadn't seen him since his second year in uni and I wondered what he looked like by now.

I went to bed early that night, planning to get a good night's sleep. But what I didn't account for was the ghoulish shrieking coming from the room beside mine.
Mom.
I jumped to my feet, hurried out of my room and burst into hers. I expected to find her lying in bed, awakened by a terrible nightmare—like the ones I was still having regularly—but that wasn't the case.
She stood upright in front of the window.
I ran to her side and grabbed her by the shoulders, asking her what was wrong. She pointed at the window.
"I saw it," she said.
"Saw what?" I asked angrily. Mind you, I was already at my limit by now because of her disturbing behavior. I was also half-asleep and I wanted a quick and clear answer, so that I could go back to bed.
"I saw the dog," she whispered.
My heart dropped. "What dog?"
"The one you told us about. After… Ashley," she said, turning her head toward me. Her eyes were wide open. She was stricken by fear, but she seemed sound of mind in that moment. "The one with the big insect eyes," she continued. "Like those of a bee. You were right, James. You were *right*."
I stared outside into the pitch darkness, trying to distinguish shapes in that cold autumn night. It was useless; it was just too damn dark. I sat on the edge of her bed and heaved a sigh. "Was it a Jack Russell?" I asked.
She nodded.
Could it be the same one? It was now fifteen years later, and the dog definitely hadn't been a pup when it came for Ashley. I would've shrugged it off as Mom having a nightmare after all, if I didn't know any better. Because who knows whether the dog was really a dog or whether it even aged? The one thing that comforted me was that she had likely seen it. Which meant that I wasn't the only one. Do you believe me now?

I wanted to ask her, but I bit my tongue. No need to kick someone when they're down, I reasoned with myself. I was going to put her in a home soon, and she didn't even know about that.

I helped her get back into bed and sang her a lullaby, much like the ones she had sung to Andrew and me when we were still little.

When she fell asleep, I went back to my room and planned to get into bed. But sleep wouldn't come. By then, I had become quite accustomed to insomnia, so I popped a movie into my DVD player and zoned out while it played. My mind was focused on the skin divers, and I kept replaying my telephone conversation with Michael in my head.

Michael called back the next morning, around 9 a.m. I was still awake and had called in sick, so I answered the phone quickly. "Michael?" I asked as soon as I picked up.

"Yeah, it's me," he said. He went silent for a moment. "Are you alright?"

"Sure," I replied.

"Alright, then. Well… I've discussed things with Stacy and we're actually pretty tied up here. I have a lot of clients on my plate, and she's juggling both work and wedding planning. There's still so much we have to decide. I just don't think that I can make time for it."

My stomach churned upon hearing his words. Was he kidding me?

"Have you tried calling Dad? He still lives with Donna on Oakwood Ave. He's a lot closer to you than I am."

"No, I haven't called Charles," I replied angrily. "I haven't talked to him in years. You do remember him leaving Mom, right? Why would I ask him to come and help us?"

"Because you're his son," he said coldly. He paused for a moment. "Look, I really do want to help you, and I would if I could. I hope you know that. But it's a near six-hour drive, and I'd have to take several days off, which I can't really afford right now. I'm still building my business and I cannot have it fail. Our livelihood depends on it, you know. I mean, Stacy works, of course, but it's mostly auditions and small roles in local theater. It's not putting food on the table."

"What about my table?" I snapped back. "I'm working six days a week to keep our heads above water. Charles's alimony isn't cutting it, it hasn't in a long time. I'm doing all the housework, the groceries, everything! And we are barely getting by. And now, all this shit that's been going on. I'm going absolutely crazy here, Michael. I'm at the end of my rope. You've got to help me, man."

He was silent for a moment before he asked, "Does she still drink?"

I swallowed. "Yeah…" I responded hesitantly. I thought I had told him the whole story—well, except for the skin diver, of course—the night before, but I wasn't sure anymore. My sleep deprivation was fucking with my memory.

He heaved a heavy sigh. "Well, that's quite the mess. Look, here's what you're going to do: you're going to call the local nursing home and talk with them. No, before that, you need to call the doctor."

"But the money," I sputtered, seeing the bills pile up in my mind's eye.

"Don't worry about the money. I've got you covered, alright? I'll send you a check in the afternoon. For now, just call the doctor and let him help you. You're still with Stephen, right?"

"Yeah," I replied. Stephen had been our doctor since Andrew's birth.

"Alright, he'll get you sorted out. Just give him a call and he'll help you put her up in a home. I'm sure of that. If there's any trouble, call Dad. He'll be happy to help you, I'm sure of that too. And I'll send a check your way, so don't worry. Okay?"

I felt the anger rushing through my veins. It wasn't okay. I still felt completely alone, abandoned even, and I didn't want to get my father mixed up in all of this. I didn't want him back in my life. I did, however, want to see Michael. I truly, desperately wanted to see him again, and it was only in that moment that I realized so. "Fuck," I said out loud.

"James?" he asked.

"You gotta come over here, man. I'm at a loss… I'm…" I wasn't able to finish my sentence. I broke down and started sobbing like a little boy. Michael waited for a while, just listening to me cry. "I'm sorry, dude," he said eventually. "This is all I can do."

"No," I replied with a cracked voice. "This is all you *want* to do." I knew I was going to regret the words I was about to utter, but I couldn't hold back. "You fucked me, man. You really fucked me. You were all I had, even before Dad left, and then you left as well. I always thought you

would come back. But you left me here. You left me to take care of her
and Drew. Oh, and I don't know if you knew, but he's a crackhead now!
Yeah, he ran away from home because Mom apparently made him wear
dresses and locked him up in the shed, and his life went down the drain
right there and then. Pretty fucked up, right!? So then it all came down to
me. I wasn't able to run away, like the both of you. I wasn't able to find
someone to marry."

I thought of my break-up with Daisha and also recalled the phone
conversation with Michael, the year before—that call was the reason I
drove past William's and Dorothy's house and got myself into that giant
mess. "I had to see it happen again because of you," I blurted out. I
knew my rambling probably didn't make much sense to him, but I was
venting all of it. I yelled at him for another few minutes and even went
as far as to call him a useless asshole.

He hung up the phone right after that.

I tried calling him several times over the next few days, but he wouldn't
pick up.

On Tuesday, his check came in the mail.

Chapter 3

It wasn't difficult on a practical level, getting Mom into the nursing home, but I found it hard nonetheless. I went through all the stages of grief, for some ridiculous reason. It's not like she was dead or anything, but she felt less and less like my mom—even after her years of drinking. She morphed into this whole other persona and it got increasingly tough to visit her. I started off by visiting her three times a week. After two months, it decreased to once a week. After five months, I had moved into my new place, and I'd visit her just once a month.

I was tired. I was just too damn tired. I couldn't do it anymore. 2008 was around the corner and I was about to turn 26. I didn't want to be tied down by the phantom chains of my youth any longer. So, I decided to change it all up.

I quit my job. I sold my car. And I sold the house.

I had been stuck in that brick prison for too long. Taking care of mom. Wishing my father would come back—in the early days, that is. Hoping Michael would come back. And hoping Andrew would find his way back, now that Mom wasn't living here anymore.

Michael had a friend from uni take care of most of the process for me. He lived close-by and his girlfriend was a real estate agent, which was super helpful. I felt blessed that Michael still tried to help me, even after all that I said to him on the phone that time. We never really talked about that conversation.

After the house got appraised, it took a few months for it to sell and it was already 2008 by then. Christmas had passed and January had been cold as fuck.

It was now mid-February and the asset distribution started. Michael, me and Andrew would all inherit, but Andrew couldn't be tracked down at first. It took close to two months before he was found, by sheer dumb luck, near a dumpster on Kensington Ave. He was nearly frozen to death and high as a kite.

Both Michael and I were wary of letting Andrew inherit a large sum of money in his current state of living, even though he had every right to.

So, we took it upon ourselves to get him help. Proper help, this time. Offering him a sofa to sleep on, at a guy's house who reminded him of his molester, wasn't my greatest idea.

Michael teamed up with my father to make sure Andrew wouldn't get the money before beating his drug addiction. Andrew found that to be complete bullshit, of course, and resisted with force. But he did give in in the end and went to a nearby rehab facility. Maybe it was the newfound love from his family that did the trick. Who knows.

I was just surprised my father showed up for him at all. Nancy and Pam, his twin daughters, were 5 years old now, and he seemed to have his hands full. His marriage with Nicole was crumbling as well. The one thing he had going for him was the money he made. He had always been a successful businessman and he never really worried about finances. It made me jealous, honestly.

But now, it was finally *my* time to make a clean start. I moved states in April and bought a small house in Dover, New Hampshire. Roughly 28.800 people lived there, compared to the 2.300 in Greenville, and the city was nearly ten times as big, which made for some much needed hustle and bustle. I was in my mid 20s and I wanted to *live*.

There were a lot of people around my age and I met my first group of friends there. There were also plenty of beautiful women. Which meant no more slim pickings for me, with all the best to Daisha.

Before making the move to Dover, I actually considered buying a house in Allenstown. The place was cheap and the area was peaceful and quiet, with plenty of nature, which I liked. But there weren't many job opportunities and I needed money.

Dover was also closer to Michael's, who now lived only an hour's drive away. I figured we would start hanging out again, like the good old days, but I was naive in thinking so.

I was still obsessed with the skin divers and I took all of my findings and drawings with me to my new place, as well as my gun, machete, and the other stuff I had bought to prepare for another run-in with the skin divers. I couldn't be sure if they would show up anywhere else—maybe they only existed in Greenville—but my gut told me I'd run into one of them again. Sooner rather than later.

I still had frequent nightmares—Ashley was in some of them, even sixteen years after the fact. For a while, William and Dorothy played the lead roles in my nightly self-made horror movies. But nowadays, most of my nightmares revolved around dogs with gigantic bee eyes. They were all around me. Swarming like a hive and buzzing. They'd rip into me, and I'd be lucid as they controlled my body and made me do things I didn't want to do.

Killing William and Dorothy with a butcher knife, for example. Charging at Ashley with het father's lawn mower. Choking Michael in his sleep. Running Andrew down with a blue Ford Escort and even shooting him in the face, right between his eyes. The skin divers also made me kill my father and my little half-sisters plenty of times in the most horrendous ways. Sometimes it involved my machete, sometimes a raging fire and other times it happened with my bare hands. I watched the life drain from the little girls' eyes as I drowned them in their backyard pool.

I'd always wake up in cold sweat after, feeling sick to my stomach and disgusted with myself—as if I was in charge of what happened. I was too ashamed to talk about it to anyone and thus I found my comfort in other things.

I had my job at Dover Wheels, which I really loved. They mostly repaired and customized American cars, like Mustangs and Corvettes, and restored classics. But every now and then, they also worked on Japanese muscle cars and I was the one they asked for those kinds of jobs. Repairing, tuning and customizing cars like a Mitsubishi Evo, Honda Type R and a slick black Nissan GT-R. It was a dream come true for me.

Within two months of working there, I was able to buy my own dream car for a good price, purely by chance. A guy had brought in his Nissan Skyline and I was just all over the beauty. It was midnight black with 18-inch rims and tinted windows. *Sick as fuck.* He kinda laughed at my enthusiasm and we got to talking.

He told me he had another Skyline, a silver one, just parked in his garage, collecting dust. It had broken down a few years prior and he couldn't be bothered to bring it to the shop—different standards of living, I guess.

He said he'd sell it to me for a good price, but I'd had to replace the engine and some other things.

After checking the car out and popping the hood, I agreed. He even lowered the price a tad more, for which I was insanely grateful. I mean, I was all for it, I would've eaten stale bread for the next six months if it meant I could drive that beauty.

It took me several weeks to get her up and running, and later on, I wrapped her with chameleon color and put on 18-inch rims. I was hella proud. She was my baby.

My car was my main comfort in those days. I just loved driving her around town, checking out girls and being checked out by them. I loved the cool breeze rolling over my arm with the window down. I loved the thumping of the bass from the audio system I built in. I also loved driving to quiet parts of town and just chilling with a beer and lighting up a joint—yeah, that was still a criminal offense back then.

I also hooked up with two girls at that time, Amy and Kimberley, mostly in the back seat of my Skyline.

Life was good for a while.

That summer was all about the beach, having sex with Amy and Kimberley at their place or in my car, and fixing up other people's rides in the sweltering heat. It was incredible.

One night, at Amy's birthday party, I took her up to her room, and made her scream so loud, the people outside could hear her over the music. Another night, Kimberley had brought some curvy, foxy-looking girl with her, and they drove me absolutely wild, taking turns on me, and nearly making me pass out. Yeah, those were the good days.

Consequently, I nearly forgot about the skin divers.

Until one afternoon, when the sun was particularly strong, and my AC was busted. It would take a good two weeks for someone to even look at it. Kimberley offered me a spot on the bed in her condo, which her father had bought for her a year ago. The place was pretty neat, and I happily agreed.

30

I was too anxious about parking my Skyline out in the open for several
weeks, since she was safely tucked away in my garage, which was like a
third of my living space in size. So, I borrowed a bike from my new
friend Thomas. From Kim's place to my work took only twenty minutes
by bike, compared to the roughly fifteen minute drive, so that was fine—
it's just that I loved driving my baby around and I would definitely miss
that for the next two weeks.

I grabbed my bag, stuffed some clothes in there, plus an extra pair of
shoes, and took a look around my room. My walls were plastered with
the drawings of the skin divers, the painting of the Jack Russell with the
giant eyes, and scribbled notes about my findings. At that moment, it
seemed like it was the room of a child—a little child with an unhealthy
obsession. My life had changed too much to still have these things up on
my walls. If I were to bring one of my girls home, they'd probably run
away, screaming. I didn't want people thinking I was insane. Plus, I had
so few clues to go on, I might as well cease my search, I figured.

Before leaving for Kimberley, I ripped all the skin diver-related papers
off the walls, stuffed them into a spare drawer in my closet, and tucked
the painting behind my desk.

I locked the house, had another look at my baby, and made sure my
garage was locked tight. Then I jumped on Thomas's bike and headed
down the road.

It was hot as hell and my shirt stuck to my chest, but the smooth breeze
while biking was pretty nice. It was also a good way for me to stay in
shape because I drove my car any chance I got. I was still pretty fit, but I
wasn't nearly as muscular as I was when I was still taking martial arts
lessons, back in Delaware.

I was thinking of finding a gym in my new town, when I turned a corner
without paying attention to my surroundings.

Something passed me in the corner of my eye. It took me three full
seconds to grasp what I had just seen. I hit the brakes on the bike and
nearly twisted my neck to look at the four-legged creature roaming the
sidewalk. When I stopped and looked at the thing, the thing also stopped
and looked back at me.

It wasn't a Jack Russell this time. It wasn't a Cocker Spaniel. Heck, it wasn't even a dog. It was a damn cat. It had white fur, a little black spot on its head, and those bee-like eyes that I had come to despise. They were the eyes of a hunter, scouring the streets for its prey, and it seemed like it had just locked onto me.

I panicked and started pedaling as fast as I could. I wasn't prepared for this. I didn't have a weapon on me, and I was on a fucking bike, of all things—why didn't I just table my anxiety and take my car!? But I wasn't about to die. I had crossed paths with two other skin divers before, and I wasn't going to let my third time be my last.

Man, when I look back at it now... I was lucky to just have survived *two* of them. But I didn't know what they were capable of at the time. I was blissfully ignorant. And maybe that saved my life once more on that sunny day.

I pedaled and pedaled, without so much as glancing behind me, nearly crashing into an oncoming convertible with a man in his late fifties behind the wheel. Adrenaline soared through my body. Sweat gushed down my back and chest. My calves cramped up and my lungs wheezed as I tried to get away from the monster.

A loud screeching sounded. Then, a ground-shaking *BANG*.

The sound nearly made me jump from the bike and I looked back. I gasped, halted and looked at the grisly scene behind me. The convertible, that had just passed me, had crashed into the porch of the house on the other side of the street, scraping the back of the Chevrolet that was parked on the driveway. The mailbox lay in the grass, knocked over by the car, and the person who had been sitting on the porch lay on the grass as well—he had jumped away from the car in whichever direction his body decided on in that split second, right over the balustrade, and onto the lawn. The man in the convertible had his head on the airbag. As I watched in horror, the cat's head started to emerge from the man's back. It leaped from his body in such a casual way, it freaked me the fuck out.

I was afraid the cat would focus on me next, so I started pedaling like a madman. I couldn't resist glancing back though, and when I did, my stomach churned. The cat had moved over to the person lying in the grass.

I looked back once more but by then the cat was gone.

I kept cycling, not slowing down until I reached Royal Drive, where Kimberley lived. My legs gave out as soon as I got off the bike and I collapsed onto the concrete, struggling to catch my breath. Sweat drenched my clothes and my heart pounded like it was trying to break through my ribs. My vision blurred, and for a moment I swear I saw those little stars, like the ones you see in cartoons.

I stayed there, sprawled under the blistering sun, until I could finally force myself back to my feet.

I knew I had to call emergency services. I didn't know what havoc the cat might have wreaked, but maybe, just maybe, the one from the porch was still alive. Maybe I could save them, if I acted fast.

I ran inside the condo building, ignored the people greeting me, got into the elevator, and impatiently tapped my foot as it went up. I rang Kimberley's doorbell five times in quick succession. She opened the door, clearly startled by my frantic behavior, and I bolted inside, grabbing her phone.

I dialed 911 and told the operator what had happened—everything except the part about the skin diver. I said that someone had crashed into another person's porch and that they might both be injured. The operator asked for the address and then for my current location, sounding skeptical. She questioned why I hadn't called from a nearby house instead of from miles away, but I didn't feel like explaining.

I just told her to hurry and hung up. Guilt gnawed at me for fleeing the scene and not calling emergency services right away, but in that moment, all I could think about was staying alive.

When I turned around, Kimberley was staring at me. She looked dumbfounded. "What's going on?" she asked. "Did you witness an accident?"

I nodded.

"Near Lake Street?"

"Yeah."

"Then why'd you come all the way here?" She looked genuinely puzzled. "You should've rung a neighbor's door or something."

I sighed. "I panicked, alright?"

"Well, sure, but still… If you see someone get hurt, you have to help them," she said, her tone growing sharper.

Her words pissed me off. She had no idea what had really happened, yet here she was, judging me. "I know," I snapped. There was no way I could tell her about the skin diver. Just like I couldn't even talk to my own brother about it, the one person I trusted most.

Her expression softened. "Alright then," she said in a soft voice. "Sorry, I just… I don't know." She sighed and glanced away. "It must have been awful to see that happen. Let me fix you a drink." She guided me to the couch, took my bag from my shoulders and sat my soaked ass down, before grabbing me a cold beer from the kitchen.

I let my head tilt back and only then noticed how comfortable it was with the AC blowing. So much better than at my place, that had turned into a personal sauna. As my head cooled down and the beer soothed my throat, my mind became clearer. I thought of the skin diver that had looked like a cat this time around. A horrifying realization hit me: the skin divers could be anywhere. Any-fucking-where.

Kimberley was watching the news quietly on her plasma TV, sipping her favorite wine.

Under normal circumstances, we'd be ogling each other for a while, then start kissing, before moving on to the R-rated stuff. She was wearing an appropriate outfit for it too—a miniskirt and a bikini top, even with the AC blasting. She knew exactly what I liked.

But at that moment, my mind was closed off for absolutely everyone and everything. Upon the realization that any pet—heck, maybe even any animal—could be home to a skin diver, I had another realization. One that made me sick to my stomach. The cat had been chasing me. It wanted *me*, but the driver of the car was in the wrong place at the wrong time. He would never know that he saved my life today. And I would never forget that I cost him his.

I staggered to my feet and headed to the bathroom. I made my way to the toilet, crouched down, and unloaded my breakfast. I got up and looked into the mirror. My face looked flushed, my shirt still hadn't dried, and my hair was messy. I definitely had looked worse, but it was the way I felt inside that made me seem like a wreck. I brushed my teeth, splashed some water in my face, and went back into the living room. Kimberley looked up. "Feeling better?"

I nodded. "Yeah, thanks."

She gave me a soft smile before her eyes flicked back to the TV.

I tried to watch as well, but I couldn't shake the thoughts in my head. The images of that damn cat and what it had done still haunted me. I cleared my throat, feeling a lump form as I tried to find the right words.

"Kim… there's something I need to tell you." I hesitated for a moment.

She looked at me, her brow furrowed in concern. "What's wrong?"

"It's about what happened." I ran a hand through my damp hair. "It wasn't just… an accident. That cat…" I swallowed, "it wasn't a normal cat."

Her eyebrows shifted up. "What do you mean? A stray?"

"No," I replied, my voice dropping. "It was something else. Something… I'm not even sure how to describe it. It's like this… thing, that takes the shape of dogs and well, cats, but it's not really them. It's dangerous."

She stared at me. Her eyes widened slightly as if she was trying to figure out if I was serious. "James, what are you talking about? You didn't hit your head, did you?"

I sighed. "No, I didn't. I'm being serious. It wasn't just a cat. It… it did something to that driver. Like, it dove right into his skin, and just… disappeared."

She frowned and bit her lip. "That sounds… kinda crazy, James."

My frustration bubbled up. I felt like the little kid in front of my father all over again. "I know how it sounds, alright? But I'm telling you, that's what happened."

She looked at me for a while longer and then her eyes softened. She leaned forward and placed a hand on my arm. "Babe, I think you're just really stressed out."

My chest felt like it was about to explode. Once again, I was trying to open up to someone, and they just wouldn't listen to me—the way she was looking at me, like I was losing it, made my stomach tighten. I really wanted her to believe me, make her understand. But how could she? It all sounded insane, because it *was* insane.

I felt like I had to bury the whole skin diver situation deep inside me, far away from the light. It had put a distance between my father and me and it even caused friction between Michael and me. I didn't want it to wreck the thing I had going with Kimberley, as well.

"Listen," she started. "I'm sorry about before. I didn't mean to stress you out and berate you or anything. It's just that…" she paused for a moment and looked at me, "my sister got hit by a car a few years back. She was flung ten feet through the air, and her bike was totally trashed. She watched the car take off, without so much as checking on her, and passed out. We don't know how long she was out for, but a while later, another car came by, and the driver took her to the hospital. She didn't break anything, luckily, but her ankle was badly bruised and it turned out she had a severe concussion. If that guy hadn't helped her…" She swallowed visibly. "She would've had to walk to the nearest house to call for help, which was over a mile away, on a single leg—in a state of shock. It likely would've killed her, the doctors said."

"That's horrible," I replied. "A hit-and-run is never okay. How is she doing now?"

"She's good," she replied. "She even married the guy, you know. Called him her savior." She smiled and looked at me in her usual playful way, with a sparkle in her eyes.

I knew it made her happy when I listened to her and showed her compassion. She'd often return my basic kindness with passion. I don't think she was used to the basics. Sure, she seemed to be doing well, with her daddy gifting her a condo, and her graduating with honors from McIntosh College, before the place closed in 2009. But she had quite a range of issues. Her mother left when she was only 5 years old and her dad, well… he paid her bills, but he never paid her attention. She was close with her sister, Sarah, who was 4 years older, and they had a good thing going, but their dad did pay attention to *her*. He'd often take her golfing and let her go on boat rides with him—things Kimberley enjoyed as well, so she felt jealous, hurt and overlooked. The only upside was, it never really put a strain on her relationship with her sister, which I had a lot of respect for.

Just as my mind started wandering back toward the skin divers, Kimberley leaned over to me and kissed me on the cheek. I turned my head and smiled at her.

"Enjoying the AC?" she asked coyly.

"Damn right I am," I responded with a lecherous stare.

"Wanna make it a little hotter?"

She didn't even have to add in the teasing lip-bite because I was already hard, but it was a nice touch. She always knew how to turn me on. While we were doing it on the couch, my mind was blissfully blank. It was just me and her, our skins touching, our voices moaning. We then moved to her bedroom for round two—I was completely in the moment with her.

But it wouldn't take long for my thoughts to boomerang back to my new revelations about the skin divers: any pet could be a potential skin diver. Kimberley didn't have any pets, luckily, but Amy did. She lived with her parents, after all, and they had three big-ass dogs: a Mastiff, a Cane Corso and a Saint Bernard—yeah, the one like Cujo. If they were to become skin divers… Heck, maybe they already were. Then again, all the skin divers had been relatively small so far, since they were able to fit inside a person's body. Based on the ones I'd seen, Amy's dogs might be too big to be skin divers.

And what if they don't just take on the form of cats or dogs, but even smaller animals as well? Like your typical household rabbit or a pesky mouse.

I pondered the many possibilities as I sipped my third beer for the day, with Kimberley's head resting on my chest. I still had too many questions, too few answers, and I wanted to know what the hell was going on. Sure, I wasn't going to solve anything by continuously running away from those monstrosities. But how was I going to get close enough without exposing myself to danger? Life-threatening danger at that. My limited experience in martial arts wasn't going to save me in a one-on-one confrontation, I learnt from my run-in with the cat. And if I didn't have a gun on me…

I heaved a heavy sigh without noticing and concluded that I'd have to start carrying a gun from this point on. I left the damn thing at home. I guess I just kinda forgot about it because my mind had been pre-occupied with other stuff lately. My Skyline. Kimberley and her curvy friend. Amy. My best friends Thomas and Riley. My job.

Kimberley raised her head. "You okay?"

"Yeah, I'm fine. I just realized I left something at home."

"Do you need to go get it?"

"I think I should."

"What is it?"

I went silent. I didn't know what to tell her. I didn't even know how she felt about guns, let alone having one in the house—especially when I was just a temporary guest. But I wanted to protect her as much as I wanted to protect myself.

"You're going to Amy, aren't you?" she continued.

"What? No. I really did leave something at my place."

"So, tell me what it is."

I hesitated for a moment and then bit the bullet. "My gun."

Her eyes widened. "You own a gun?"

"Yeah…"

She made a face, kinda like a pouting one. "Why do you wanna bring it here?"

"Because…" How was I going to explain this without mentioning skin divers? I thought, frantically trying to think of a good excuse.

"You got yourself into hot water, didn't you?" She sighed. "I knew you'd be trouble, the moment I saw you."

To my surprise, she smiled as she said that.

"Well, alright then, go and get your fancy little gun. I mean, I'm going to assume it's little. Is it?"

I nodded. "It's just a handgun."

"Just a handgun," she repeated. "So, you're not going to Amy?"

"No, not today."

She pouted again and got off from the bed. "Are you going to keep seeing her?"

"I don't know. Probably. Why? It's not like we're going steady, are we?"

38

She looked at me for a moment. "Well… you *are* staying here for the
next few weeks."

"Yeah, that's because my AC's out, remember?"

"I'm not a fool," she bit back at me. "I know that's the reason, but come
on."

"You're the one who said you just wanted to fool around, Kim. And I
went with it. Look, can we do this later? I really need it with me."

"I need an answer," she urged me. "Are you going to keep seeing her?"

I looked at her silently. I really liked and respected her, but I wasn't *in love*
with her. I couldn't give her an answer she'd be happy with, unless I lied.
But lying for the sake of lying wasn't my style. "Yeah, Kim," I said finally.
"I'm going to keep seeing Amy and you can either kick me out right now
or be fine with that."

She stomped out of the bedroom.

I sighed. I definitely could've worded that better.

I grabbed my shorts from the ground and put my clothes back on. Since
I was going to go back out in that blistering heat and ride Thomas's bike,
I wasn't going to put on fresh clothing. I walked into the living room and
looked at Kimberley.

She lay curled up on the couch, buck naked, seemingly moping. She
often had mood swings and usually I could handle them quite alright, but
at that moment, I was beyond annoyed. I felt like I had more important
shit to take care of. Like picking up my gun to keep us both safe—
hoping a gun could hurt a skin diver, because what if they couldn't?

"I'll be back in a bit, alright?"

She said nothing.

I looked at her for a while longer, shrugged, and walked out. I got back
to the bike and started cycling back to my house. Which route do I take?
Do I go back the same way and see the aftermath, possibly running into
that fucking cat again? Or do I take a different route? There was only
one different route and it was just as long—since the streets were parallel
to each other—but still, I went with the same route I took on my way to
Kim's. The cat was probably long gone by now and it could be anywhere.
Plus, my morbid curiosity got the best of me.

I turned onto New Rochester Road, past Indian Brook Drive, past Willand Pond Road. I could see two patrol cars in the distance. I passed Newton Street, then Auburn Street, and started to slow down. I slowly passed Sherman Street and was finally able to make out the three officers on-site. I casually passed Lake Street and looked at the house on the corner. One of the officers looked back at me from what was left of the porch—the convertible was still jammed in there, but the two people were gone.

I faced forward and continued my way home. My fingers crossed on the handles, as I prayed for the man on the porch to have survived. I prayed for the driver as well, although for different reasons. The guy was dead— I could feel it in my gut.

I got home, parked the bike and went inside. The sweltering heat inside my home hit me like a concrete block. I quickly got to my bed, grabbed my gun from under my mattress and a handful of bullets. I figured seven were enough, for now. I stuffed the bullets in a sock, put it in my pocket and stuffed the gun in my other pocket.

I took a look at myself in the mirror. It would've been better if I'd taken my backpack with me, which was now at Kim's, so I could transport the gun in there, because now, I stuck out like a sore thumb—messy bed-hair, wet shirt, dirty kicks. Half a sock dangling from my one pocket, the grip visible from the other. It was hardly concealed and I'd have to pass the cops on my way back to Kimberley. I did have my license, but I still had Pennsylvania's policies in mind and wasn't aware that New Hampshire's laws were a tad looser, even before enacting the permit-less carry law.

I walked back to my front door, opened it and froze.

Right before my feet sat a white furry animal with a black spot on its head. A cat. *The* cat.

My heart skipped a beat and I quickly slammed the door. "What the fu —?" I said out loud. I grabbed the gun from my pocket and loaded it quickly.

Was I going to open the door and shoot it? Or should I try so from one of the windows? The heat inside was suffocating and I had to think fast before my brain melted. My hands trembled as I opened the door to just a crack and tried peering outside, while aiming the gun through the crack.

The cat just sat on my doorstep, gazing up at me with normal-looking eyes.

Was it the skin diver? Because if it wasn't, I was about to shoot a random, innocent cat. What if the skin diver wasn't actually this cat, but just used it as a vessel before ditching it? Was that possible? I stared at the beast with one eye—I wouldn't open the door any further—waiting for something to happen.

Meow.

I stared at it. It just meowed. "The fuck do you want?" I responded in a coarse voice, trying to hide the shakiness.

Silence.

"Leave, or I'll shoot you," I said.

The cat still eyed me with its normal cat-like eyes and it wasn't about to move.

"Alright then," I continued. "If you plan on staying here, I'm going to assume you're trying to kill me."

I took a deep breath, opened the door with my muscles tensed, and took aim.

"Hey, James!"

My body jolted. I looked up and quickly hid the gun behind the doorframe. "Hey… Peter."

Peter, the mailman, casually walked up to my mailbox and dropped a letter in. "Is that your cat? I didn't take you for a cat person."

"Yeah, no, it's not mine. It's… trespassing."

"Trespassing!?" He laughed loudly. "Well then, now I get why you were holding him at gunpoint. Listen, if you don't like it…" he started walking up my driveway, "my sister loves cats. I bet she'll take it in if nobody owns it."

I struggled to respond. I wanted to tell him to back off and stay the fuck away from this murderous cat, warning him that it could kill him in an instant. But thus far, the cat hadn't made any move other than meowing and its eyes hadn't changed. Their morphing eyes were a sign, I had concluded quite early on—a sign of them going into attack-mode.

"Yeah, I don't know man," I finally said. Peter was now close enough to be within its danger zone. "I think it belongs to somebody, after all."

"Alright. Then don't shoot it, will you?"

"Yeah, yeah." I scratched my head. This *fucking* cat. Why is it here? Did it follow me? And why won't it do something? Because if it changed right now... yeah... That's it! If its eyes were to morph and it were to attack me, I'd shoot it dead and Peter would be my witness!

"Let me check for a tag," I said quickly, since Peter was already turning around to continue on his route. He stood still and watched me bend over to the white cat with the black spot on his head—the presumed skin diver, guilty until proven otherwise in my eyes.

I reached out to its neck to feel if there was a collar hidden under its fur, but I didn't get the chance.

It bit me and ran off.

"Fuck!" I exclaimed, dropping the gun by accident and grabbing my wounded hand. Blood started seeping.

"Oh jeez," Peter responded. He walked up to my side. "You gotta disinfect that, man. Maybe even get a shot."

"I should've taken the shot," I sighed, visibly annoyed.

He laughed again. "Yeah, maybe you should have. Well, good luck with that." He nodded and turned around, going on his merry way.

"Yeah... thanks for that." I picked up my gun, unloaded it and put it back into my pocket. I disinfected the wound, put on some antibiotic ointment and stared at it. There were two tiny puncture holes. What happens when you're bitten by a possible skin diver? And why didn't that damn cat just morph, like it had before? Maybe one of my theories checked out—maybe the skin diver had changed hosts. Why else would it just sit on my doorstep, meow at me and then bite me when the mailman walks up. If it were a skin diver, it would've taken the opportunity to kill us... right?

Confused by the entire situation, I left the house, locked it up and got back on the bike. The bite-wound stung a little and I knew I'd have to go to the doctor with it. Kimberley was probably going to wonder what was taking me so long, but I wasn't going to risk infection. That shit's serious.

You could get blood poisoning and even bacteria that can get to your heart. Heck, that cat could even have rabies, as far as I knew.
So, I cycled to the local doctor's office and walked in. The lady at the front desk told me I had to wait, but that the doctor could squeeze me in in about 30 minutes. I was just happy for him to see me without an appointment, so I sat down in the waiting room and let my head rest against the wall. At least there was AC in here.
The sweat on my shirt had already dried from the cooling wind, when doctor Patel called me in. I had seen him once before since I moved here, for a little problem down south—courtesy of Kimberley's curvy friend. He was nothing like Stephen, our doctor from my hometown. He had a stern expression, didn't shake hands and spoke in a rather cold way. But he was good. He looked at the wound for a while and gave me a tetanus shot, saying it was better to be safe than sorry. I paid the 40 bucks, which I would've rather spent on beer or the upkeep of my Skyline, or condoms even, and finally went back over to Kimberley's.
I half-expected her to open the door with red eyes and an angry frown, but she had a broad smile plastered on her face and she hugged me as soon as I stepped in. "Sorry it took a while," I said. "I got bit by a cat."
"Oh no," she responded. "Are you alright?"
"Yeah, the doc gave me a tetanus shot, so it should be fine."
She looked at my hand for a moment, then kissed me on the lips. "I'm sorry, babe. I'm sorry about before."
"Don't worry about it," I responded. "You're great," I added.
She suddenly took me for round three—which had a rough start since my mind was elsewhere—and when we were finished, it was already dark outside and my stomach was growling.

I barely slept that night, even though it was nice and cool inside Kim's condo. My mind buzzed with questions and I couldn't get over the guilt I felt from steering that skin diver toward the oncoming convertible, effectively ending the life of the man behind the wheel.
There was a slight discomfort in my hand as well.

Chapter 4

The next morning around 8 am, right when I was about to head off to work, Kimberley's phone rang. She picked up and after a few seconds, handed the phone to me. "It's the police," she said promptly.

My heart skipped a beat and I answered reluctantly. "Hello, this is James Hunter."

The officer on the other side of the phone introduced himself with a raspy voice. "Hello James, this is William Abbott."

My heart skipped a beat. William… *Abbott?* I vividly saw the old man sitting at his dining table, moments before the Cocker Spaniel took him.

"So, we meet again," the raspy voice continued.

I gasped for air.

"It's been a while, hasn't it?"

Kimberley stared at me with a confused expression as I tried to find the words to react to the dead man on the phone.

There was an awkward silence.

"Y-yes, sir," I finally stuttered.

"You do remember me, don't you?"

"Of course I do… sir," I answered breathless. How couldn't I? But what the fuck was going on!? Dead men don't talk, let alone make a phone call.

William laughed softly. "You called emergency services yesterday because of a car accident that you were a witness to, is that right?"

"Y-yes, sir." I couldn't help but stumble over my words—my pounding heart squeezed my throat and made me dizzy.

"I'd like to talk to you about that and take your statement. Are you able to come in today?"

I hesitated for a moment. I had to go to work and I was still completely baffled by being called by William Abbott, of all people. And it wasn't a freak coincidence that his name was William Abbott because he clearly knew who I was. We had met before. Although… how would he know my name?

"James?"

"Yes, sir. I can come in after work, around five. Is that alright?"

"That's alright," he responded. "Just ask for William at the front desk when you walk in."

"Alright," I responded, quickly adding "sir".

"See you in the afternoon then. Goodbye, James Hunter." He hung up.

I put the phone back in its place.

Kimberley had made herself a cup of coffee and was staring at me from her kitchen table. "What's gotten you all jumpy, this morning? You look like you've seen a ghost."

I smiled crookedly. I could say I did not *see* one and I'd be telling the truth, but I felt a knot in my stomach, so big that I could hardly speak. "Barely slept," I muttered. I walked over to her, gave her a kiss and headed out the door.

I always enjoyed my days at the garage. I really didn't mind working because it felt more like a hobby to me. But that particular day—I was working on a newly brought in Acura CSX, trying to loosen the caliper bolts with a wrench—was excruciating. I couldn't wrap my head around the whole situation.

Did William survive? No, it was in the paper after all, next to a few missing persons notices. Did the skin diver take over his body and now pose as him, luring his next victim, much like a bodysnatcher? But people would surely recognize him and freak over seeing a dead man being up and about. Although, he was in New Hampshire now. But why was he here? Did he *follow me?*

I put some more force on the wrench because one of the bolts was stubborn as hell. But I was so caught up in my own head, the wrench slipped from my grip. My arm jerked forward and scraped the sharp metal edge of the brake rotor. I felt the sting as it slid through my skin.

"Fuck," I hissed. I pulled my arm back and looked down at the cut. It wasn't too deep, but it was pretty painful.

This was definitely not my week.

I got out from under the car and pressed a clean rag from my toolbox on the wound to stop the bleeding.

"Yo, Jamie, what'd you do?" Eddie asked as he looked up from under the hood of a red Dodge Challenger.

"Nothing," I responded quickly. "Just a tiny cut."

He showed a crooked smile. "Well… that's not going to cut it."

I laughed out loud as I walked over to the first-aid kit on the wall and wrapped a bandage around my arm. Eddie's dark humor was one of the things I loved about him.

Everybody called him Crazy Eddie. Not because he was some kind of sicko, but because he nearly died because of his crazed love for cars. Back in the 70s, he was a name to be reckoned with in the underground drag racing scene. They'd often gather in secluded places where they could race without much interference, although police crackdowns were pretty common. He drove a purple Plymouth Barracuda, or so I was told, which was stripped to its bare weight with some modifications to amp its power. Eddie often won, but didn't always come out unscathed. One day, he was about to race against his sworn rival, whom everybody called Buster, in the area near the Cocheco River, when a patrol car pulled up and attempted to stop them. Instead of forgoing the race, Eddie and Buster took it as a new challenge: to outrace the patrol car. As they sped away, they had an unfortunate run-in with fate. Their cars collided and Eddie swerved off Dover Road. He slammed his brakes and tried steering back onto the road, hitting a mailbox along the way. He couldn't get control over the car and crashed into a large sugar maple tree.

Paramedics had to amputate his right leg to free him from the wreckage and rushed him to the hospital. He had lost a whole lot of blood by then and the chances of him making it were really slim. They were able to save his life, but he had damage to his spine, which sentenced him to a life on heavy painkillers and he lost the use of his left hand—at least, for the most part.

Now, he walked around Dover Wheels with one crutch and a balled-up hand, which he had become quite skilled with. Colleagues often called him *handy* when talking to customers and it always got a laugh out of Crazy Eddie when the customers awkwardly tried to salvage the situation.

Eddie had been the lucky one on that faithful day, though, because
Buster had crashed into a tree on the other side of the road and was
killed on impact.

I walked back to the Acura and replaced the worn-out brake pads, my
mind still millions of miles away.

I got off work a little over 5 p.m. I cycled to the police station and felt
my heart beating rapidly the entire way there. My shirt stuck to my body
and the bandage around my arm was soaked in sweat. I was constantly
eyeing the sidewalks, nervously scanning for signs of another cat or dog.
Yes, that's what my life had come to: I was suspicious of every cat and
every dog I saw.

I locked the bike and stood in front of the police station. My throat was
dry as sandpaper and my legs felt heavy, like I was stuck in cement. I was
scared of going inside. Scared of seeing the man who was supposed to
be dead. William Abbott.

After a little while, I took a deep breath and stepped inside. I told the
lady at the desk whom I was meeting and she asked me to wait by the
chairs in front. I sat down and fidgeted on my seat. Every other second,
I looked at to the door behind the lady.

Finally, after what seemed like hours, the door finally opened and a man
came out.

I looked at the man, but it was not William Abbott. I lowered my gaze
and stared at my twiddling thumbs.

"James?"

I looked up at the man now standing beside me. It took me a moment to
recognize him. It was William, alright, but not the William Abbott I had
in mind. It was the man who had interviewed me after my very first run-
in with a skin diver. The officer who had mainly spoken to my father,
instead of Ashley's parents. He looked just like he had sixteen years ago,
though his hair was now graying. "W-William," I responded. "I mean,
officer… Abbott."

He smiled. "You can call me William, that's fine. We go way back, after
all. Can I get you something to drink? Some water, maybe?" He eyed me
up and down.

I felt the sweat drizzling from my back and nodded. "Yes, please." The AC inside the station wasn't cranked up nearly as much as Kimberley's. "Follow me, please." He guided me through the door he had exited earlier and led me into a small room. The temperature in there was alright—at least better than it was outside.

"Take a seat," he said. "I'll be back in a bit with your water." He left the room.

I sat down on one of the chairs on the left side of the table, my heart beating like a woodpecker on a tree. On the other side stood a fancy looking chair with a monitor in front.

Two William Abbotts… what an ironic, gut-punching coincidence. Both had played a role in a skin diver story, yet neither had been aware of that. William came back into the room, handed me a cup of cold water, and sat down opposite me with a steaming cup of coffee in his hand. He moved the monitor a little to the side and looked at me. "What happened?" He nodded at the bandage around my arm.

"My stupidity." I grinned.

He kept looking at the bandage, not saying a word.

The uncomfortable silence made me elaborate. "An accident at work. It's just a little cut, though. The bandage makes it look much worse."

"What kind of work do you do?"

"I'm a mechanic at Dover Wheels. I do repairs, tuning and modding. Stuff like that."

"Oh, yeah?" He frowned. "So you became a car enthusiast. That's… admirable."

I looked at him, puzzled.

"How is your mother doing?"

Ah. The car remark suddenly clicked. "She's… not well. Got diagnosed with Wernicke-Korsakoff, so she's in a home now."

"I'm sorry to hear that. Do you visit her often?"

"Not anymore. She's in Philly."

"That's quite a drive."

"Yeah. Michael, ehh, my older brother, he's looking to transfer her to a nursing home in Boston. But it's quite a hassle, apparently."

"Michael," he responded with glee. "Yeah, I remember him. He wanted to be a big time lawyer, didn't he?"

I nodded.

"How did that work out for him?"

"Well, he got his degree and he's quite busy—got his own business and everything. So, I guess he's doing well."

"You guess? Meaning you don't talk to him regularly?" William pried.

I shook my head, wishing he would just get on with taking my testimony about the car crash on Lake Street.

"You know, I ran into your father a few years ago. When was it? Ah, yes, three years ago, just before Christmas." He paused and took a sip of his coffee. "He told me he divorced your mom, not long after what happened to that little girl. That reminded me…" He paused again and looked at me intently. "I've always remembered your testimony from back then."

I swallowed and reached for my cup of water.

"You had quite the fantasy. I was sure you were going to be a writer, or something." He laughed, as if he said something funny. "Anyway," he continued. "Back to what you came here for."

I took a big gulp of water and put the half-empty cup down in front of me.

"Can you walk me through what you saw yesterday? Starting from right before it happened." He pulled the monitor closer toward him and hovered his fingers above the keyboard.

"Well… I was on my way to Kimberley and I was cycling down New Rochester Road. And…" I had already decided on not telling the police about the skin diver this time around, so I wasn't going to mention the cat, but I wasn't sure what else I could say.

"Who's Kimberley and why were you going there?"

"She's…" I paused, "a girl I know. We're kind of hooking up, you know."

"So, she's your girlfriend?"

"No."

William stopped typing and peered at me over the top of the monitor.

"Lucky boy," he said under his breath, then started laughing. "Man, I wish I was young again. Hitting the streets, picking up the girls…" he sighed, "instead of sitting at home with the old ball and chain."

I resisted the urge to frown and call him out. I needed the police on my side, even just a little.

"But alright, you went to see your breeze for a quickie, I take it?"

I blinked. "N-no. I'm staying over at her place for a few weeks because my AC is busted."

"But you had sex, right?"

I shifted in my seat. He was really starting to irritate me—what the fuck was up with his questions? "Does it matter?" I asked after a short silence.

"Well, I'm not going to type it up, if that's what you're worried about. Why? You got a girlfriend and you don't want her finding out about this Kimberley chick?"

I shook my head, feeling increasingly uncomfortable.

"Come on. Off the record. What did you and Kimberley do? Walk me through it."

I stared at him in silence. *What the actual f—?*

He started laughing. "I'm just yanking your chain, man. You should chill, James."

Did this middle-aged dude just tell me to chill? I gritted my teeth, but reminded myself that he was a police officer and he could make my life very difficult if I wasn't careful. Especially since I wasn't entirely innocent in regard to the car crash. So I smiled, cringing on the inside.

"Anyway, back on record now. You were cycling down New Rochester Road and then what?"

"I saw the car heading my way. It was a convertible and there was a man behind the wheel. He was in his late fifties, I think. He passed me and then I heard his tires screech, like a moment later, and this loud *BANG*. When I turned, I saw the car'd crashed into the porch of that blue house on the corner."

"I see. And did you see something before that? Maybe a dog he was trying to avoid?"

I thought for a moment. I should probably mention the cat now, I figured. "Y-yeah, maybe. I think I did see something from the corner of my eye. A cat, maybe."

"A cat?"

"Yeah, I think so."

"What did it look like?"

If I were to describe it, it could come back to bite me in the ass, I figured. Peter might have told his friends about me trying to shoot a cat on my doorstep, turning it into some hilarious anecdote—and those kinds of stories traveled fast. Plus, I had basically claimed I hadn't seen it clearly, leaving me some room to wiggle. I shook my head. "I don't know. I just saw something move. It was small. And it didn't attract much attention." That was a big fat lie.

"Alright. So what happened next?"

I bit my lip. "I stopped for a moment and then I realized I had to call 911. But I don't have a cellphone, so I figured I'd use Kim's phone."

He nodded slowly. "You know, I checked out her home address and yours as well. You live a lot closer to Lake Street. Why didn't you just cycle home? Heck, why didn't you ring a neighbor's doorbell?"

I stared at him silently, with a pit in my stomach.

"I mean, I'm not trying to berate you or anything. But that was really fucking stupid, kid."

I fidgeted with the bandage on my arm and drank the rest of my water.

"Yeah, it was stupid," I admitted. But I was trying to survive, I added in my mind.

"Did you see anyone else around? Another car, pedestrians, anything unusual?"

I shook my head. "No, I don't think so. I mean, other than the guy on the porch. He's always sitting there, just drinking beer."

He typed for a bit, then stopped.

Silence filled the room.

He took another sip of his coffee, which was likely lukewarm by now. "I would usually ask whether you stayed until the first responders arrived, but… you know."

I nodded, feeling the pit in my stomach grow.

"You were really lucky that another neighbor noticed what happened and called right away," he continued. "The driver died, but at least they were able to save the other person."

My heart skipped a beat. "He survived?" I blurted.

"Yeah…" William looked at me, studying my face for a moment. "He's in a coma, though."

Without noticing, I had placed a hand on my heart. I wanted to scream, but bit my tongue. Keep it together, James, I urged myself. You can do a victory dance once you're outside and out of view.

"Anyway, I appreciate you coming in," William continued. "We just need to piece together what went down. Your statement might help us understand what exactly caused the accident."

I nodded slowly.

"That's all, for now. But if you remember anything else, give me a call, alright? Or just come walking in and tell Tammy that you're here to see me."

I nodded once more, feeling a weight lift slightly from my shoulders. I had been wrong. The man on the porch survived. Someone had survived a skin diver. It was possible! I suddenly felt ecstatic.

William stood up and showed me the door. "Take care, James. And for the love of God, buy a cellphone, will you?" He laughed again—he sure considered himself quite the comedian.

"Yeah, I will," I responded sheepishly. "Thank you."

I walked out of the hallway and headed to the front desk. I checked out Tammy, who had asked me to wait earlier, and noticed she was quite the catch for a woman in her 40s. She wasn't in an age group I'd normally go for, but her brown eyes held a deep, inviting glow. She smiled at me coyly before I walked out and grabbed Thomas's bike. I stood still for a moment, hesitating. For some dumb reason, I wanted to walk back in and ask her for her number.

All kinds of scenarios played out in my head, with one even ending in her bent over her desk, drooling on her keyboard. I shook my head in annoyance. Why was I horny at a time like this? Damn hormones.

When I arrived at Kimberley's, she immediately started asking me about my bandage. I told her what had happened and gave her a recap of my conversation with William Abbott, the officer who had interviewed my

10-year-old self. I left out the fact that he had the same name as the man I watched die.

The next few days were pretty uneventful. We watched some movies at night, went to the beach outside of working hours and just did what young people do.

By the fifth day, living with Kimberley was starting to get on my nerves. It wasn't like we were fighting or that she nagged at me for leaving the toilet seat up, but it was more like… she was there constantly—I didn't have room to breathe.

So, on the sixth day, a Friday, I stayed out with Thomas and Riley, drinking beer and kicking back at Seapoint Beach. Around this time of year, it was difficult to park there because of restrictions for non-residents, but we managed to snag a spot nearby.

We sat on the sand and watched the women walking by in their swimwear. There were a few girls playing volleyball a little farther down. Riley commented on their looks, but we soon realized they were jailbait and we redirected our attention. A group of women around our age sat down in front of us, within talking distance.

Thomas started asking me about Kimberley, loud enough for the women to hear. I knew he liked Kim because we were attracted to the same types of girls. I kept my answer short and respectful, also loud enough for them to hear.

One of the women turned her head and looked at us. She whispered something in her friend's ear, who also took a second look at us.

"Hiya, lovely ladies," Riley said with a charming smile—he was a looker with his square jaw and bright blue eyes. "Why don't you come and join us, huh? We got some cold ones, if you're thirsty."

The women laughed, looked at each other and then walked over to us.

"Let me guess," one of them said. "You all ditched your girlfriends to ogle some women at the beach?"

"You don't know me at all," Riley responded, grabbing a pack of Marlboros and offering them a cigarette. "When I'm in a relationship, I don't even *look* at another woman. Let alone talk to them. And these two

guys right here? Single as they come. Well, James does have a good thing
going, though."

I laughed and gave him a look.

"Well, James, tell me all about this good thing," another woman said as
she promptly sat down in front of me, leaning against my leg.

The other women sat down as well, two next to Riley and two next to
Thomas. We gave them beer from our cooler and talked until the sun
started to dip toward the water—although it was still hot as hell.

We soon got into the water, swimming and playing around for a while.
Brittany, the woman who had sat with me, started touching me under the
surface. I took a gander at our surroundings and moved us further into
the water, far away from the children and the other adults, as the sun
started sinking into the water.

The booze and the warmth were getting to us, and with nighttime
approaching, Kimberley would not be happy.

I got to Kimberley's late that night, drunk. At first she wouldn't open the
door and when she finally did, she scowled at me.

"What's wrong?" I asked.

"People talk, James." She crossed her arms. "You're practically living with
me, yet you go out and fuck some random bitch."

"We're not together, Kim. We agreed on that."

"Yeah, you made that clear, already. Crystal clear. And I'm done with it."

I looked at her questioningly. "I don't get it. You were totally fine with
just fooling around, up until a week ago, that is. You were the one who
brought in what's her face… that curvy chick. And you even told me that
you didn't care who I'd get with."

"Well, maybe you should've read between the lines, James. And her name
is Nicole."

I sighed. "What's this about, Kimberley?" I reached my hand out to her
and patiently waited for her to grab it.

She eyed my hand, but wouldn't touch it.

"Did your dad call, or what?"

She nodded silently.

"What'd he say this time? Hm?" I took a step toward her, gently putting a hand on her shoulder.

She shook her head. "I don't wanna talk about it."

"I sense that. But you do wanna fight about it."

She bit her lip.

"Come on, baby. Talk to me."

Her eyes started watering and then she hugged me. It was always like that. She would get angry at me—sometimes for legit reasons—and then mellow out again.

"Do you *want* to be my girlfriend?" I asked. "Just to be clear, I'm not asking you out right now, but I'm asking what you want."

"I don't know," she whispered.

"When you figure it out, tell me, alright?" I rested my chin on her head. "Because this isn't good for the both of us. I should be able to go out and do whatever, without feeling like shit afterwards."

"I know… I'm sorry." She pulled her head back and looked at me. "But could you keep it in your pants when you're here, at least? I mean… we're living together right now."

I sighed silently. I wanted to correct her and say I was just crashing here for two weeks because of my busted AC, and because she volunteered— I could just as well have crashed with Thomas or Riley. Heck, I could've even crashed at Amy's—although her parents haven't been too fond of me ever since I embarrassed them at Amy's birthday party with those loud noises.

"Alright," I finally said.

She smiled. A tear rolled down her cheek. "Thank you."

I nodded. "Can I go to sleep now? I'm tired."

A week later, my AC was finally fixed and I went back home. Kimberley and I had barely touched each other since that Friday, and I knew we were basically over. I was pretty bummed out about it because we really had a great thing going and I liked her a lot. She was sexy and in for anything. She used to be so free-spirited, even introducing me to my first threesome. But now, months in, both our issues were surfacing —her commitment and abandonment issues, and my issues of not wanting to be a caregiver and wanting to do whatever I wanted and whenever I wanted. Oh, and the added trauma of the people dying around me. Paranoia regarding cats and dogs. Nightmares—although I barely experienced those when I stayed at her place, I realized later on. I did plan on working things out with her, but by that time, Thomas had already wedged himself between us. That kinda took me by surprise, but I decided to put our friendship first nonetheless.

I tried visiting the skin diver survivor at the hospital, who was in a coma, but only family members were allowed to see him.
He would spend another few months in the hospital before waking up and returning back home.
And he would remember everything.

Chapter 5

On my way to work on a Wednesday morning, I was nearly out of gas. I usually filled my baby up at the station at the intersection and sometimes grabbed a sandwich from across the street. I waited patiently while the tank was filling and casually looked around me. It was now mid-September and the days started getting cooler. Women swapped out their skirts for pants and dressed in layers. Some men wore fleece jackets or vests in the early mornings and evenings and I would soon be one of them.

I breathed in the morning air and looked at the trees around the gas station. They were beginning to change color. There were hints of yellow, orange and red. I had always loved the fall foliage. It was breathtaking.

The pump clicked and I went inside to pay for the gas. When I came back out and walked over to my Skyline, my attention was drawn to the cat walking the pavement. It was that damn white cat with the sharp teeth. I stopped in my tracks and stared at it. It paid me no attention and just went its merry way—its eyes looked normal enough.

I heaved a heavy sigh and only then noticed that I had been holding my breath for the past minute or so. I unclenched my jaw and shook my arms in an attempt to ease my adrenaline rush.

It was around 4:45 p.m. on a Friday afternoon when I was putting up storm windows. It was getting dark outside and I wore a thick fleece vest to keep warm. I still had a lot to do for the upcoming cold months: check my heating system, chop and stack enough wood to last through the winter, buy ice melt and stock my home with essentials in case I got snowed in. I had already raked the leaves and cleaned the gutters, so at least that was done. I'd try to get as much as done as possible in the next few weeks, before the end of November, but my social calendar had gotten quite busy.

This weekend, I'd be driving back down to The Keystone State to visit my mom in the nursing home.

Next weekend, I'd go apple picking at a local apple orchard with Amy, Thomas and Kimberley—they were now openly dating, Riley and Heather. Heather was Riley's breeze—they were together in the way Amy and I were, and the way Kimberley and I used to be.

I finished putting up the last storm window on the outside and walked back to my front door, taking a gander at my surroundings. The fall foliage was incredibly beautiful this time of year.

I headed back inside, grabbed my already packed bag and locked up the house. I got my Skyline out and locked the garage up as well. My boss Chris let me go home early today, so that I could drive down to Philly before midnight. I'd booked a cheap hotel near Race Street, which was about a 6.5-hour drive from home, and the nursing home was within walking distance of the hotel, which was great.

I arrived in Philly around 11:15 pm, after two piss breaks, and checked into the hotel. I was tired as hell and I definitely wasn't looking forward to tomorrow, but I felt obligated to visit mom—it had been way too long already. I went to my hotel room, hit the bed and fell asleep as soon as my head touched the pillow.

The nursing home seemed great and they took good care of my mom. She seemed to be doing pretty well, although her eyelids were still drooping, her legs shook slightly, and she was telling me all these strange stories once again. Some seemed plausible at best, others were complete bullshit. The nurses also warned me that she might not remember my visit because Mom had memory issues. That wasn't new to me, honestly. For a moment I wondered why I was even there, if she would likely forget about me, but then I realized: *I* would remember. And she was still my mom, after everything. After years of being the adult around the house and working my ass off for money, which she would sometimes steal to feed her addiction. When I just wanted to live a life… well, pretty much like the life I was living now. Friends. My car. Girls. Freedom. Plus, as little responsibility as possible. It would have been nice to add family to that list, though.

When I saw families like Amy's, all gathered around a table, feasting on food and wine, sharing stories and laughs, it always made me jealous.

And I'd always compare them to my own family. I mean, every family has their problems, but some more than others. That's for sure.

I sipped a black coffee as I was sitting by the window in the large restaurant. My mom sat opposite me and was drinking jasmine tea. It seemed strange, seeing her drink from a regular glass.

She started telling her fifth nonsensical story. The first story was about a lady in the supermarket, who had presumably thrown a wine bottle at her for standing in the way—I knew Mom wasn't allowed to leave the facility and the shopping was done for her.

The second story was about a man in the pool, with whom she had gotten frisky, but he had to move homes when his wife found out—I mean, it was possible, but yikes, Mom, don't tell me this kind of shit. The third story was about a meatball-stealing vigilante on the third floor, and her fourth story included a murder mystery, a conspiracy theory and an ambiguous cover-up.

This fifth story seemed to be about a bird that had it out for her.

"I mean, you should've seen him, Michael," she muttered—oh yeah, she'd been calling me Michael all day. She also believed she had only two children: Michael and Andrea. Yeah, her make-believe daughter… the fantasy that had messed up my little brother. Apparently, I'd been completely erased from her memory.

Me, the one who'd taken care of her the longest.

"The bird just kept coming at the window and it was so fast!" She put her hand on her heart and made a weird noise. "It tried to get inside like its life depended on it. It was angry. Trust me, baby, I know anger. I have seen it all my life. This bird was *so* angry." She shook her head.

I sighed silently and looked out of the window. We were pretty high up and I doubted any bird would prefer knocking on windows in the sky over snatching the low-hanging fruit in the parks below. I watched the people, tiny as ants, move around the streets, as my mom kept blabbing on about the angry bird.

"But that wasn't even the scariest part," she continued. "It changed, Michael. It changed like that little dog, back then."

I turned my head and stared at her. "What?"

"Yes, I'm telling you."

"What do you mean, it changed?" My heart started beating faster.

"Its eyes," she responded, looking at me fiercely.

"What did they look like?" I pressed.

She shifted her gaze around the room, suspiciously eyeing the nurses and some people sitting close to us. Then, she put her hands in front of her eyes, mimicking large circles. "They were big, like this, and completely black. They bulged out of its skull, as if they were spilling out. It was very uncanny, you know."

I gasped. Could it be? Did the skin divers take to the skies as well?

"I've never seen a bird like that," she muttered. "I was really scared. I thought it was going to break the glass!" Then, she eyed me intently. "You were right, James."

I held my breath. "Mom?" I murmured.

"What's wrong, pumpkin?"

"Do you know who I am?"

"Of course I do, sweetheart. Don't be silly." She laughed like a child would.

"That bird… can you show it to me?"

"It only comes at night," she responded promptly.

"Then, can you film it?"

"But I don't have a camera."

"I can get you one. I can go and buy it right now."

She looked at me questioningly. "Is it that important?"

"Yeah, Mom. It's really, really important. Can you do that for me?"

She thought for a moment, then nodded. "Sure, pumpkin. I would do anything for you. You know that. But I don't know if the bird will come tonight. It doesn't come every night, but every so often."

"Either way is fine," I answered.

I went outside a little later, passing several missing persons posters on lampposts, and bought a digital camera that put quite a dent in my paycheck for the month. I handed it to her and told the nurses that she wanted to photograph the scenery from her window, so she could make a photo album for my younger brother—they seemed to buy that. I just hoped the quality of the camera was good enough to catch a black bird on film, or even on a photo, in the pitch-black night sky. It's in your hands now, Mom, I said to myself. Please, come through for me, just this one time.

I grabbed a bite to eat and then did what I never thought I would do: I called my father.
On Sunday morning, I had breakfast with him at his house. It was fucking weird. I hadn't seen him in years, even though he had helped Michael and me put my mom in the nursing home and he had been supporting Andrew with rehab. He had gained quite a bit of weight and looked tired and shabby.
He still lived inside the house that he had bought for him and Nicole—I chuckled at her name, now that I associated it with Kimberley's curvy friend.
Apparently, he and Nicole split last year and he now called her 'the bitch'. She had apparently been screwing the neighbor for over a year and she'd married him last month. My father coped by burying himself in his work, eating and drinking. I heard all about it at the breakfast table. He sure was bitter toward his newest ex-wife.
He still saw Nancy and Pam every other weekend, who were now 6 years old. From the way he talked about them, I could tell that he cared, but he was also tired. Tired, like I had been, after taking care of Mom for so long.
He also complained that dating was hard, now that he was in his 60s. Pickings were slim.
"But Dad," I started.
He looked up from his bacon and egg sandwich.
"You've got plenty of money. There are certain types of women who dig just that."
He frowned for a moment, then started laughing. "Maybe you're right. See, I can still learn a thing or two from my children."
I smiled faintly.
"So, tell me about you. Busy chasing tail over there? What do the women look like? Are they hotties? They must be hotties. You're still young, you get to enjoy all of that."

"Yeah, they're good," I said and I told him a little about Kimberley and Amy, without going into too much detail.

The more questions he asked, the more awkward I felt. It was all so superficial and there was one subject that always burned on my mind whenever I saw the guy or talked to him: the skin divers—the way he had rejected my truth.

"Dad," I said, swallowing hard.

"Hm?"

"Do you remember about that day? With Ashley, I mean?"

He gobbled down his bacon. "Can we not talk about that?"

I shrugged. "We don't *have* to. But I want to ask you something."

He sighed and put his fork down. "Alright. Ask away."

"Do you remember what I told you that day? About the dog?"

His eyes narrowed as he stared at me. "Why?"

"Do you remember?"

He nodded slowly, without uttering a word.

"Did you believe me? Even just a little? Ever?"

"Look, James," he started. "Any kid would be traumatized after witnessing something like that. I mean, your own mother killed a little girl, nearly Andrew's age. How could that *not* mess up someone? Look at Andrew, he completely went down the drain because of your mother. I should've never left you kids with her."

I bit the inside of my cheek so hard, I tasted blood. I'd had enough. He didn't know a fucking thing about our lives after he left. He only knew the small parts we told him when we visited him every other weekend— and we always made sure that we'd have something positive to share, because we wouldn't hear the end of it otherwise. He had always just taken the revised stories of our shallow lives and left us to deal with the brunt of it.

I could hardly hear him talk over my own thoughts, but I did hear him casually mentioning that he visited Andrew twice a week. Apparently, my little brother lived up near Cooper Point, not too far from where I was staying. He was working at the local aquarium and seemed to have his shit together. That, at least, made me happy.

I took the opportunity to thank my father for his help with Andrew—
and even with mom—and took my leave. I drove back toward my hotel,
but decided on a little detour. I wanted to pay my little brother a visit.
Now that I was down here, I'd better make the most of it.

For some reason, seeing Andrew was even stranger than seeing my dad,
even though I felt a lot closer to Andrew and we had spent such a large
portion of our lives together. Maybe it was because of the way things
had gone down. Maybe it was because he looked so… clean. His hair
was neatly combed back, his shirt was tucked in his pants, and his house
—small, but comfortable—was incredibly tidy. He even had a girlfriend,
her name was Brooke. She was a few years older than him and that was
probably a good thing. He could really use a responsible person in his
life, especially after all that he'd been through.
The visit was short and sweet and he promised to come up to Dover
when he was able to take a week off. He didn't mention the money
incident and neither did I. Somehow, that didn't seem to matter anymore.
I was just happy to see him like that.

In the early afternoon, after kicking back at the hotel for a while, I went
back to the nursing home. My heart was racing as I was imagining the
videos in which the bird got exposed as a skin diver. I sincerely hoped
that it wasn't just another non-sensical story.
When I arrived, my mom was pretty out of it. Apparently, she had
fought with a lady from across the hall yesterday, who had wanted to
borrow the brand-new camera to take pictures of her grandson, who
only visited twice a year. The nurses had confiscated the camera before
nightfall, and when the bird came to the window, my mom had nothing
to record it with.
I begged the nurses to give her back the camera. They did, but I was still
angry. I could've had the evidence in my hands at this very moment. I
could've taken it straight to the police. *Really*? I thought to myself. What's
the police gonna do with a video from a bird with big eyes?
I went back to the hotel, checked out, and started on my journey back to
Dover in the late afternoon.

It was almost midnight when I finally laid my head on my pillow.

That night, I had a nightmare of a bird coming to my window. Its eyes morphed to those of a giant bee.

The busy weekend took quite the toll on my sleep and I felt kinda down the entire week after. But on Saturday, I plastered on a smile and went to pick up Amy.

I parked my Skyline in front of her house and waited for her to come out. I didn't feel like going up to the front door and having a possible confrontation with her father. She came out in a short pink dress, with winter tights and a thick coat. Her hair was tied up in a playful way. She looked cute as hell.

We drove down to the apple orchard and waited for Thomas, Kimberley, Riley and Heather to show up—the four of them arrived in the same car. Seeing Kimberley clinging onto Thomas's arm as they got out of the car kinda formed a lump in my throat. I swallowed it down and greeted them.

We went inside the orchard and picked the finest apples we could find. I tried to focus my attention on Amy as much as I could, but it was hard not to look at Kimberley. She was wearing long leather boots and hot pants—yeah, even in this kind of weather—and a furry coat. Her makeup was plastered on thick and when she saw me glance at her, she smiled coyly.

Fuck, I thought to myself. I sincerely hoped Thomas didn't catch that.

Amy and I filled up our basket pretty fast and walked back to the parking lot. We would wait for the others, but we decided to do so from the comfort of my car. Nice and warm. I put on some music and we watched the people walk by.

"You wanna come back to my place?" I asked suddenly.

She turned to me and look baffled. "Your place?"

"…Yeah."

"Sure." She still looked surprised and it made me chuckle.

"What's up?" I asked.

"Well… you've never invited me to your place before."

"Oh." That was true, I realized. "It's not much, you know. I mean, not compared to your house."

She laughed. "I don't mind. I can do cosy."

I looked at her for a while and smiled. I wondered what it would be like to be part of her family. Sitting around that table, feasting on food and wine, sharing laughs and stories. But in order to even have a chance at that, I would have to put in effort. And I'd probably have to start with her dad. I sighed. Then again, maybe Amy wanted a guy with a big family like hers, in the long run. So that they could join together for even larger feasts and harder laughs. I had nothing to offer on that part.

I stared outside and watched Kimberley and Thomas enter the parking lot, both smoking a cigarette. In that way, Kimberley was like me. She was like winter—cold and erratic, while Amy was like a summer breeze. Maybe you shouldn't mix those temperatures.

Winter was especially cold that year and I got snowed in twice. I did little more than work, scour the internet for possible information on skin divers and visit the hospital to see whether the skin diver survivor had awoken from his coma yet. I had Amy over several times and went to her house on Summer Street a few times as well. Her father still wasn't a fan of mine, but we got along a little better. He mostly liked to talk about sports. I liked to talk about cars. We had found a sort of common ground in racing.

One afternoon, after watching a race together, I slowly drove back home. I turned onto Indian Brook Road and carefully navigated the slippery street. I was about to turn onto Old Rochester Road when something inside me told me to take the next left, onto New Rochester Road. So, I did. I passed the same streets I used to pass when I was still going over to Kim's.

I was nearing Lake Street, slowed down a little more and drove by the blue house on the corner. The porch was still largely destroyed—courtesy of that skin diver—and inside, lights were burning.

My heart jumped. He's back, I thought. The survivor has awoken!

I came to a stop and eyed the windows. The curtains were closed. Was I about to just walk up to that front door and knock? The man inside didn't know me, although maybe from passing. What would I even say? I couldn't just open up about the skin divers, nor could I tell him that I was indirectly responsible for his months-long comatose state and his shattered porch. He'd probably shoot me dead if I did.

I'd have to be patient and wait for spring to come around. He'd be sitting out on his porch and it'd probably be easier to approach the dude. Plus, he'd have some more time to heal the fuck up. That's what I told myself. Although, I was probably just afraid in that moment.

Around the holidays I bought myself a cellphone and decided to give both my brothers a call.

"Hello?" said Andrew in an uncertain tone.

"Sup, Drew? It's me."

"James? Is this… your number?" He sounded clearly surprised.

"Yeah, man. Finally got myself a cell," I replied with a wide grin.

"Damn, it's been ages."

"I know, right? How you've been?"

"I'm good," he replied. "Been clean for over six months now, since my last relapse. Job's going well. This place is finally starting to feel like home, too. Things are… you know, looking up."

"That's great, man. I'm proud of you. I know it hasn't been easy." My voice softened.

He kept silent for a while before continuing. "Yeah, it's been a long road, huh. But Brooke's great, she really keeps me on track."

"I'm glad to hear that. You deserve it, Drew."

"Thanks," he said quietly. "I mean, it's still one day at a time, but yeah… So, what made you get a cell, anyway?"

"Just figured it was about time," I said, deflecting a little. "Thought it'd be nice to actually stay in touch, you know."

"Yeah, totally. I'm glad you called, dude. How's things over there? You still working at the garage?"

"Yeah, same old, same old. Just finished up a Toyota Supra, pretty cool."

"Of course you did," he laughed. "You and your Japanese cars. I still don't get the appeal, but you do you."

I laughed as well.

"We actually just got a car of our own. Bet you won't like it, though."

"Oh, shit. What you got?"

He paused for a moment. "You can't laugh."

"Okay, okay. I promise."

"Brooke picked it. She really likes them and… you know. Gotta keep her happy."

"Just spit it out, man," I responded, already trying not to grin.

"It's… a Mini Cooper."

I bursted out in laughter.

"Dude, you promised!"

"Hahaha, I'm sorry, Drew, but… that is *whack*."

"Well, at least we're mobile now, you know." His voice sounded like he was trying to muffle his own laughter.

"I can tune that shit up for you, if you want. Just bring 'er around."

"Nahh, dude, Brooke's gonna kill me." He laughed out loud. "You know what they say. A happy wife is a happy life."

My smile faded. "…Wife?" I asked.

"Yeah… I was meaning to tell you, but… yeah. That's where we're at. I wanna get engaged, like Michael, and enjoy life as a married man, as soon as I have the money saved up."

I was silent for a while. Michael had already popped the question? That was news to me. Not that we spoke often, but… man, I really wished he had told me.

Somehow, I felt a little left behind. Michael had gotten out of our situation quickly enough and it made sense for him to have this whole other life. But now, it seemed like even Andrew had surpassed me—and he'd been worse off than I was. I took a moment to gather my thoughts.

"That's great, man. That's… wild, even. I'm really happy for you."

It was his turn to be silent.

"So, how do you plan on asking her?"

"I was thinking of either the Longwood Gardens or the beach at Cape May. You know, with the sunset."

"I bet she'd love that."

"I really hope so," he said before keeping silent again. "…Thanks, James."

"Yeah, man. Anyway, I wanted to wish you guys a merry Christmas. Tell Brooke I said hi."

"Thanks, you too, dude. Got any plans?"

"Not really," I lied. I didn't want to talk about my complicated relationship with Amy—which was still meant as a fling and nothing serious, but it was starting to get more and more serious as time went on.

"Alright, well, take care."

"You too, Drew."

I hung up and stared in front of myself for a while, before calling Michael. He broke the news about his engagement within the first ten seconds, which eased my frustration a little. He also told me he was still working on getting Mom into a nursing home up in Boston. Things were in order, but there was a waiting list and it would probably take a few more months.

I thought of the camera I had given her and all the months that had passed—I hadn't driven down to visit her, not even once since the last time.

At the end of the call, he said he'd come and visit me in April. I very much looked forward to that. An entire weekend with my big bro, some cold ones, chilling along the Cochecho River and cruising around in my Skyline together.

I celebrated Christmas with Amy and her family. I'd put in quite a bit of time and effort to get her dad to like me and so far, it seemed to pay off. It was pretty nice to experience the warm atmosphere that filled their home, but it also made me feel more and more out of place. Especially now that my older brother was preparing his wedding and my little brother was working up the courage to pop the question.

Marriage had never been on the horizon for me. Dating, maybe. But I like the no strings attached kind of thing. Just… casual. Luckily, Amy wasn't looking for a boyfriend at the time. Although, she did treat me like that in front of her parents, which was confusing at times. I guess she didn't want to explain to her parents what was really going on.

Thomas and Kim, Riley and his new chick Tess, and Amy and I had a little get-together at New Year's. We drove down to Portsmouth in two cars and went downtown to hit the bars and check out some live performances. Afterwards, we set off some small fireworks and toasted with champagne. Around 4 a.m. we crashed at Riley's uncle's place—Riley's mother died when he was twelve and his dad was out of the picture—drunk out of our minds and stoned as fuck.

Honestly, it was a damn good night. I took it as a premonition for the year to come. But little did I know, 2010 would take a serious toll on me.

Chapter 6

Winter had passed and spring came around. By April, the town felt much more alive. Kids were outside playing in yards and adults were prepping their gardens and fixing up their houses.

Every week I'd take the little detour toward my work and drive past Lake Street, looking at the blue house on the corner. Every time, the porch was fixed up a little more. But I hadn't seen the guy once.

Until one afternoon, around 5:40 p.m. I drove back from work and decided on the detour, in hopes of catching a glimpse of the skin diver survivor. And there he was, sitting on his now completely fixed porch, with a small table on his side. He held a beer in one hand and a cigarette in the other.

My heart started beating faster as I turned the corner and parked my car. I got out of the car, locked it, and slowly made my way back around the corner. I casually eyed him as I walked by.

He looked back at me.

I softly cleared my throat. "Nice day for a beer, huh?" I asked with a slight grin, trying to sound as friendly as possible.

"Depends on who's askin," he grunted, looking at me with a piercing stare.

He was a skinny dude, who looked to be in his late 50s or early 60s. On his head was a faded, frayed baseball cap with an ugly greenish color and the logo of a local fishing store plastered on it. The logo was sun-bleached, but I could still make out the words: *On the Hook, Dover Supplies.* The brim was curved and dirty, showing obvious signs of wear and tear, and his messy white hair peaked out from under it. I didn't know it at the time, but that cap was a part of him. It was almost like a uniform and it's rarely seen off his head, even when he's just sitting inside his house.

"James," I responded with a hesitant smile. "I live a few blocks over." I waited for him to respond and stood still in front of his lawn.

But he remained silent.

"At Strafford Road," I added. "I moved here about a year ago."

Still no response.

Thoughts raced through my head. How was I gonna talk to this guy? He sure didn't make it easy. I had to figure out if he remembered anything from that day. I had to know if he remembered the skin diver—or the cat, rather.

"Sorry about your porch," I said, as I casually started walking toward him, carefully maneuvering around his truck, which looked to be a 1980's Chevrolet C/K, an old, rusty workhorse, with chipped blue paint and several dents. "You did a damn good job at fixing it, though. Barely see the damage anymore."

"Fuck you want, city boy?"

I froze. As I got closer to him, I saw the handgun lying on the table next to him. His hand was still clutching the beer bottle, resting on the table, just a few inches away from the gun. Would he shoot me if I got too close? I didn't want to find out, either way.

"I just thought I'd introduce myself, is all," I said.

He eyed me suspiciously. "Introduce yourself, huh? What for?"

I had to think quickly. "I'm a mechanic. I work at Dover Wheels, on Japanese imports, mostly."

"Figures," he muttered. "You that guy that drives the souped-up rice rocket?"

"Yeah," I admitted with a grin. "A Skyline. You know your cars?"

"Enough to know I wouldn't be caught dead in one of those," he said, scowling. "Give me a good ol' American truck any day."

I turned to his truck and saw the messed up back bumper, which had had an unfortunate collision with the convertible. My attention was drawn to a sticker on the back window that read *Live Free or Die*.

"Fair enough. That a 1980's Chevy?" I asked.

He grunted. "What's it to you?"

"Well, just thought I could fix that up for you." I nodded at the bumper. It was partly my fault, after all, as well as the part where he almost died —although he didn't know that, luckily.

"Don't need anything from you," he grumbled. "Thing's built to last, not like that plastic toy of yours."

"Well, that toy can outrun just about anything on the road," I shot back
with a smirk.
He snorted. "Speed's for idiots and teenagers, little city boy."
I nodded slowly. "Alright then. Well, I just wanted to offer."
"You done?" He took a gulp of his beer and smacked it back down on
the table. The gun moved a little.
"Yeah, yeah…" My eyes shot back and forth. "I just wanted to say that
it's good to see you up and about. I heard you were in a coma for quite
some time."
He narrowed his eyes and stared at me. "You listen to me, kid," he
hissed. "I don't like people poking around. You keep to yourself and we
won't have any problems."
I raised my hands in mock surrender, which wasn't the brightest idea,
looking back. "Fair enough, fair enough. I'm not here to cause trouble."
"Then get the fuck off my lawn." His fingers slid toward his handgun.
"Alright. Have a good day," I said quickly. I turned around and walked
back toward the sidewalk, trying not to seem in a hurry.
He kept silent and eyed me suspiciously from under the brim of his cap
until I was finally out of his sight. That little walk around the corner
seemed to take forever, I tell you.
I got back into my car and heaved a heavy sigh. Alright, I thought. That
did not go as planned. That grumpy old fucker was impossible to talk to.
I should try again some other time, but I had to figure out how to break
the ice first. Maybe Michael would have some brilliant insight.

On a Saturday, early in the morning, Michael drove up my driveway in a
silver Cadillac CTS. It was such a telling car for him.
I was already out on the little stairs in front of my house, smoking a
cigarette. It was a nasty habit I'd recently picked up from Riley.
Michael got out of his car, carrying a bag, and looked me up and down.
"Get out of here," he said.
I grinned.
"You're not smoking in my car, that's for sure."
"It's good to see you too, bro."

He smiled and walked over, dropping his bag on the grass. He gave me a firm hug. "It's been too long, little brother."

"It has, it has."

"Move over." He sat down next to me on the steps and looked at the road. "It's pretty quiet here."

"Yeah. It's great."

"I can imagine you like it."

"You don't?" I asked.

"Never been much of a fan of silence," he admitted. "Heard enough of it."

I nodded. I knew he was talking about the prolonged silence in our home, back in the day, often following fights between our mom and dad, before they split up.

"So, how's Boston treating you, then?" I asked as I blew smoke up in the air.

"Busy as always. Work's been pretty hectic, but you know me, I like to stay on top of things." He deflected a little as he looked at me. "You should come and visit, you know? You haven't even met Stacy yet."

"Yeah, that's… Let's plan something."

He frowned. "That's the third time you've said that, you know. I mean, I drove up here, this time. But I really want you to meet her. We're getting married, after all. She's going to be my wife."

"Yeah, and I'd love to meet her, man."

He kept looking at me, but said nothing. Something in his eyes conveyed disappointment.

"In two weeks, over the weekend, I'll come to Boston. That okay?"

He nodded slowly. "The weekend might get busy, though."

"Yeah, you inviting lots of people over for your birthday?"

He smiled. "Yeah, we're throwing a party on Saturday night. You should be there."

"Wouldn't miss it for the world," I responded and stared in front of myself.

There was a long silence, in which the chirping birds were the loudest of all.

"Still working on those Japanese cars?" he asked.

I nodded. "Yeah, still tuning and fixing up some pretty slick rides. The guy that sold me his Skyline brought in his, a few days ago. It's incredible. I mean, you should see it, really. It's black as the night sky with 18-inch rims and tinted windows."

"Oh, yeah?"

"We can drive by the garage later, if you want. I can show it to you."

"Sure," he replied. "But first, I wanna see yours."

I smiled and stood up. "Roger that."

I showed him my car and we took her for a spin toward Cochecho River that afternoon, where we enjoyed a cold beer on the waterside.

"So, you still running the firm?" I asked.

"You bet. It's all suits and briefcases." He sighed and stretched out his legs. "I'm actually thinking of taking a step back, though."

"For real? Why?"

"I don't know. Just take on some smaller cases. Shake things up a little."

I raised an eyebrow. "Smaller cases? You, the big-shot lawyer, doing grunt work?"

He laughed. "Sometimes that's where you find the real stories, you know." He took a sip of his beer. "Plus, I've been missing the simpler stuff, I guess."

"Well, cheers to that," I said, clinking my bottle against his. "But what's keeping you?"

"Stacy," he muttered with a smile. "Weddings are expensive, little brother."

"Bet they are. But she's got a good income, now that she switched to real estate, right?"

He eyed me. "You can't think like that, James, if you're to ever keep a woman for longer than a few months."

"Hey, I'm doing great, just cruising."

He smirked. "Sure you do. I'm just saying. Once you're planning a life together, you can't just go around making selfish decisions. You have to think about the other person."

"But she wants you to be happy, right?"

"Of course. And I want her to be happy as well. So that's why I'm not saying a word about the whole thing until I'm sure it's what I want. *After the wedding.*" He gave me a look. "Please keep it to yourself, will you?"
I nodded.
"I mean it. Don't tell Drew, either, 'cause you know he'll blab."
I laughed. "That's for sure."
"So, how are things with the ladies? Still having fun?"
"You know me."
He put down his empty beer bottle and looked at the water flowing through the river. "Still juggling two girls at once?"
I shook my head. "Nah, Kimberley's with Thomas now."
"Oh, shit. For real?"
"Yeah."
"Man, that's got to sting."
I shrugged. "He's good to her."
"Well, yeah, sure. But that's your best friend, little brother."
"It's fine."
He looked at me for a moment and sighed. "If you say so."

As soon as we got hungry, we drove into town and grabbed a bite to eat. We went home afterwards.
"You've really made this place your own," Michael remarked as he looked around at my vintage car posters and shabby furniture that had seen better days but still held a certain charm.
"Yeah, it ain't much, but it's home," I said. "And it's got everything I need."
"A garage, most importantly," he laughed and sprawled on the worn-out couch.
"You want a beer? Or something stronger?"
"Beer's fine," he replied.
I handed him a beer and sat down next to him. Our conversation started flowing smoothly, much like it used to, despite the years and distance.
We sat on my couch, reminiscing about old times—the good ones—and laughing over our childhood antics. Like that one time we drew fake tattoos on each other with a marker and convinced Andrew that they

were real. He believed us right up until the shower washed them off. Or
when we pissed off our father by changing the TV channels with a
remote control from behind the backdoor window.
Later in the evening, I tried to bring up the one topic that always had a
seat in my mind. "I haven't told you about the last time I visited mom,
have I?"
He shook his head. "What about it?"
"Well," I said hesitantly. "She told me something interesting. Something
about a bird coming to her window every night."
"Oh, yeah? What kind of bird?"
"I don't know. A bird. But anyway, that bird had really big eyes. Like,
huge, you know. And sort of… insect-like."
He slowly put his beer down on the table and turned to me. "Is this
about those skin divers again? You still haven't given up on those
delusions?"
I kept silent, waiting for him to either give me room to talk about them
or to shut me down completely.
"You do know her memory isn't right because of the disease, right?"
I nodded.
"She's told me plenty of stories. Even one including a guy who'd strip
down naked in the middle of the dining hall and swing on the
chandeliers." He sighed. "There were no chandeliers. And the nurses
would never allow it."
"Yeah, I heard a few funny ones as well. But this one…"
"It fits your narrative," he said promptly. "I mean, I'm not surprised,
honestly. You've told her about the dog, that one day, and it was probably
a Hail Mary for her—meaning she wouldn't have to take responsibility
for what she did." He blankly stared in front of him. "And you told me
that she saw the dog in our yard, years later. But the disease had already
kicked in and messed with her brain, by then."
"Can you just keep an open mind about this? Please?" I looked at him
with a serious expression. "Please…"
His eyes shot back and forth. "Okay. Well, what about the bird?"
"She told me it tried to break the window and that she was scared of it.
And if it really is a skin diver, well… I need that evidence, Michael."

"Sure," he said in a soft, unsure tone.

"So he bought her a camera and asked her to film it or even take a photo or something."

He raised his eyebrows. "Okay…"

"I really hope she did. Especially since she's going over to Boston soon."

"She moved last weekend, actually," he said abruptly.

"Really?" I looked at him in surprise. "Did you see her?"

He nodded.

"And the camera? Did she have that with her?"

"I don't know. It's not like I went through her stuff. Who knows what I'd find." He shuddered, smirking faintly.

I got up from the couch and reached for my car keys. "I have to go see her."

"Dude, what? No." He grabbed the keys and held them by his side. "You're not going anywhere with this much booze in you. Visiting hours are long over. Plus, I'm here, remember."

I hesitated, but sat back down anyway.

"Just check in with her when you're in Boston, in two weeks. Okay?"

I nodded slowly.

"I'm being serious, Jamie."

I've always hated that nickname—it made me feel like a little kid. "Yeah, yeah. Now give me back my keys."

"Why? You afraid I'll steal your car?" He smirked.

"As a matter of fact…"

He tossed the keys on the table and laughed out loud.

The rest of the weekend went by pretty fast and we talked casually. I didn't mention the skin divers again. I'm glad he seemed to be more willing to listen than he had been in the past, but he still wasn't convinced. Not in the slightest. I figured the only people I could talk to about those fuckers were my mom, of all people, and the grumpy old dude on the porch, whose name I didn't even know. Yet.

On my way to work, I stopped for gas and noticed a familiar face approaching.

"Lovely morning, isn't it?" William said as he walked over to me from his patrol car. His voice was calm, but there was an edge to it.

"I guess," I replied, keeping my tone neutral.

He stood beside me, watching as I filled up the tank. "There's something I've been thinking about," he said slowly.

"Oh, yeah?" I asked. "What's that?"

"Your statement…" he started. His eyes narrowed and he looked me up and down. "I still can't quite wrap my head around why you didn't call 911 right away."

I tried not to show any reaction, focusing on the gas pump instead. "You still on that? Thought that thing was closed shut."

"You'd like that, wouldn't you?" he replied abruptly.

I gave him a questioning look.

He smirked, stayed silent for a while and then continued with a probing tone. "It's odd, don't you think? Fleeing the scene of… an accident. Most people would've called for help, right away. You could've gone up to any house nearby. But you didn't."

"Yeah, well," I said, forcing a shrug, "I didn't have my cell and I was just heading to Kimberley's. It was stupid, I know."

"Stupid," he repeated. "Sure. But it's not exactly *normal*, is it?"

I finished filling the tank, hastily returning the nozzle. "No, it's not," I admitted, trying to sound casual. "I guess car accidents just throw me off."

He smiled, but it didn't reach his eyes. "So, what? Trauma?" he asked, watching me closely.

"I don't know," I said, avoiding his gaze. "But I'm late for work." I started to head toward the cashier.

He followed, not letting up. "Gotta make these dollars, huh? Standing around gas stations isn't part of the job description, I take it?" he said, trying to lighten the mood, but his eyes stayed on me. "Could be great advertising, if you ask me." He laughed at his own joke.

I paid quickly, aware of his eyes on me the entire time. As soon as I was outside, I got into my car and drove off, catching a glimpse of him in my rearview mirror.

Later that week, on a Wednesday afternoon, I took a stroll along New Rochester Road. I walked on the sidewalk opposite the blue house. I looked at the grumpy old dude and nodded, but he didn't acknowledge me. I tried again on Friday. Then on Tuesday and once more on the next Friday. That time, he gave a long glance. To me, that meant victory.

On Saturday morning, around 6 a.m. I got into my car. I had been way too nervous to sleep and had drunk five cups of coffee by then. My fingers slightly trembled as they reached for the steering wheel. Tomorrow, I'd find out if my mom had come through for me and if I'd finally have some evidence to back up my words, since people were quick to judge them as bullshit.

The drive down to Boston was pretty chill and I decided in that moment that I should drive down there more often. Not just to visit Mom in the new home, but to visit Michael as well—he was right, I should've met Stacy a long time ago.

After about an hour and a half, I arrived in Wakefield. I drove down Main Street, past Lake Quannapowitt, and stopped in front of a big white house with a large porch. I parked my baby on the side of the road, got out and looked at my surroundings. The houses around here were pretty big and they looked hella fancy. The view from Michael's lawn was gorgeous as well. He could see over the lake and the park surrounding it. There was a bit of hustle and bustle and cars passing by, but it was pretty peaceful. I wondered why Michael had commented on the peace and quiet in my street.

I grabbed my bag and the present I'd bought Michael from the trunk, crossed the street and waited for a jogger to pass. She gave a slight nod. I hid the present behind my bag, walked up the porch and silently knocked on the front door. I didn't know if he was awake already. We'd agreed on 9 a.m. after all and I was nearly two hours early.

To my surprise, he opened the door and was already fully dressed.

"You're early," he said with a smirk. "Broke the speed limit, or what?"

I laughed. "Nah, bro, just couldn't sleep."

"Oh, you're that excited, are you? Well then, where's my present?"

I handed him the gift.

"Oh, damn, you did?" He laughed and gave me a hug.

"Open it," I said.

"Right now?"

I ushered him to tear off the wrapping and so he did. He stared down at the book in his hands. For a moment, he was completely silent. Then, he laughed so hard that a couple, walking on the other side of the street, gave us a curious look.

"The firm, by John Grisham," he read out loud. "That's excellent, little brother. I've been meaning to read this for a while now. Thank you." He then guided me inside and that's when I first saw his wife-to-be, Stacy. She was absolutely drop-dead gorgeous and I hadn't expected anything less from Michael, to be honest. She was funny as well.

He did good, I thought to myself, standing inside that enormous house, shaking the hand of a woman who could've easily made money off her looks but had opted for real estate instead—though *something* must have led her to quit acting.

Michael was all smiles that weekend and, seeing him like that, I started thinking that maybe a serious relationship could be a good thing after all. Look at what it did for him and Andrew. They both had a purpose. Meaning. Someone to rely on. Someone to talk to on the cold, dark nights. Maybe, just maybe… that actually beat picking up random women and fucking them for the sake of it. Like in an alley, or on a bench in the park, for the thrill of getting caught. Or in the sea, just hours after meeting them.

I made a silent commitment to myself to try and explore this with Amy. If it had to be anyone, it had to be her, I thought. She was steady, level-headed, warm, bubbly. Pretty much the opposite of Kim, who was with Thomas now, anyway.

To try and test my own commitment that night, I didn't even sleep with Jill, the crazy hot woman at Michael's birthday party, who was apparently a friend of Stacy's. Maybe I could do this, after all, I figured.

The next day, I was pretty hung over still when I said goodbye to Michael and Stacy. I drove over to the nursing home, which was only ten minutes away from his house. I figured he probably went to see Mom all the time and I felt a little guilty over that.

I introduced myself to her nurses and got impatient as it seemed they were going to give me the entire tour around the home. It wasn't that different from her old home and I just wanted to see her and ask about the bird.

"Pumpkin!"

I turned around and saw my mom, already stretching her arms out for a hug. Finally freed from the nurses, I walked over to her and hugged her.

"Hey, mom. How are you?"

"I'm well," she responded.

I was surprised to see her looking so brightly. Even her eyes seemed present.

"How are you?"

"I'm good," I said quickly. "Do you have the camera?"

"What camera?"

I stared at her blankly. "The one I gave you."

"Don't be silly. What would I do with a camera?"

"Well…" I looked around nervously. "Because of the bird, remember?"

"The bird," she repeated my words. "I don't like that bird."

She remembers, at least, I thought. "Can you show me your new room?" I asked, still nervously watching the nurses.

"Sure, pumpkin."

I followed her down the hallway, into her room, which was slightly smaller than her previous one, but there was a little desk inside this one. I started going through her closet.

"What are you doing?" she asked in surprise.

"I need that camera, Mom." But there was nothing in the closet and I was getting really annoyed. I moved to the desk, opened the drawers and heaved a sigh of relief. There it was, stuffed inside one of the drawers like it was stationary or some other cheap shit. I took out the camera and tried to turn it on, but it was all out of juice. "Damn it," I sighed.

"Language, sweetheart."

I ignored her and stuffed the camera in my pocket—it made it look like I had a huge bulge.

"Do you think I'm safe now?" she asked.

I looked up and only then noticed the look in her eyes. She looked terrified. "Yeah, mom," I said. "I mean, you haven't seen the bird since moving here, right?"

"No."

"And it's like seven hours apart," I continued. "They don't follow you like that. I've never seen the Jack Russell or the Cocker Spaniel again, either. Nor the cat."

She eyed me for a while. "He hasn't come to visit me in years, you know."

"Who?" I asked.

"Your brother."

I thought of Andrew and how he was too traumatized to even show his face in front of her. "Well, yeah, mom… that's the way things are right now. But, maybe someday. Who knows."

"I don't think it's fair," she responded abruptly.

"I'm sure you don't, but-"

"He was with me the longest. He should come and visit me."

I frowned.

"You should tell your little brother to come over."

"Mom… do you know who I am?"

"Well, that's a silly question, isn't it?"

"Answer me."

She looked at me with unsure eyes, but didn't answer me. She didn't have to—I knew enough.

Later, when I was back at home, I called Michael and told him about my visit to Mom and her still obvious gaps in her memory. We talked about her inconsistent recognition and the stories she had come up with this time. The nurses had told me that these symptoms weren't uncommon and that there was still a chance that she could improve.

Michael didn't ask about the bird or the camera and I didn't tell. I had to charge the damn thing first—it took well over an hour before I could even turn it on and I waited impatiently.

When the camera finally turned on, I looked on in surprise and utter disappointment as I saw what was on it. I skipped through photos and videos of random people—some I had noticed when I visited her in the old home. They were all doing random things. There was some sort of birthday party. A bingo. Someone's children had come to visit. There were some questionable pool photos and even one of my mom in a bathing suit, which I didn't need to see.

As I kept on going through the saved files, I felt my heart sink. This can't be it, I thought. I was nearly at the end and there was absolutely nothing of value on there. Not to me, anyway.

I was about to smack the camera down on the table in frustration when it showed me the final bit of media on there. It immediately caught my eye because the screen was pretty dark and I could hear my mother breathing heavily. For a moment, I prayed that it wasn't anything like what her bathing suit photo had implied.

I was in luck.

My eyes squeezed as I stared at the little screen. The only light source was the moon outside and I could faintly make out the shape of the window and a shape sitting on the window sill. I heard its frantic pecking on the window. The shape disappeared for a moment and then it flew against the glass with a loud *BANG*. I heard my mother gasp and that's where the video ended.

It was thin. Heck, it was practically nothing. But it was more than I had before and it could help me in the long run.

Before going to bed, I cleaned out most of the memory on the camera and copied the video to my computer. Now that the camera had plenty of free space, I could use it myself. Although I didn't fancy carrying that thing around all the time, just in hopes of catching one of those fuckers in the act *and* having to outrun them at the same time.

No, my gun would be the thing to keep handy. My life meant more than a sliver of evidence after all.

Chapter 7

Over the next several weeks, I exchanged some glances with the old grump on the porch, before finally mustering up the courage to try and talk to him again. I knew I'd have to cut to the chase with this guy.

"Hey," I said loudly, waiting in front of his driveway.

"What you want, kid?" he shouted.

"I wanted to ask you something."

He took a puff from his cigarette and eyed me.

"Is that alright?"

"Depends."

I took a few steps onto his driveway. "It's about that day. When that car crashed into your porch."

"Speak up or step closer, city boy," he barked.

If I was gonna tell him that I was there that day and that I was pretty much the reason that he almost died, I wasn't gonna take one step closer to him—I knew he had his handgun on the table next to him and I didn't want to find out how good of a shot he was.

"Did you see a cat?" I shouted back at him.

He went silent.

"It was a white cat with a little black spot on its head. It was walking on the sidewalk over there." I pointed.

"So?" He slowly stood up.

I wondered if this was the point where I needed to run. "Did it seem normal to you?" I pressed.

He visibly tensed and his eyes narrowed, then slowly started walking down the stairs. "Why?"

"Because I saw it. And I saw what it did." My voice softened as the guy was now close enough to hear me normally. "It jumped into that guy in the convertible and it killed him."

His eyes narrowed further. "So, you're the kid on the bike, huh?"

I swallowed and nodded.

"That fucking cat was chasing you, you know." It wasn't a question, the way he said it. It was a statement. He had taken notice, alright.

"Yeah, I think it did," I responded with a slight quiver in my voice. "I tried to get away from it."

"Why?" He was now in front of me and I could count the wrinkles on his face.

"Because it seemed dangerous."

He looked me up and down.

"I knew it wanted to attack me because there was something about it. Its eyes were huge and insect-like, like those of a bee," I continued, trying to remain as calm as I could while the guy was staring me down. I was also trying to sound sane, but now that I was telling all this to a complete stranger, I suddenly understood why it had made Michael awkward. "I had seen it before," I confessed. "In a dog, though."

He raised an eyebrow.

I hesitated for a moment. I hadn't been able to confide in Kim or Amy, but here I was, spilling my guts to this guy. There was something about the way he looked at me that made me want to keep talking—as if he hadn't written me off as some disturbed mental patient right off the bat. "I was ten years old when I first saw it. It was this small Jack Russell, just wandering the street like any other dog. Until its eyes changed into *that*," I mimicked my mom, "just like that cat. It then jumped into this little girl, right in front of our house, and smacked her into the back of a moving car."

"She alive?"

I shook my head.

"That's messed up, kid."

I hesitated about telling him about the Cocker Spaniel and how it had killed William and Dorothy.

"What do you know?" he asked slowly, squinting his eyes. Something had piqued his attention.

"Not much," I said. "But I think something's going on."

He snorted. "You wouldn't last a damn minute if you knew what was really going on, kid. You're just a cocky shithead from the city with a fast car and no brains."

I grinned. "Well, I may come off as cocky, but I ain't stupid."

He just kept staring at me. "You keeping something from me, boy?" he
asked slowly, in an awfully menacing tone.
I bit my lip and my eyes shot back and forth. Was I going to continue?
"Spill it."
Well, here goes nothing. I took a deep breath and told him what more
had happened that day with the Jack Russell. Right there on the sidewalk.
A few people passed by in the meanwhile and gave us a strange look—or
him, rather.
I told him about my mom, having possibly seen the dog in our backyard.
And then I told him about the elderly couple, without going into too
much detail. I, for sure, wasn't going to tell this guy that I had crapped
my pants.
All the while, he was silent.
Then, I told him about moving here, with as little information as
possible, and about the cat. How it had shown up on my doorstep after
and bitten me, and how it had gleefully passed me by while I was filling
up my car at the intersection.
After I was done talking, there fell a deep and meaningful silence. I
wasn't sure whether he'd believe me, but it felt so fucking good to get all
of this off my chest.
He put his hands in his pockets and stared at me. "That's some story,
kid."
"You're the sole survivor," I added. "From what I've seen, anyway. Who
knows how many there are out there."
"And why's that, you think?"
I looked at him. "What do you mean?"
"Why'd I survive, kid?" he grumbled.
"I… I don't know, really."
"It's 'cause my mind is strong, kid. I can't be controlled." He stared at me
with his fierce grey eyes. He didn't blink once. "But what about you? You
a city dweller who goes along with everyone and everything, never
having a fucking mind of your own, huh?"
I slowly shook my head. "If I did, I wouldn't have told you all this, just
now."

He was silent for a moment, then slowly nodded. "So, now what? You want my help, is that it?"

I bit my tongue. I wasn't even sure what I wanted from him. Just for him to believe me was something. If he did believe me, that is. "Yeah," I responded after a short silence.

"You do know you put me in a fucking coma for months, huh? You're in no place to be asking me for a fucking favor, kid." He glared at me. "I think it's time you got lost."

I paused, then nodded. "Alright. I'll go, for now." I had to conjure up some major balls in that moment. "But I'll be back," I added. "I think we're going to need each other."

"We'll see about that."

I felt a shiver down my spine as he stared through me with his piercing eyes. I turned and started walking down the sidewalk, desperate to get home and lock the door behind me.

"Hey, kid!"

I turned, half-expecting him to be aiming his gun at me. But the only thing he aimed was his stare.

"Name's Scott," he grumbled. He turned around and walked back to his porch.

I'd just gotten home when my phone buzzed.

It was a message from Riley:

James, meet me @ frog pond. Need to talk.

The Frog Pond? Not our usual bar—it was way across town, mostly deserted, and the walls outside were littered with graffiti and missing posters—both pets and people.

I pulled into the parking lot of the Frog Pond, which was half-empty during this time of day. I spotted Riley standing by the side of his car, staring off into the distance. His posture was more rigid than usual and he clutched a bottle of Knob Creek in his hand.

"Riley," I called out as I approached.

He turned slowly, his face revealing a mix of relief and sadness. "Hey, thanks for coming."

"Yeah, sure," I replied, taking in his disheveled appearance. "What's up?
You look… like shit."
He gave a small, weary chuckle and gestured for me to follow him inside.
He tucked the bottle in his pocket, barely concealing it. We made our
way to a quiet corner of the bar, away from the few regulars who were
scattered around.
As we sat down, he slumped into his seat, visibly exhausted.
"What's going on?" I asked, trying to maintain eye contact—he was
fidgeting and his eyes looked distant.
He took a deep breath as he tried to find the right words. "It's… it's my
uncle," he finally managed. "He's got cancer."
"Fuck," I said under my breath. "I'm sorry, dude. What's… How's it
looking? Is he gonna be alright?"
He shook his head, slow and defeated. "Stage four," he replied. "Not
much they can do, just trying to make him comfortable for what time
he's got left."
"Fuck, man, that sucks… I'm really sorry."
"Thanks," he said, barely audible. "It's been rough. I've been… trying to
keep busy, but it's fucking hard to focus on anything else, you know?"
I nodded. "Well, I'm glad you texted, man. You wanna talk about it?"
He hesitated for a moment. "Not really. Just want a drink and I didn't
want to drink alone."
"Then drink we shall," I said, gesturing to the waitress.
We knocked back quite a few—with him slipping some from his pocket
—and I had to ask Amy to come and pick me up. I'd have to come back
for my Skyline later. I didn't feel good about leaving my baby out there
on the parking lot, but I wanted to be a good friend foremost.

The next time I saw Scott was purely by chance. I had gone into the local
hardware store to pick up some supplies for work, when I spotted him
near the paint section, glaring at a rack of paint cans. It was almost
funny, the way he stared at them with an angry scowl. As if those cans
had murdered his cat and he was planning his revenge.
He turned his head and saw me looking at him.
I nodded casually. "Scott."

He grunted and mumbled something, before staring down the cans of paint again.

"You painting something?" I asked as I walked over to him.

"What's it look like?" he snorted. "Some idiot crashed into my porch, remember."

"Yeah, sorry about that…"

He looked at me and narrowed his eyes. "You here to bother me or buy some shit?"

"I'm just picking up some oil for the shop. But, you know, if you need help with the paint-"

"I don't need help," he barked, cutting me off. "Last thing I need is some city boy fucking up my porch even more."

I grinned. "Fair enough. Just thought I'd offer, since… you know. What color you thinking?"

"Not that it's any of your business, but I'm thinkin' something that don't look like shit."

"That's solid," I responded, laughing.

"You done talkin' yet?"

"Yeah, I'll go. Good luck with the paint."

"Luck's got nothin' to do with it, kid," he muttered.

I walked over to the oil section, grabbed my supplies and headed toward the cashier. I put my stuff down on the belt and took a few steps forward to make room for the guy behind me. When I noticed who it was, he had already put his cans of light-blue paint on the belt, right next to my oil.

The lady looked at me as she was scanning the oil.

"Ring it up," I said with a smile.

After I paid for Scott's paint, he grumbled and took off with the cans under one arm. He walked up to his Chevy and opened the tailgate, which squeaked loudly. He threw in the cans, slammed the thing shut and drove off without so much as looking at me.

After my run-in with Scott, I turned to the internet to try and see if I could find clues on the skin divers. I couldn't be the only one ever to have witnessed them. And maybe Scott wasn't the sole survivor in the entire world.

I searched: *Unusual animal behavior shapeshifting* and got a lot of hits. I went through the first few websites one by one. There were some articles on werewolves and lycantrophy, detailing the legends of humans turning into wolves, but that didn't match the skin divers as I'd seen them—they weren't just dogs, although close to wolves; they were cats and even birds.

I read about Loki from Norse mythology and the Kitsune—fox spirits— from Japanese folklore. Neither fit the skin divers.

I read about aliens and Bigfoot and saw videos and photos of supposed evidence. There were massive forum threads with in-depth theories.

Then, I stumbled upon the black dog legends. My eyes hovered for a moment. They were apparently unnaturally large dogs with glowing red or yellow eyes. No, that didn't quite fit it either, I thought.

I went on to the next website and my attention was immediately drawn to the word 'skin'. My heart jumped.

Skinwalkers. This must be it, I thought, and I started reading.

Skinwalkers were figures from Navajo culture. They were malevolent witches, typically, with the ability to transform into, possess or disguise themselves as animals. According to the legends, they'd gain this ability through immoral acts, such as murdering a close relative. The animals they transform into were usually associated with death or ill omens, like crows, wolves and foxes. But, they could take on the form of any creature they chose.

A crow is a bird, a wolf is close to a dog, and a fox is similar enough to a cat, I reasoned, heaving a relieved sigh. Could this be one and the same? Further down on the website there was something about their supernatural abilities. Skinwalkers had abilities like mind control, speed, strength, and the power to curse or harm others with rituals. I bit my lip. This sounded less like the skin divers.

Also, they could mimic voices, making them even more dangerous. Well, as of yet, I hadn't heard any of them talk—but who knows?

I yawned and stretched my arms as I pondered the possibilities. Skinwalkers had magic powers, according to these forum posts. As for skin divers… I wasn't sure. So far, they could morph their eyes and take over people's bodies to kill them. That could be magical, sure. But I read nothing about Skinwalkers diving into people's backs.

I left the website open and turned off the monitor

Maybe I should make a website of my own, I thought, then laughed at the idea.

Summer was around the corner and Amy and I were about to go on a little camping trip. I had loaded up my car and was driving down Silver Street to go and pick her up, when my cell started ringing. I slowed down, grabbed the phone from my pocket and answered it.

"Sup, bro?" I said gleefully.

"James, you sitting down?" Michael's voice sounded gruff and his tone was dead-serious.

"Eh, yeah, driving though. Give me… thirty sec, I'll be parked then." I turned the corner and drove onto Summer Street, then took the first turn to the right and parked on Amy's driveway.

All the while, Michael was breathing heavily into the phone.

"Alright, I'm parked. What's up, man? You sound panicked."

"It's Dad," he said. He paused for a moment. "There's something wrong with his heart. He's been rushed to the ER."

I turned off the engine and sat there, silently.

"He's had high blood pressure for years, and apparently, his medication didn't quite take—or maybe he just failed to take his pills… I don't really know."

"O-okay," I stuttered. "So what do you want me to do?"

He was silent for a moment. "What I want you to do? What the fuck do you mean, dude? I'm calling you to say that our father's in the fucking ER. What the fuck do *you* want to do?"

"Bro, I don't know. I didn't even know he had high blood pressure. I barely talked to him."

"Well, fuck me," he snapped. "Look, you can do whatever the fuck you want. I just thought it'd make sense if we'd go and visit him. Together, you know. He's our father."

"Well, yeah, fine. I mean…" I tried to gather my thoughts. "What about Drew?"

"Yeah, he knows. He's at the hospital right now, waiting. He's the one who called me, actually. He was having breakfast with him when he suddenly collapsed. He just… went limp. Hit his head on the table and everything. Said it was a bloody mess. He had to call 911 and take Nancy and Pam into the other room and distract 'em with some cartoon on the TV. This was his weekend with them, you know. It's fucking awful. Seeing your dad collapse like that, when you're *that* young."

Andrew appeared before my mind's eye—he was only six years old when everything went to hell.

"So yeah, get your ass over here, little bro. Fix something with your boss. We're not sure if he'll make it…" his voice died away. "So, just… be prepared, you know."

"Yeah, alright, I'll-" I saw Amy stepping out the front door with a suitcase and a giant bag. "I'll work something out. See you in a bit, okay?"

"Drive safely," Michael said, nearly out of breath, and he hung up right after.

I got out of the car and looked at Amy. She could see tell something was wrong from the look in my eyes.

"What's wrong?" she asked.

"It's my dad, hon."

"Oh no, what happened?"

"Something's wrong with his heart, and he's in the ER. I gotta drive down there. Like, now."

She let go of her bags and quickly walked up to me, hugging me tightly. "Are you going to be okay? Do you need company?"

"I'll be picking up Michael. And Stacy, probably."

"I can go with you. I really don't mind. I want to be there for you."

I sighed and shook my head. She'd never even met my father and I wasn't sure if now was the right time. "Thanks, but…"

She eyed me a little nervously, then nodded. "Alright, baby. Just… call me, okay?"

"Yeah, I will." I got back into my car and watched her turn around with her shoulders slumped. "I'm sorry," I added loudly.

"Don't be. Go and see your dad, James. Give him my best."

So, instead of enjoying the summer breeze and swimming in Ricker
Pond with Amy, I drove down to Boston and picked up Michael and
Stacy for an awkward road trip toward Philly. Destination: the hospital
near Whitman Park.
"What'd you need a fucking tent for?" Michael asked as he sat down in
the passenger's seat and looked back at Stacy.
"I was gonna go camping with Amy."
"Oh." He suddenly chuckled. "Figures. Why didn't you bring her along?"
I shrugged. "I don't know. You guys've never even met her, neither has
Dad."
"He wouldn't have minded. The house is big enough."
"Let's just go," I sighed.
Michael nodded. "Yeah, before we set up camp here."

The 6-hour ride seemed to take forever. We took two short breaks,
during which Michael joined me for a cigarette. He wasn't a smoker—
never had been—but today, he was.

When we arrived in the hospital, we spotted Andrew pretty quickly.
Brooke was sitting by his side in the waiting area, holding his hand. We
greeted them with warm hugs and poured ourselves some coffee from
the machine.
I looked around. There was no one else, just the five of us. It was quiet,
except for the hum of the fluorescent lights above and the occasional
murmur from the nurses at the nearby station. A large window offered a
view of the courtyard, but none of us were paying attention to that.
Michael was slouched in a stiff-backed chair, his foot rhythmically
tapping on the floor. His eyes were glued to his phone, but I don't think
he was seeing anything. Stacy placed her hand on his knee, gently
reassuring him without a word.
Andrew was pacing around the room, holding his fifth cup of coffee
since Michael and I arrived. Every few seconds, his eyes darted toward
the door. Brooke kept glancing at him, biting her nails.

I regretted not bringing Amy with me. Sitting there, I felt like the odd one out. This whole situation felt off—I had the least connection to our father. In my mind, we barely had a relationship. Not since he walked out. Those weekend visits every other week? They were never enough to building something real, something lasting. And then, of course, he had his new family.

After that realization on that uncomfortable chair in the waiting room, I felt more connected to Kimberley than ever. We both had fathers who barely paid attention to us. And if they did, they directed it elsewhere. For her, it was her sister. For me, it was my older, more responsible brother and my younger brother in need.

Time seemed to stretch on endlessly in that fluorescent-lit waiting room, and I hated it. The clock ticked like a fucking bomb, while we just kept on waiting, hoping for some news. Hoping for the doctor to get his ass out here and tell us what's what.

Finally, the door swung open and a man in doctor's uniform entered. All eyes in the room snapped to him and Michael immediately got up. His expression was calm but serious.

"Mr. Hunter?" the man addressed Andrew, recognizing him as the one who'd brought in my father.

"Yeah," Andrew responded with a small voice.

Michael walked over to them. "I've got this. Sit," he said, softly patting Andrew on the back. He shook the doctor's hand, who introduced himself as Dr. Phelps.

"Your father has made it through the initial assessment," Dr. Phelps said with a reassuring nod. "He experienced a significant cardiac event, likely due to arrhythmia, which is why he collapsed. We were able to stabilize him and he's now out of immediate danger."

A collective exhale echoed between the walls. Brooke squeezed Andrew's arm.

"The good news is that he's conscious and responsive," the doctor continued. "But, his heart condition is serious." He gave a stern look. "We're recommending a pacemaker to help regulate his heart rhythm and prevent other episodes. It's a relatively common procedure, but there are

risks involved, as is with any surgery. We can go over those in detail
before we start."
Michael nodded slowly. "Thank you, doctor. Can we see him?"
"Yes, certainly, but it has to be brief. He's still quite fragile." Dr. Phelps
smiled, then led us down the corridor to the room where our father lay.
Michael was one step in front of us all the way and he was the first to
reach the door. He put his hand on the handle and hesitated for a
moment. He exchanged looks with Stacy, took a deep breath and opened
the door.
Inside, Charles lay in a hospital bed, propped up with some pillows. He
looked awfully pale and exhausted, and there was an IV stuck in his arm.
On his chest was a heart monitor, and around him were monitors
beeping softly. His eyes lit up when he saw us.
"Hey there, old man," Michael said softly as he approached the bed, his
voice nearly cracking.
Our father smiled weakly. "I must've scared the shit out of you all, huh?"
Stacy moved to the other side of the bed, taking his hand in hers. "You
bet you did, but you're okay now. That's all that matters."
Andrew stepped a little closer and Charles reached out to him.
"Come here, son." He took Andrew's hand and squeezed tightly.
Andrew broke down, right then and there, as Brooke gently stroked his
back.
I stood back a little, observing the whole situation, until my father finally
looked at me.
"I'm glad you're here, boy," he said, his voice low.
I nodded, swallowing the lump in my throat.

Michael had a thorough talk with the doctor later that day while Andrew
and I just sort of listened. The doc explained everything about the
procedure, and Michael gave the go-ahead.
Our father would need to stay in the hospital for three to five days, so
that they could monitor him. After that, he'd have to rest at home for
several weeks to regain his strength and adapt to the pacemaker.
I took a full week off work to be there with everyone, sleeping in the
study at our father's house. Michael and Stacy took the second bedroom,

which had been intended for Nancy and Pam. Andrew and Brooke slept at home, since they lived nearby anyway.

After that week, I drove back up to Dover by myself. Michael and Stacy wanted to stay longer and told me they'd catch a cab or something. I figured Charles was doing well enough by now, and honestly, I just wanted to get away. Even when there were four of us, I still felt like the fifth wheel.

Back in town, I hit the gas station to fill my baby up. That's where I spotted Scott across the lot, standing next to his worn-out truck. I got out of the car and glanced at him. He seemed to be struggling to open the gas cap.

"Need a hand with that?" I asked.

"I can manage." He glared at me for a moment.

I walked over to him anyway. "It looks like it's stuck."

"No fucking shit, Sherlock."

"I can-"

"I said I can manage, damn it!" The cap finally gave way and he grumbled. "Don't need no help. Especially from some kid from the city." He looked at my car. "Thinking he knows it all," he muttered under his breath.

"I don't know it all. I just know about cars."

"Well, ain't you special?" he replied sarcastically.

I smirked. "Yeah, I get that a lot."

He put in the gas hose and started pumping gas. "You done tryin' to make friends yet?"

"I wouldn't say friends," I said with a shrug. "But if you ever need a hand-"

"If I need a hand, you'll be the last fucker I ask. Got it?"

I bit my lip. "Got it."

"Now, fuck off in that plastic toy of yours."

"Have a nice day, Scott." I walked back to my car and started filling her up. I glanced at Scott, who slammed the cap back on. If I was gonna crack this dude, I'd have to come up with other methods, I thought, or just be even more persistent.

A few days later, I went to the grocery store to buy food. I wanted to stock up on some canned goods, just in case. I walked through the aisle and grabbed some beans, corn and tuna. I wandered over to the next aisle and as I rounded the corner, I spotted an all too familiar figure in front of the pickles section.

"Didn't peg you for a pickle guy, Scott," I said with a grin.

He glanced up, clearly not amused. "You followin' me now?"

"Nah, just doing some shopping," I responded casually. "Didn't know this was your turf."

"It ain't. Just don't like bein' bothered. Seems you forget that."

"Not trying to bother you. Just wanted to say hi."

He gave me a hard look, sizing me up. "Why, you think we're *pals* now, 'cause you spilled some sob story 'bout your murderous mommy? Or 'cause you think there's some monster goin' around killing people?"

I felt my hands ball into fists. There were some things you didn't joke about—my family and the skin divers topped that list. "You ever get tired of being a grumpy old bastard?" I blurted out before I could stop myself. *Fuuuck.* He was probably going to kick my ass—or worse. I was pretty sure he carried a gun everywhere, and he seemed like the type who wouldn't hesitate to use it, even in a grocery store next to a row of canned pickles.

His eyes narrowed. "You got a death wish, kid?"

"No, I'm serious." I decided to push through, half-expecting to end up as tomorrow's headline: *Death by Pickles.*

He studied me for a moment, then shrugged. "If you're bored, go pick up girls. Got the face for it."

"Why, thank you," I replied with a smirk.

"Wasn't a compliment, kid."

"I'll take it anyway."

He snorted. "You would."

When I got home, I kicked off my shoes and grabbed the last beer from the fridge. I cranked up the AC, sank into the couch, heaved a heavy sigh, and took a long sip.

I replayed the grocery store encounter with Scott in my head. That was reckless of me—he could've easily killed me right then and there. I was lucky he seemed to almost appreciate the insult.

I took another gulp.

I got off Scott-free, I thought to myself, and nearly choked.

Chapter 8

On Monday afternoon, I went to buy groceries. I had run out of pretty much everything, including beer. Just as I was reaching for a Budweiser six-pack, I heard a voice next to me.

"Budweiser, huh? Yeah, I took you for that kind of guy."

I looked up, slightly agitated, and saw William, standing just a foot away.

"Well, you got me," I said, raising my hands in mock surrender.

He stared at me. A faint smile began to unfold on his face. "Not yet, I do," he muttered.

I narrowed my eyes. "What's that supposed to mean?"

"I keep going over your statement," he replied. "A cat…" He looked at the beer on the shelves. "You *think* it was a cat." His fingers brushed the Budweiser price tag. "Why a cat, James? Why couldn't it have been a dog?"

"It could've been," I answered, trying to keep my tone casual.

"Indeed it could. But that's not what you said. You insisted it was cat."

"Yeah, well, it was on the loose, so-"

"So?" His eyes locked onto mine. "We get the occasional call about a dog off its leash. Not common, but it happens."

"Well, maybe it was a dog then," I said, feeling a tightening in my chest. "A small one, though."

"Did you see it cross the street?"

"No, it was on the sidewalk," I replied, my pulse quickening. "It was close, so it must've been why driver swerved. Don't you think?"

He squinted, then smiled again. "Who knows what I think?" He glanced around the isle. "You have a history of mentioning dog-like creatures in relation to car accidents."

"What do you mean? It was just the one." I grabbed the six-pack and eyed it intently, getting increasingly nervous. What the fuck was up with this guy? Why was he grilling me like that? Did he know something?

"The guy woke up from his coma," he continued, dodging my question. "Did you know that?"

"Yeah, I've seen him on his porch."

"I bet you have." He eyed me intently.

I froze for a moment, then forced myself to look at him. "Is there anything I can help with?"

"That's what I'm trying to find out," he replied in a sharp tone. "I think there's more to the story. There's something you're not telling me, and I'm going to find out what it is."

I grinned, though my hands tightened around the six-pack. "Good luck with your investigation," I said, turning away from him.

"Don't need it," he responded as I walked way from him. "Just need a sharp mind, James."

I inhaled slowly as I made my way to the cashier.

I replanned my outing with Amy and picked her up in the early morning, the next weekend.

She seemed happier than ever and was constantly laughing at my jokes—even though they weren't all that funny. I appreciated her efforts nonetheless.

We went swimming in Ricker Pond, made lunch together, went for a hike and visited a waterfall. I fucked her against a tree near the waterfall before we headed back our cabin—no tent this time—and took a shower.

Later, we made dinner and ate it on the little porch, complemented by a drink—beer for me, wine for her. We watched the stars that night and had sex again before falling asleep.

The next day, we went for a long hike and took a break near a large rock. We sat down to have some food and water. Before resuming our walk, I went down on her. The birds flew up from the trees around us as she came.

We drove back home that evening.

If this was what a serious relationship was like, you could count me in, I thought. I considered asking her to be my girl as I dropped her off at her place, but I bit my tongue. I didn't want to fuck up what we had. And what we had was sweet. Damn.

As I drove back home, I naturally took to New Rochester Road. I'd
gotten so accustomed to this route, trying to get Scott warmed up to me,
that I didn't even consider taking my old route. My stereo blasted as I
drew near his house. He was sitting on his porch, probably watching the
sunset, with a beer and a cig. He looked up and shook his head.
I turned the volume down, parked my car to the curb and got out.
"Tryin' to make me go deaf?" he barked at me.
"Just enjoying some music, Scott," I hollered back at him.
"You call that music? You're a fucking idiot. It's garbage, that's what it
is."
I walked up to him. "Porch looks good."
"Tends to be like that, with no cars in it," he said as he eyed me. It wasn't
a glare, for a change.
I scratched the back of my head.
"Why you here, city boy?"
I shrugged. "Just saw you out."
"And figured you'd come and annoy me, instead of letting me enjoy my
sunset in peace." He gestured toward the sky with his beer. "Isn't that
just abso-fuckin'-lutely fucktastic," he added sarcastically.
"Yeah, it does look fantastic," I replied, feigning ignorance.
He snorted. "Y'know… If you keep coming 'round here, I might need to
start chargin' you for the privilege. I don't do no charity."
For a moment, I thought of telling him to enjoy the sunset by his lone
fucking self, and taking off. But I was headstrong. "Mind if I sit here for
a bit?"
He looked me up and down, squinting his eyes. "Long as you don't talk,"
he grunted.
"Fair enough." There was no other chair, so I sat down on the little
stairs, basically at his feet.
We sat in silence, watching the sky turn bright red and the world go by.
Some guy walked his poodle and nearly let it shit on Scott's yard, until he
saw him glaring at him.
A young couple drove by with the windows down, blasting their music
louder than I had, which was followed by some swearing on Scott's part,
which I won't repeat.

A bird landed on the roof of his truck and then hopped onto the driveway as Scott threw down old pieces of bread.

After nearly half an hour, he said his first word to me. "Beer?"

"Yeah, if you've got some."

He stood up from his chair, groaning softly, and walked inside. He came out with another Bud and handed it to me.

"Thanks."

"I'll put it on your tab," he muttered. "So, what's your endgame here?" he asked. "Wear me down with your constant whining or just hope that I'll eventually find you tolerable?"

"Would that work?" I smirked.

He shrugged. Then he suddenly jumped up. "Fuck me with a fiddlestick!" he yelled. He ran inside the house.

My eyes widened. "What the—?"

The floorboards creaked as he stepped back onto the porch, cocking his hunting rifle.

I jumped up and nearly fell over my own feet as I stumbled off the porch, trying to get away from him.

I was halfway to my car when I saw what he had seen. My body froze. The poodle.

It was right in front of me. The leash was still attached to its collar, but its owner was nowhere in sight. And I—no, we—already knew his fate because we saw the eyes of that poodle.

"Move!" Scott yelled in my ear, shoving me to the side.

I fell down on the grass and heard the crack of his rifle as he fired. The poodle… screamed.

It didn't bark or yelp; it screamed in a primal, harrowing wail, like a harpy gone berserk.

I covered my ears and looked on as Scott fired a second time.

Blood splattered on the streets, as dark-red as the sky had become, and the poodle twitched in its final moments. Its eyes slowly morphed back to their regular size, the uncanny bulge disappearing with its final breath.

I scrambled to my feet, my heart pounding, as Scott rushed forward. He kneeled down and inspected the scene from up close, his face grim.

I staggered over to him and looked down at the poodle.

"You alright?" he asked with a rough voice.

"Yeah, thanks. That was-" I swallowed hard, trying to steady my voice.

"That was close."

He grunted and put his rifle down as the neighbors flocked out of their houses toward us.

"Why'd you stand there looking like a fucking idiot?" he barked at me. "You blocked my aim."

"Sorry, I just-"

"You nearly got yourself killed, kid. Again." His tone softened a little. One of the neighbors approached us—she was an elderly lady, who looked to be in her 80s. "What is going on here, Scott? Why'd you shoot the poodle?"

"Nothin' to see here, Betty. Just a stray."

"But that looks like Donald's dog."

Another neighbor chimed in. "Yes, it is. I saw him walking it just a while ago."

"Well, Donald's got a rabid dog. I did you all a favor, so get the fuck off my back," Scott snapped at them.

"You okay, Scotty?" Betty asked with watery eyes.

I looked at her with confusion and amazement. *Scotty?* For a second, I feared he'd grab his gun and empty it on her.

"Fine, Betty. Go to bed," he grumbled.

She put a hand on his shoulder and pinched, then turned to the other nosy neighbors. "You heard the man, go back inside. Nothing to see here." She urged them all to go back to their houses, and so they did. She looked at Scott. "I'm sorry you had to do that."

He shrugged. "Night, Betty." He grabbed his rifle and walked back to his porch.

"Excuse me," I said to the elderly lady, Betty.

She looked at me with big doe eyes. "Well, aren't you a handsome young man. What's wrong, looker?"

I wanted to ask her why she called him Scotty, but changed my question. "How long have you known him?"

"Donald? Well, he moved here about five years ago, and that dog of his… ah, it just kept yapping and yapping. You like dogs? Never get a poodle. Don't. Ever. Not in a million years. Damn dog would shit on everybody's lawn. And it stank, oh Lord. The stink! Not sure what it ate, but from the way it smelled, you'd think it was long dead before." She nodded at the dog.

I intended to interrupt her at first, but I was baffled.

"Until Scott learned him a lesson, that is." She pointed at me with her finger. "Don't you ever get on his bad side, sugar."

"Wasn't planning to. But what about you and Scott? How long have you known him?"

"Scotty and I go back ages. Even before the military. After, he was just… someone else, I guess. Oh, the horror he must've witnessed—my heart hurts for him. But I must say, it's pretty rare to see him have company over." She looked at the porch. "Best not make him wait, though. When it comes to anything else, he is patient like a saint. But not when it comes to people."

"I'll keep that in mind."

She nodded. "I'm sure we'll talk again soon. Take care now, sugar," she said with a wink before shuffling off.

I stared at the poodle and turned around, only to be shoved out of the way again by Scott, who was carrying a cardboard box.

He kneeled down, put the box next to the poodle and started shoving it inside with the tip of his rifle.

"What are you doing?"

"What's it look like, kid? It's a dead one." He got up and carried the box inside his house.

I walked up to his front door and hesitated, the tips of my feet touching his doorway. He hadn't ushered me in and I didn't see him anymore. I figured he was the type of guy who'd shot you if you stepped foot inside his house, uninvited.

"Kid!" he shouted from somewhere farther away.

I stepped inside, quickly glancing around. I walked through his living room, trying not to eye his stuff too much, and made my way into the kitchen. The back door was open, so I stepped outside into his backyard. Under the dim light of the fading sun, I saw a shooting range— improvised, it seemed—a garden, and a large shed. The shed doors were open and the lights were on. Scott was inside, standing at a workbench and emptying the contents of the box onto it.

I walked over to him.

"Close the doors," he barked.

I pulled the doors shut and stood beside him, feeling the wind ruffle my hair. This shed was anything but isolated.

"Took you long enough."

"I was talking to Betty. She seems friendly."

He turned to me and stared me dead in the eyes. "You nearly died just now and your first fucking instinct is to get chummy with the neighbors?" He shook his head. "You're a weird one, I'm telling you. Or just an idiot. Either way, grab a knife, will you." He gestured to a plastic box on top of a cabinet.

Inside the box were several different knives: small ones—probably meant for gutting fish, given the fishing poles on the wall; large ones, like a machete—possibly used for clearing overgrowth or splitting wood; and medium-sized ones. I grabbed one of those and handed it to him.

He looked at it. "Hm. Maybe you ain't dumb, after all," he muttered. He brought the knife to the poodle's neck and started cutting.

I took a step back, disgusted and in awe. "Why are you cutting into it?"

"Ever see survivalist movies?"

"Some."

"Figures. Kids nowadays get all their wisdom from that square box." He grunted, pulling back the poodles skin.

I turned away, my stomach churning.

He laughed loudly. "Ain't got the stomach for it, huh? Well, I'll let you know when the coast's clear, princess." His laughter lingered as I found myself inspecting the back of his shed, which looked like it had been converted into a personal gym.

I did so, not out of curiosity, but out of sheer necessity. If I didn't direct my attention elsewhere, I was gonna puke all over the damn floor. I resisted the urge to put my hands over my ears, wanting to block out the nasty, spluttering sounds. I really didn't want to give him more ammo for name-calling. Knowing him, even just a little, he'd stick with whatever nickname he came up with until the end of time. I just hoped 'princess' wasn't one of them.

"You can look now, kid."

I turned around and stared at what was left of the poodle.

It was completely skinned, its fur lying in a pool of blood.

"The fuck you do?" I gasped for air.

"Gotta see what's inside. Ain't you curious? You finally got your skin eater, didn't you?"

"Skin diver," I corrected.

"Whatever."

"So, is there anything different? I mean, different from usual?"

He gave me a look. "What do you mean, usual? I don't go around skinning dogs, you fool."

I heaved a heavy sigh. "You know what I mean."

"Not sure yet. Gotta cut it open first," he replied, shoving the knife into its neck and slicing its flesh open all the way to the belly.

I was too slow to turn away. My knees buckled, and I had to catch myself as I puked.

He laughed, then grumbled, "I ain't fucking cleaning that."

I wiped my mouth, shaking my head.

"What the…" he mumbled.

"What's wrong?"

He didn't answer.

Even though I really didn't want to, I took a deep breath and turned around to look at the horrific scene. Scott stood frozen in front of the workbench, just staring down at the poodle's corpse, his hands stretching the sides of its cut-open belly.

I suppressed another round of nausea and looked inside the gaping hole.

He turned his head and looked at me, puzzled.

"What *is* that?" I asked, covering my nose and mouth.

"It looks like…" he began, before sliding one hand into the hole and pulling it back out. "Ash."

He opened his hand, letting the ashes from the poodle's inside scatter onto the workbench. The flakes were mostly black and they swayed in the wind.

106

"Is it safe to touch? What if you breathe it in?" I asked, concerned.

"I've breathed in far worse than this, kid," he replied in a gruff voice. He forcefully pulled the flaps of the belly further until the poodle was nearly turned inside out.

I turned away and retched again.

This time, he didn't laugh. He just silently continued inspecting the bloody corpse. "There's nothing in here," he muttered. "No organs. No bones. No nothing. Just fuckin' ash. The hell's going on?"

I came to his side and took a closer look at the ash. Then I remembered the Cocker Spaniel diving into Dorothy—it had emitted a cloud of black ash. "Should we store some?" I asked, hesitantly.

"What for? It's ashes," he barked.

"I don't know. Maybe we can have it tested or something. See whether it really is ash or whether it's something else."

"Who's gonna test this shit?"

"I dunno. Don't you have someone from your military days you can reach out to? I mean, you must have some old buddies who could… help." I tried to keep my tone light, as I knew so little about Scott's past and he never said a damn word about it.

His shoulders stiffened and his eyes narrowed. "Why? You think I'm just sittin' on a fucking Rolodex of people I can call up for favors?"

"No, that's not—I just figured, with your background, maybe you know someone who could analyze something like this. Someone you trust."

He let out a sharp breath, more of a grunt than a sigh. The muscle in his jaw twitched. "Trust," he repeated, the word heavy in the air. "You don't just throw that around, kid."

I looked at him and waited patiently for him to elaborate.

"There was a time," he continued, his voice lower now, almost a growl, "when I thought I could rely on the people I served with. We were supposed to have each other's backs. But that… trust… it gets broken. Sometimes in ways you can't come back from."

I listened thoughtfully and wished I understood more. "So, you don't think any of them would help?" I asked carefully.

He shook his head, a bitter smile tugging at the corner of his mouth. "Help? Maybe. Just not for the right reasons—and that's a risk I'm not willing to take. Not with this."

I nodded slowly. "I get that," I said quietly. "We'll figure it out another way. I'll see if I can ask around. Discreetly, of course."

He didn't respond immediately, but after a long pause, he nodded once. "Fine. Grab some cans from over there," he said, as the top layer of the ash got picked up by the wind and blew into the sky.

I followed his gesture and gathered a couple of empty cans—the ones that looked at least slightly clean.

"C'mon, hurry up, kid. Shit's blowing all over the place."

I handed him the glass jars, and he swept the remaining ash into them, screwing the tops on tightly before handing one to me.

"Here, keep this safe. I'll take the rest."

"Why split it?" I asked.

"You never know who's watching," he grumbled. "If anyone else is onto these skin eaters and they want a piece of this, they'll be coming for it. It's your precious proof, kid. Though, it'll hardly prove shit."

I looked into his eyes, my hand tightening around the jar. "Yeah, alright," I replied.

He grabbed a trashcan and wiped the poodle's remains off the table as if it was nothing more but some faded candy wrappers.

"What do you think happened to David?" I asked.

He shrugged. "Dead, probably."

I bit my lip. "You survived…" I started.

"Told you, my mind's strong like that. David's ain't. Keep up, damn city boy."

"And how would you know?" I snapped back.

He flared his nostrils. "Anyone who goes around buying poodles and letting 'em shit on other people's lawns ain't got a penny for a brain." He then opened the shed doors and hurried back inside the house with the other jar in his hand.

I stepped outside as well and looked up at the night sky. Apart from the light of the moon, it was completely dark. It had been a clear sky all day, but there were no stars to be seen tonight.

Scott came back outside. "Well, what are you standin' round for, idiot?
Go home!" He brushed past me, turned off the lights inside the shed
and locked it.
"Scott," I started.
"Hm?"
"Thanks."
"What for? Saving your ass?"
"That too," I replied. "And for believing me." I swallowed. "So far,
everyone has made me out to be crazy person, including my own family."
He shrugged. "Don't seem as crazy as the other idiots out there, to me."
I smiled.
"Now, go home, kid. I ain't running a hotel."

When I got home, I stored the jar in a heavy wooden box under my bed,
next to where I kept most of my ammo. I thought of Scott's hunting
rifle and how the bullet had blasted through the poodle like it was a stick
of butter. That rifle packed some serious power. I grabbed my handgun
from my nightstand and cursed myself for not keeping it on me. If it
hadn't been for Scott, I would've been dead right now.
The grumpy old dude had saved my fucking life today.
I sank down on my bed with a sigh. At least now I knew that those
fuckers could die—by normal means, even. But how? The poodle didn't
have any intestines to burst, no heart to pierce, no lungs to collapse, no
veins to rupture. So why did it die? Heck, why did it even bleed?
I lay down and cradled my head. I had so many questions—even more
than before. And it felt like I wasn't going to get answers any time soon,
unless I had help.
A lab, I had said. I would ask around to have a lab look at the jar of
ashes. It sounded like a really dumb idea now that my fear had taken a
back seat to my rationality. No lab was going to take this shit. They'd
probably even block me from waltzing inside. But it was the only thing I
could think of back then.

The next day was a work day and I had trouble staying focused. The
images from the night before kept playing over and over in my head, like

a short clip on a loop. It was annoying and exhausting, and Chris, my boss, took notice.

"You doin' alright, James?" he asked, giving me a once-over.

"Yeah, I'm fine," I replied quickly. "Just a little tired."

"You look like a corpse, if you ask me. Sure you're not coming down with something?"

I shook my head. "Nah, just tired, really."

"Alright then. Just make sure you keep an eye on yourself. Don't want another accident like last time." He pointed at the scar on my forearm— courtesy of the metal edge of that rotor. I probably should have gotten stitches, but… eh.

"Jamie's got it covered," Crazy Eddie said in a leisurely tone, hopping over to us without his crutches. "Plus, the bandages are all stocked up. Gotta use 'em on something, right?" He laughed out loud while Chris frowned.

"It's not a laughing matter, Ed," he responded. "These sorts of things, if they happen on my watch—in my shop even—I'm the one responsible."

"I know, C, I know. But you're way too serious. Lighten up," Eddie said, waving his lame hand like it was nothing. "It's not like he lost a limb, like me." He gestured at the place where his right leg used to be. "Only got one left." He winked at me and his laughter filled the shop.

Both Chris and I couldn't keep a straight face.

Damn, if only Scott would have Crazy Eddie's attitude, I thought. It'd be a lot easier to get along with the guy. Then again, I knew nothing of Scott's past, except that, according to Betty, he had been in the military —I wondered if he'd ever tell me about that.

I was at my usual gas station, filling up the tank, when a patrol car pulled up next to me. My heart sank as soon as I saw who it was. Seriously, *again*? What the hell does this guy want now?

William parked right beside me and stepped out. "Fancy seeing you here, James," he said with a casual nod.

"Not too fancy," I replied. My nerves were on edge, but I tried to keep my tone light.

"You know, funny thing about this town—people talk," he continued. His gaze was on me, steady, as if he was monitoring my every reaction. "They mention the strangest things sometimes. Like, how you always seem to be around when something… unusual happens."

I placed the nozzle back, turning to face him. "You know how small towns are. Rumors spread faster than facts."

"True," he said, almost thoughtfully. "But where there's smoke, there's usually something worth looking into. Especially if it involves death…"

My throat tightened and I forced myself to shrug. "I see. Well, have a good day, officer." I turned to head inside to pay.

"It's *detective*, actually," he corrected me in a cold tone. "I guess I forgot to clarify when we met at the station. But you can call me William, if you prefer."

I gave a slight nod, hoping to end the conversation.

He studied me—his eyes narrowed. "You know… you've been looking a little rough around the edges lately. Everything alright?"

"Yeah," I muttered. "Just work and life. You know how it is."

"Sure," he said, a hint of skepticism in his voice. "But you know, stress can do funny things to a man. Makes him see things, hear things… maybe even remember things differently."

I let out a heavy sigh, feeling cornered. "Look, I know you're just doing your job, but it's getting old. Yes, I am stressed. I witnessed a car crash, Kimberley and I broke up, my father was rushed to the ER. How could I not be stressed?"

His expression softened, just slightly. "Is your dad alright?"

I nodded stiffly. "He's recovering."

"I see," he said slowly. "Kimberley, huh? Thought you said she wasn't your girlfriend."

"She wasn't," I snapped. "Doesn't mean it wasn't a breakup."

He held my gaze for a moment longer than I was comfortable with. "Alright then. Well, give my best to your dad. Spend time with him while you can." His voice dropped just a fraction. "You never know when life can take a turn."

With that, he nodded and got back into his car.

As I watched him drive off, eyeing his license plate, a shiver ran down my spine—I couldn't shake the feeling that this was far from over.

Back home, I took the camera from my desk and looked at the video of the bird. I looked at it again and again before turning on my computer and going back down the rabbit hole.

Animals turning into ashes upon death?

I got several hits on cremation processes. I kept scrolling and read about some myths, including the tale of the phoenix.

Next, I tried: *Ashes instead of bones inside dead animals.*

This led me to forums discussing supernatural phenomena, occult rituals and witchcraft, where people talked about using ashes instead of bones for certain ceremonies.

A search for *Dog no bones no organs* brought up scientific and veterinary articles about rare medical conditions—though the bones weren't completely gone; they were either underdeveloped or only some of them were missing. I also stumbled upon a platform where people wrote about horror stories and urban legends.

But so far, nothing matched the skin divers.

My last attempt was: *Skinwalkers turn to ash dog.* Since Skinwalkers seemed the closest match to what I was researching, I hoped this would give me something to go on—but again, I found nothing about them turning to ashes upon death.

I sighed. Creating my own website started to make more and more sense, but I had zero understanding of how to build one. Again, that was something I'd have to ask around for. Maybe Thomas or Riley knew someone. I could ask them without getting too many questions in return, which wouldn't be the case with Amy. I didn't need more questions, and I sure as hell wasn't going to explain the skin diver phenomenon to her. Then, it hit me—Chris would know. Dover Wheels had a website. He'd either built it himself or had someone do it for him.

The next day was a Friday, and I was happy to go to work. If it had been a Saturday and I'd had to wait until Monday to ask Chris… Nah, I was too impatient for that.

112

I went into my garage and looked at my Skyline. I'd had her for almost two years now and she had never let me down. Until today.

I slid into the driver's seat and turned the key, expecting the usual powerful roar of her engine. Instead, I heard a sluggish whirring sound. The engine wouldn't turn over. I frowned and tried again. The dashboard lights flickered and the whirring noise sputtered, followed by a clicking sound.

"Damn it," I said. "Not now!" My hands gripped the wheel tightly. I let out an annoyed sigh, got out of the car and grabbed the jumper cables from the workbench in the corner. Except, I didn't have anything to use them on. My Skyline was my only ride.

I took out my phone and called Riley—he lived closest to me out of all my friends who had cars—but he didn't pick up. That wasn't unusual for him.

Next, I tried Thomas.

"Sup, dude?" he answered.

"Sup. You off today?"

"Nah, man. I'm at work. Why?"

"Ah, never mind. Car won't start."

"That sucks. I'd say use my bike, but you'd have to walk all the way. Don't Amy's folks have a car?"

"Way too far, dude. Might as well walk to work."

"Damn."

"Yeah, well… Anyway, talk to you later."

"Alright, man. Good luck."

"Thanks." I hung up. Now what? Maybe cycling wasn't the worst idea. Kimberley had a bike as well, nowadays, since she'd often go cycling with Thomas, so I figured I might as well ask her. I dialed her number, which was still in my favorites, below Amy.

"James!"

"Hey Kim, what's up?"

"I'm surprised you called. What's going on?"

"Well, my car won't start, so I'm in a bit of a bind."

"Oh no," she replied. "Not your baby," she added in a teasing tone.

"Hehe, yeah. Think you can help me out? If I could borrow your bike today, that'd be great."

"Sure, come on over. I just got out of the shower."

I swallowed, trying not to picture her naked. "Alright, be there in about thirty."

"Alright, babe."

I frowned.

"Ah, sorry…" she said in a soft voice. "Force of habit. See you in a bit." She quickly hung up.

I started walking, taking the fastest route via New Rochester Road while calling Chris to let him know I'd be in late.

I was nearing Lake Street and I glanced over at Scott's place, which had become a bit of a habit for me. He wasn't on his porch, but his truck was parked in the driveway.

Without giving it much thought, I walked up his driveway and onto his porch. "Scott?" I said loudly as I approached the front door.

It took mere seconds before he opened it—I hadn't even knocked yet. "What?" he barked at me.

I nearly flinched. "You busy?"

"Fuck you want, boy?"

"Car trouble." I glanced at his Chevy. "I need a jump. Could you help me out?"

He stared at me for a moment and then started laughing, loudly. "Rice rocket finally gave out, huh? Told ya, if you got somewhere to go, you do it steady." He walked back inside.

I heard the dangling of a set of keys and a moment later, he stepped onto the porch and vigorously locked the door behind him.

"Plastic ain't made to last," he grumbled as he walked over to his truck. "Nothing reliable about it. Take my Chevy, though, sturdy as a horse." Before he got in the truck, he gave me a look. "Well, you comin' or not?"

As soon as I opened the passenger door, I could smell the old leather and tobacco stench. I shoved some trash to the side, sat down and buckled up. The seatbelt looked tattered, and for a moment I thought I was probably insane for even getting in a car with this guy. The engine sputtered for a moment before he turned the truck onto the street.

The thing rattled and groaned as we drove. And you call *my* car unreliable? I wouldn't be surprised if we got stuck on the side of the road with this rusty old thing. I wondered when this car had last gotten proper maintenance—but I couldn't comment on any of that, given the situation.

Scott drove directly toward Strafford Road—I found it freaky that he remembered my street name from just that one conversation. "Where?" he asked.

"Number six," I replied, pointing at my house.

"Hm," he responded, as if that was a full sentence. He drove up to the garage and I got out of the Chevy.

I opened the garage door, popped the hood of my baby—I heard Scott do the same—and grabbed the jumper cables from my workbench. I turned around, only to see Scott already connecting his clamps.

"I've got…" I started. But it didn't matter.

"Try it," he barked.

I slid into the driver's seat and turned the key. This time, the engine roared to life. I let out a sigh of relief.

Scott quickly disconnected the cables, slammed both hoods shut and tossed the cables in the back of his truck.

I got out, ready to thank him, but he was already backing out of the driveway, so I had to shout my thanks and wave.

He gave a small nod and drove off.

I finally sped down to Dover Wheels, knowing I'd have to replace the battery real soon.

When I arrived at work, I suddenly remembered Kimberley.

I shot her a quick text that said: *Got help. At work. Thanks.*

I got a reply almost instantly.

Yay! Glad to hear it. We still on for bbq on Sunday? X

We had agreed on doing some grilling and drinking with our little club: Amy and me, Thomas and Kim, Riley and his newest fling Jane. I shot her a text back to confirm.

"You made it," Chris said as he walked over to me, tucking a cigarette that he was about to smoke behind his ear. He put his hand on my shoulder. "Battery?"

"Yeah. Thought I had more time on it."

He nodded. "Might've been faulty. Go and pop a new one in."

I looked at him questioningly. "Right now?"

"Yeah, the Lexus can wait. Guy's on holiday now anyway, won't be able to pick it up until September." He walked away.

"Thanks, Chris." I smiled, feeling a weight lift off my shoulders. I was able to fix my car today *and* save myself time and money—that's always welcome. "Oh, Chris!" I yelled, running after him.

He turned around. "No running, James."

"Could you tell me how you got the website up and running? For Dover Wheels, I mean? I'm kinda looking into making a website, but I don't know shit about it."

He raised his eyebrows. "I thought you knew. It's Eddie's handiwork."

"Wait, for real?"

He nodded. "He'll be in right before lunch. Got a new round of pain meds."

"Alright, thanks." I walked back over to my workplace, cleared out the vermillion Lexus LC 500 and drove my Skyline in to give her some much needed maintenance. Under normal circumstances, she would've had my undivided attention and I would've picked up on the battery running out. But these weren't normal circumstances. These were strange and chaotic times.

Yet, looking back now, they were actually pretty peaceful and uneventful.

Chapter 9

During lunch I asked Eddie about the website and he said he'd fix something for me—just the basics, but that was all I needed. He was going to try and have it ready for me somewhere in the next two weeks —his new pain meds were taking him for a spin and he had difficulty adjusting.

On my way back home, I saw Scott's truck parked at the local post office, with him alongside it. He was cursing so loudly, I could hear him over my music. I parked a few spots over and got out. "Everything alright, Scott?"
He turned to me and glared—though his glare seemed a little friendlier than before. "Mind your own business," he said in a gruff voice.
"I was just checking. You looked a little heated."
He snapped. "Damn package is late, and they're givin' me the runaround."
"That sucks, man. Need me to talk to them?"
"Yeah, I'm sure they'd listen to you, Mr. City Slicker," he said sarcastically.
"Can't hurt to try, right?"
"Already hurtin' just talkin' to you," he grumbled.
"Glad to know I have that effect," I replied with a grin.
"Just get me my damn package and let me get the hell outta here."
I walked in with him begrudgingly following behind me.
Three minutes later, we walked out with his package. He muttered something under his breath before getting into his truck and driving off.

The next day, I swung by Scott's house with a bottle of scotch, to thank him for jump starting my car.
He didn't even bark at me this time around.
We spent some time on his porch and I watched him meticulously clean his hunting rifle—apparently he'd bought a new scope for it, since his old one was busted.

I told him about my idea for the website to share information on the skin divers. He wasn't too thrilled about it, saying how anyone could post anything and how the government is always watching, but he agreed it could be useful. After all, we had so little to go on. Maybe we could even find someone who could analyze the ashes.

"Don't give away too much, kid," he grumbled. "Information is power. Use it wisely."

I looked at him and felt like there was more to his words than he'd let on.

The little get together with my friends on Sunday, complete with stacks of meat and plenty of beer, was set up to be pretty fun and relaxing. But as I sat there, zoning out to Jane talking about her mother's issues with some hair salon in town, I got this strange feeling. The sort of uneasy feeling that tells you that you're running out of time. I felt like there were more important things to focus on. There were monsters out there, threatening our lives. Just because the threat was nearly invisible, didn't mean it wasn't present. Just take that damn poodle, for example. I was vigilant most of the time, but when it truly mattered, I had to rely on Scott to save my fucking ass. If he hadn't been there, I'd be six feet down already.

All I wanted was to create that website and put up every single encounter I had had with the skin divers and every clue I could think of. Including the video of the bird and some photos of the jar with ashes.

Someone out there would know more. Someone out there had seen them too and was trying to do something about it. Maybe they were looking for me, too, wanting someone to believe them.

I was so caught up in my own head, that I barely paid attention to Riley. I couldn't see the pain he was dealing with at the time.

His uncle had lost his battle with cancer.

In the following weeks, I threw myself into my little side project. Eddie managed to get the website up and running sooner than expected. It was bare-bones, but functional: a simple forum layout where I could post media, and where others could comment and share their own experiences. That was perhaps the thing I was most curious about: how many other witnesses were there? Where did they live? Was this a worldwide thing?

It took me some time to figure out how to work the website. I was pretty proud when I made the title say: *Skin Divers—Unexplained Phenomena.*
I also made a subtitle that said:

They look like ordinary pets—dogs, cats, birds. Harmless at first. But then their eyes change. They grow, become dark, bee-like, and they lock onto you. And once they've seen you, there's no escaping. No mercy. Run, or they'll be the last thing you ever see.

I spent hours working on it. I wrote up detailed accounts of my encounters with the skin divers, without giving too much information on my personal situation, since I didn't want anyone tracking this back to me from the get go. I went over the Jack Russell incident and the death of Ashley. I went over the deaths of William and Dorothy, under the aliases Burt and Katy, at the hands—or paws?—of the Cocker Spaniel. I tried to be as clear and methodical as possible, hoping that someone, somewhere, might recognize a pattern or add some crucial information. Then, I started writing about the cat and I got to the part where Scott, alias GOD—Grumpy Old Dude, had survived. I wasn't sure whether I should make this public yet. What if Scott was an anomaly? What if the government really was watching and they were now looking for him? I shook my head. He'd gotten inside my mind lately. But he did have a point about information being power.

Following his advice, I didn't post any of the media. Not yet. I first needed something concrete. Something tangible. I needed to find other witnesses, and I hoped they'd find this website somewhere along the way. The whole process started to feel like a race against time, and I couldn't help but think I should've built this website ages ago. I could've met up with others already—others who believed me. Deep down, I knew I should be grateful for just Scott believing me, but I was greedy. I wanted more people to know the threat was real. I needed to warn them.

That constant uneasiness just wouldn't go away, and it made me drink more than I should.

Before publishing the website, I decided to walk through it with Scott. He'd likely have some adjustments and it kinda felt like we were in this together now—some strange fucking partnership. But as long as it served its purpose, I was fine with it.

I drove over to Scott's on Tuesday evening, around 10 p.m. to ask him to come back to my place, since I didn't have a laptop back then and it would be a waste of time and energy to drag my computer across the streets. But when I arrived, his truck wasn't on the driveway and the lights inside were off.

I drove back, feeling a little disappointed, and went to bed.

I was restless and distracted during my shift at Dover Wheels. Chris noticed it and he gave me a few sympathetic glances, but didn't pry. He was a good guy like that.

After work, I drove down New Rochester Road and looked out in the distance, trying to see if I could spot Scott's truck from far away.

I sped down the street, being the impatient bastard that I was, and saw his Chevy. I parked my baby in front and walked up to his porch.

"Scott," I said loudly, knocking on the door.

There was no answer.

I tried again. "Scott!"

Nothing.

Then, a shot fired.

I shrunk down and looked around. *It came from nearby.* I ran off the porch and around the house, straight into his backyard. I spotted Scott, standing with his feet apart and his hunting rifle in his hands, firing away at his practice targets.

As I started walking over to him, he suddenly turned around and aimed the scope at me.

The deadly stare in his eyes ran a cold shiver up my spine, and for a moment I believed he would pull the trigger.

"Scott," I said hesitantly.

He blinked and slightly raised his head. "Kid?" He slowly lowered the rifle. "Don't go strollin' into other people's yards, you fucktwat," he snapped.

"I heard a gunshot and I… I just thought…"

"Thought the grumpy old dude bit the dust?" He snorted.

I chuckled. He was either gonna like or hate the nickname I gave him on the website.

"What you grinnin' for? You look like a fool."

"I wanted to show you the website," I replied.

"Not now, kid. I'm honing my skills, as you can see." He gestured at a few empty beer cans he had lined up on a wooden fence somewhere halfway across his makeshift shooting range. He reloaded the rifle and took aim at the cans. He shot three bullets in quick succession and three out of five cans took a hit and fell to the ground.

"Shit," I exclaimed. "How far you shooting at?"

"About two-hundred," he replied casually.

"That's impressive."

"Ain't nothing to brag about, kid."

"Can you teach me?" I blurted out.

He turned to look at me. "You must be kiddin' me," he said, with half a scowl and half a smile.

"No, I'm serious."

He gave me a once-over. "Well, what do you know. Shit-for-brains wants to pick up *hunting*."

"Not just hunting," I said. "I want to be able to protect myself. And others," I added. "I have a handgun. Got my permit, too."

He eyed me up and down. "What're you packin'?"

"Glock 19."

He snorted. "A Glock, huh? You plannin' on takin' out paper targets, or you actually wanna stop something? Pea shooter won't do you much good if you're up against 'em skin eaters."

"It's reliable," I said defensively. "Never jams."

"Yeah, and so's a stapler, but I wouldn't bring one to a gunfight. Get yourself something with a fucking punch."

"Soon as I can shoot," I replied with a slight smirk.

He looked at me and I could nearly see the cogs turning in his head as he was thinking.

"Yeah, alright. I'll teach you, city boy. Just try not blow anyone's foot off, especially mine." He put down the rifle and walked over to the beer cans at a leisurely pace. He put the fallen cans back up and grabbed a few glass bottles from a box next to the fence, neatly lining them up beside each other. He then went into his shed and came back out a little later, carrying earmuffs, gloves and safety glasses—nearly identical to the ones he was wearing.

He walked back toward me, staring the entire way.

I felt like I was some small game about to be hunted. The look in his piercing eyes reminded me of the skin divers's stare—like a predator locking onto its prey.

He shoved the equipment into my hands. "Here, kid. Put these on. Don't want you blowing out your eardrums or getting a piece of brass in your eye. Safety first. Always."

"Thanks," I replied. "What are the gloves for?" I asked, only understanding the need for earmuffs and safety glasses, since I had worn them when getting my firearms license.

"They'll help with the recoil and give better grip. Don't need 'em for a squirrel deterrent like yours, but they come in handy for these." He grabbed his rifle, reloaded it and handed it to me. "Alright, first thing's first," he said. "Don't treat it like a fucking toy. This is serious business. Got it?"

I nodded. "Got it."

"Good. Now, put the butt of the rifle against your shoulder and aim at one of those cans."

I examined the rifle for a moment and put it against my shoulder, awkwardly trying to balance it. "This feels like I'm holding a small tree."

"Yeah, well, you're not exactly known for your firm grip. Just remember, it's heavier than it looks, and your shoulder's gonna fucking feel it."

I took aim and breathed out slowly.

"And try not to kill my neighbor," he grumbled. "I'll never hear the end of it."

I slightly lowered the rifle. "What if I miss?"

"You will. It's part of the fun."

122

"Great. I've always wanted my first handling of a rifle to be a total disaster."

He rolled his eyes. "Just pull the damn trigger."

I concentrated, took aim and pulled the trigger. The rifle kicked back so hard it made me stumble. "Whoa!" I exclaimed. "It kicks like a mule."

Scott laughed out loud. "Yeah, it's called recoil. Welcome to shooting. Now try not to let it knock you into the next county. Try again."

I tried three more times, missing my shots at all times.

"Now you're just wasting bullets," he said, although he didn't seem too pissed about it. "Try to hit this time, yeah?" He suddenly kicked my shin and I nearly lost my balance. "See, that's one weak fucking stance. Root your feet."

I followed his advice, took aim once more, pulled the trigger… and missed again. "Don't you have a scope or something?"

"There's sights on there, idiot."

"Yeah, but…" I sighed.

"Just get used to it," he mumbled, as he pulled out a steel bipod. "And use this. You ain't got the stability for this shit." He put the bipod on the ground and made me sit down.

I tried again and again, now with the added stability, until the clip was empty and popped out.

"Pick that up." He took the rifle from my hands and I thought practice was over, but he reloaded it. "Last try, city boy. Eight more rounds. Make your bullets count."

On the very last shot, I was finally in luck. The sound of a can getting hit and falling to the ground was fucking sweet.

"There you go," Scott commented. You ain't completely useless."

I pulled back my shoulder and rotated it a bit. "I'm just glad the can didn't retaliate."

"Give it time," he replied. "Those cans are known to hold grudges."

I couldn't contain my laughter and I swear I could see a smile form on his face, although he quickly concealed it.

"That's enough for now. Your princess skin's gonna bruise as it is, with the way you're handling it. We'll pick it up on Saturday." He grabbed the rifle from my hands and gave me a stern look. "That is, if you're serious about this."

"I am," I replied as I got up, looking him dead in the eyes. "I can't have another poodle fuck-up."

He squinted his eyes for a moment, then nodded. "Every Saturday. Three p.m., sharp."

"Alright. So, about the website…"

"Yeah, yeah. I'll follow you home tomorrow. Just don't think I'll be stayin' for tea and cookies."

I chuckled and walked back to my car, my shoulder sore from the kickback, with a feeling that could only be described as pride. I was a shitty gunman and it even made Scott laugh—but I felt like I was at least making some progress.

On Thursday afternoon, right after work, I sped back over to Scott's and slowed down in front of his driveway.

He was sitting on his porch, but he got up as soon as he saw me and walked over to his truck. He held his hand up and I thought he was waving at me, but it turned out he was waving at Betty, who was standing in front of her window, curiously eyeing us.

I drove down a bit and heard his truckle rattle and puff as he steered out of his driveway.

He followed me back to my place.

I parked my Skyline in my garage and closed it while Scott impatiently tapped his foot on the concrete. "Come on in," I said, ushering him to go inside.

"Don't need instructions," he grumbled. He walked in, took a gander around the place and kept standing on the little doormat. "Boots?" he asked in a gruff voice.

"You can put 'em there," I said.

He took off his boots without much fuss and followed me to my bedroom, where my PC sat on my desk. He watched as I booted it and opened the website for him.

I got up from my desk chair and offered it to him.

"Fine where I am, kid," he muttered. His eyes scanned the text on the screen with intent. "Don't call her your mom. Too easy, it'll lead back to you," he said. "How do you fix this?"

I sat back down and edited the Jack Russell story.

"Just call her your neighbor or your fucking grade school teacher or whatever." He looked on as I changed *mom* into *neighbor*. "Right, and don't call it a Jack Russell. Odds are, it'll lead back to you, as well. And why the fuck would you mention the type of car you drove? Who cares? Don't give 'em so much to go on, kid, damn. You're really kinda stupid, aren't you?"

I ignored his remarks on my intelligence and trimmed down the story. We went through the Cocker Spaniel one, and agreed on changing the breed there as well.

"What should I change it to?" I asked.

"I dunno, a German Shepherd? Something common."

"Nah, that's too big. It's gotta be able to jump in people's backs. You're definitely going to feel a German Shepherd. What about a pug?"

He snorted. "A fucking pug? Why not throw in a Chihuahua while you're at it? Really make 'em quake in their boots."

"Alright then, what about calling it a terrier?"

"Yeah, a terrier could work. Small enough, common. No one's gonna think twice about it."

I nodded and made the changes. He wasn't wrong—stripping away those details really did make the stories less identifiable. But it also made them more unsettling, like they could've happened to anyone. Anywhere. But I guess that was the point. No, not *the point*—it was *reality*.

Next, he started reading the story about the cat. About him. "GOD?" he asked.

"You really wanna know?"

"Hit me."

"Grumpy old dude," I said softly.

To my surprise, he chuckled. "Yeah, you can keep it like that. Just refer to me as GOD from now on. That ought to piss people off. Just don't mention that I woke up from my coma. Let them believe that the sole survivor is still down. I don't want no one harassing me."

After making some final changes, he finally gave the go-ahead. It was already six p.m. by the time we launched the website.

"And now we wait," I said, heaving a sigh.

"So, what's this gonna do? You get, like, people talking on this?"

"Yeah, they can respond over here. That is, after they find the site," I explained.

"Site?"

"Website."

He mumbled something.

"It can take a while," I said. "Days or even weeks."

"Ain't gonna watch the grass grow," he replied and he walked out of my room.

I hurried after him. "You want a beer?"

"I want fucking food, kid."

"I can make you some."

He took a long hard look at me, then shook his head. Without saying another word, he put on his boots and went outside. His Chevy rattled down the driveway and I watched him drive off.

I was really hungry as well, but I didn't feel like cooking—not for my lone self, at least. I'd had done plenty of cooking at Kim's condo and sometimes when Amy came over here, but cooking for one person always felt kinda off to me. I usually stuck to simple recipes that didn't require much time or effort and ready-made meals that I could just pop into the oven or microwave. Today, my poison was frozen pizza.

I shoved the pizza in the oven and sat down on my couch, tuning into the TV. I skipped past the boring channels and lingered on the Discovery Channel, where some dude was surviving out in the wild. I recalled Scott's words about getting my wisdom from this square box, and smiled.

I ate my pizza while judging the guy on the screen, wondering how Scott would react in those given situations.

Later that evening, I couldn't resist taking a peek at the Skin Divers website. Crazy Eddie had set up a notification system so I could see when someone replied to one of the posts. But there were no notifications.

I walked back to the living room, grabbed my fifth beer for the day and watched some crime documentary.

That uneasy feeling, that had left for only a little while, was back and it was twice as strong. I could feel a pit growing in my stomach.

A little past eleven p.m. I decided to go to bed, since I still had one day of work before the weekend. I took another glance at my computer, but the website was as dead as it had been before launching it. I read through the three posts that we had put out there:

Skin Diver (Dog Form) killing 5-Year-Old Girl

Back in 1992, a small dog killed a 5-year-old girl on my street. The girl was on the sidewalk and the dog crept up on her. It looked normal, at first, but its eyes suddenly started growing. They became large and oval-shaped, they reminded me of a bee's eyes. It looked unnatural and creepy. Right after its eyes morphed, the dog attacked her. It didn't bite her or knock her down or anything. No, it dove into her back. Like, it disappeared into her skin completely. A car was backing out of a driveway and the girl suddenly slammed into the back bumper. She didn't run, she didn't jump. Her body just got thrown into that car at an unnatural speed, like a limp rag-doll. The girl died before she even reached the bumper. Strange thing was, nobody seemed to have even noticed the dog, nor did they remember it. I was the only one. I really hoped to never experience something like that again, but that was just my first encounter with the creatures I call Skin Divers. Anyone else seen something like this?

Skin Diver Attack (Dog Form) on an Elderly Couple

An elderly couple (let's call them Burt and Katy) were found dead in their home after a skin diver attack. The skin diver had taken on the shape of a terrier, and again, its eyes morphed before its deadly assault. Burt actually had a pacemaker, which malfunctioned due to the presence of the skin diver, and he was practically dead on impact—as soon as that terrier leapt into his back. The terrier then emerged from his body and went for Katy. Its legs could actually be grabbed, meaning it was tangible, but it was too strong for me and it took over her body. She, too, died. The skin diver emerged from her as well and escaped by jumping through the window. This was definitely no normal dog. Anyone else got a similar experience?

Skin Diver (Cat Form) kills Convertible Driver

This one still haunts me. I was biking down the street when I saw a cat strolling along the sidewalk. It looked normal enough. Until it didn't. Its eyes were, again, shaped like those of a bee—giant and uncanny. It locked onto me, like a predator does its prey, and I knew it was going to come for me. I started pedaling like a madman and I only survived because of a convertible driving by: the cat leapt into the driver instead of me, killing him instantly. The car then crashed into a porch, nearly killing the person sitting there (let's call him GOD). The cat emerged from the driver's back and moved on over to GOD. Miraculously, he survived the attack, although he went into a coma. Anyone else experienced something like this?

I called my own profile *Hunter*. It felt fitting. Yes, it was my last name, but I figured nobody was going to guess that. And in a way, I was on the hunt.

I checked back in with the website in the morning, but there was no news. When I drove over to work, I partly considered asking Eddie if the notification function really worked, but I kept my impatience to myself. I also wondered whether he'd look at it. He knew the website, since he had built it, after all. He had the url and everything. I just hoped that if he did look at it, he wasn't going to show it to Chris or any of our colleagues. I really didn't want more people to question my sanity.

That evening, as I was washing my dishes, the notification sound of the website chimed through the doorway. I perked up, quickly finished washing the last glass, and hurried over to my pc.
There was a reply on the first post, by forum user Down2Earth:

Sorry, but this sounds like a wild exaggeration. Dogs attack, sure, but slamming a girl into a car like some kind of superpower? And those 'morphing eyes' sound like something out of a bad horror movie (though that might be your goal). Are you sure you didn't just misinterpret whatever you saw in the heat of the moment? Trauma does shitty things to the mind.

I stared at the screen in disappointment. Well, that's just great, I thought.
It was the very first comment on the website and it was from someone
who didn't believe a word I said. It was practically the same comment
that cop William had made. I sighed. I didn't reply to the comment and
shut down the PC before heading to bed.

The next day was Saturday and that meant: shooting lessons from Scott.
I promised him to be there at precisely 3 p.m. so I drove over a little
early and waited in my car on his driveway. He wasn't on his porch and I
wasn't going to surprise him like last time. If I were to do that again, I'd
get a bullet between my eyes at some point. He had locked onto me like
a predator before, aiming his rifle right at me. I was definitely starting to
become curious about his military past, but I didn't want to pry.
I saw the clock on my phone hit 14:59 and got out of the car. I walked
up to his front door and waited a moment longer before knocking,
loudly. He had no doorbell, so it was always a choice between knocking
or yelling. Since he was expecting me this time, I went with the knock
instead of a yell.
It didn't take long for him to open the door. "You can walk 'round," he
said in his usual gruff voice. Then he slammed the door shut.
I walked around the house and found him standing in front of a table
he'd dragged outside. On the table were his rifle, a scope, a torque
wrench, some rings, other parts, and a piece of cloth. I glanced at the
shooting range and noticed he'd put up a worn, metal plate as a target in
the far distance, hanging from a tree. Several other targets were set up on
makeshift platforms at varying distances. I was eager to learn what Scott
had in mind for me today.
"Watch closely," he said, grabbing the rifle from the table. He wiped off
the mounting area and inspected the scope.
"What kind of rifle is this, anyway?" I asked.
"M1 Garand," he replied in a dry voice.
"And the scope?"
"M84. Does the job." He took a screwdriver and unscrewed the rear
sight from the rifle before installing the mount base, which he screwed in
tightly. He grabbed the torque wrench for some extra tightening.

I watched closely while he placed the scope rings onto the base, aligning
them with the base's mounting slots.

He tightened the ring screws as well. "Don't overdo this," he said in a
stern voice. "Or you'll fuck it up." He then went on to place the M84
scope in the rings. "Now, you gotta align it with the bore of the rifle,
that's called bore sighting, and that's for ensurin' the crosshairs are
aligned with the barrel. You can adjust it like this." He moved the scope a
little forward and then backward before putting it in place in such a
smooth, swift movement that I could instantly tell this was second nature
to him.

"Now you check if it's mounted securely and aligned well. Always do a
double check on the screws and mountin' points." He gave it another
quick wipe, then pointed it at the metal plate. "I'll zero it, so don't worry
'bout that."

"What's that mean?" I asked curiously.

"Gotta adjust the crosshairs to align with the point of impact at a
specific distance. We're lookin' at one hundred here." He peered through
the scope and turned the elevation knob.

"One hundred yards?"

He hummed to confirm. "Cover up," he said, gesturing to the earmuffs,
gloves and safety glasses in a box under the table before handing me the
rifle. "Think you're ready for this?"

"I'll try."

"Well, of course you're gonna try, that ain't my fucking question, kid."

"I'm ready," I said, feeling my heart jump with actual excitement—I
recalled the rush I'd felt after shooting that beer can.

"So, I lined up the sights perfectly for close-range. You're lookin' at the
metal target over there, closest to you."

"Didn't we try two hundred last time?"

"And how many'd you hit?" he snapped. "You wanna learn or not?"
I nodded.

"Then you start with the basics. Can't go buildin' on a faulty base. When
you stop missing this one, you can move on to the next. No sooner. Got
it?"

"I got it."

"I mean it, kid. Don't get cocky and try shootin' farther, 'cause the scope ain't aligned for that. Rookie fucker like you will kill some poor bastard walkin' his dog over there." He nodded toward the horizon. "Might even hit Donald's corpse. Fucker still hasn't been found."

"Safety first," I said.

"Damn right, kid."

All suited up, I took aim at the metal plate closest to me. I breathed out slowly and tried to keep the rifle steady—which wasn't as easy as Scott had made it look.

I took the shot and missed.

I looked at him with a questioning expression.

"Well, what're you lookin' at me for? Target's over there," he grumbled.

I tried again, then heard the metal clanking. I'd hit the plate, but nowhere near the middle.

"Alright, let's try this again," he said. "Remember, you're aiming for the *center* of the target."

"I was," I retorted defensively.

"No, 'cause if you were, that bullet'd be in the middle now, wouldn't it?"

I bit my lip and tried as hard as I could to steady my aim. I took the shot and hit the plate—dead in the center.

"Crap on a cracker," he commented, nearly giddy. "Kid's got spunk."

I smiled and kept on firing the rifle until the clip popped out and hit the ground. I didn't hit the center any of the bullets and several even missed the target completely, but still… I felt proud enough.

"Alright, next up is two hundred," he said, grabbing the rifle from my hands. He froze for a moment, staring into the distance.

I had just grabbed the empty clip from the ground and placed it on the table when I noticed his alert stance. I looked at him and then into the distance, half-expecting another skin diver, but there was nothing to see. He suddenly moved again and shoved the rifle back in my hands. "You reload," he said as he handed me a new clip. He stepped back, pulled out a worn leather pack of cigarettes from his pocket and tapped it against his palm, dislodging a single cigarette. He expertly tapped it into his mouth and lit it with a silver zippo lighter.

I looked at him, drawing a deep breath as the tobacco caught, and inspected the clip. It held eight rounds. "How do I do that, exactly? I mean, I know with the Glock, but this…"
He exhaled a cloud of smoke. His face relaxed for a moment. "Nothing like a smoke on a day like this," he muttered. "Well, kid, first thing's first. Make sure the rifle's clear before you load it. Always a good habit."
I carefully tilted the barrel downwards and checked both the chamber and the clip.
"No strays?"
I shook my head.
"Good. Now, just push it in. Slides as smooth as a pussy."
My eyebrows shot up in surprise. I aligned the clip over the magazine and pressed it down. There was some resistance, but it slid right in there with a firm push. A satisfying *click* sounded as it locked into place. I looked over at Scott, hoping for approval.
He leaned forward, took another drag, and let the smoke escape slowly through his nostrils. "M'kay, now put the bipod in place." He gestured at the steel bipod in the box under the table.
I didn't question him and did as I was told.
"You're gonna realign the scope next. Just do it like I showed you. You're aiming for the red plate over there."
"Is that the two hundred?"
"Hm."
I turned the scope's elevation knob carefully as I peered through the scope, aligning the crosshairs with the metal plate. I took a deep breath to steady myself. "Alright, let's see how this does," I muttered, making a final adjustment.
I fired a shot. The report echoed across the range and the metal plate rang out sharply. A broad smile crept over my face.
"Not bad for a rookie," Scott called out, his tone begrudgingly approving. "But try 'nd hit the center, yeah? Kinda the only shot that counts. Especially if we're up against those skin eaters."
"They're skin divers," I corrected. "Even the website's called that."
"Potato, potato," he responded in a blunt tone.

It took several tries, but I managed to hit the center. With the added stability from the bipod, it seemed harder to completely miss the target. When the clip popped out, I wanted to quickly replace it with a new one.

"Don't rush it," he barked at me.

I froze.

"Make sure everything's in place," he grumbled. "Rushing leads to misfeeds and jams. You don't fuckin' want that."

"Roger," I replied before patiently repeating the reloading steps.

"Alright, on to the next," he muttered.

I continued with the adjustments, moving to 300 yards. This time, the target appeared even smaller through the scope, and I had to be precise. I squinted my eyes and aligned the crosshairs as best as I could.

After some deep breathing, I took another shot—and though the metal plate didn't ring as loudly, it was a hit nonetheless. I felt a surge of confidence.

"Looks like you're getting the hang of it," he said. "Just remember, hitting's one thing, but being consistent is another."

I nodded and wiped the sweat from my brow. "Thanks, Scott."

"Just call me GOD," he said. His rugged laughter filled the air.

Chapter 10

When I got home I turned on my PC and saw that there were a few new replies on the website. My heart skipped a beat as I started reading, but I quickly sighed with disappointment. Most of the comments were in line with what Down2Earth had commented—dismissive and skeptical, suggesting my experiences were tall tales and too far-fetched. Also, some seemed pretty pissed that I used GOD as an acronym.

But there were also comments like the one by UrbanHunter:

Jesus, that's terrifying. I've heard stories like this from some of the older folks in my town. They say that when a creature's eyes shift, you're looking at something that's not really there—a demon or spirit in disguise. Burt and Katy didn't stand a chance.

The buzzing of my phone made me jump up. I checked it and saw a message from Riley:

Frog Pond, you coming?

I stared at it. Fuck… Riley… I'd hadn't been there for him over the past weeks, even though he was dealing with his uncle's death. I'd been so caught up in my own shit, that I'd become a shitty friend. I quickly texted back.

Meet you there.

I entered the bar and spotted Riley in the corner where we'd sat last time. "Riley," I said as I walked over to him, trying to keep my voice steady despite the unease and regret seeping through.

He looked up, his expression shifting from distant to cold. "James," he replied curtly.

I sat down, searching for the right words. "How are you holding up?"

His face tightened and his fingers gripped the glass of whisky in front of him. "Barely," he retorted.

"I should've been there," I started.

"Yeah, you should've," he shot back, glancing at me. "Why weren't you?"

"I'm sorry, I…" I bit my lip. "I had a lot on my mind, and-"

"Fuck's sake, James," he interrupted in a harsh tone. "We all have a lot on our minds. Just look at Thomas. Did you know Kim's pregnant?"

My eyebrows shot up and my mouth fell silent. I stared at him in
disbelief.
"Yeah, how 'bout that?" he said rhetorically. He chugged his glass and
slammed it back down on the table. "I really could've used a friend," he
continued, more to himself than to me. "But you couldn't even be
bothered to call or stop by. So, yeah… fuck you."
My throat felt dry and I had trouble swallowing. "Riley, I'm-"
"Save it. I don't need any useless fucks around me who don't give a damn
about me." His eyes flared with rage before he got up and left the bar.
I sat there, left with nothing but silence.

The next time I went over to Scott for target practice, I brought him
another bottle of scotch. I'd gotten used to the reloading process and I
started gaining more and more confidence.
Somewhere halfway through our practice, my phone had already bleeped
four times—indicating a new message. Now, it bleeped again.
"Shut that fuckin' thing off or I'll use it as a fucking target," he barked at
me, scowling.
"Roger," I replied and quickly turned it off.

After practice, I saw that Amy had tried to reach me. I texted her back,
telling her I'd be over in thirty and she'd better be ready for a big meal
and a beautiful sunset.
I guess I hadn't been around much lately—only swinging by once after
work for dinner and a movie. She was becoming impatient and I knew I
had to step up my game. I still hadn't asked her to be my girl and I wasn't
sure what was holding me back. Later, I concluded that I had been
afraid. Afraid of losing her. And as long as I wasn't with her then, in a
way, I couldn't lose her. Naive, right? Yeah, I could be stupid like that.
I drove home and jumped into the shower.
Before leaving the house, I took another quick look at the website. The
newest comment, by SilentWitness, wasn't a skeptical or sarcastic one—it
was one that I could actually show to Scott. Finally. I smiled faintly.

I drove over to Amy's, caught up with her parents, and then took her out to a steakhouse. She didn't really look like the type, but she loved herself a nice bloody steak.

"I don't get it," she said after her third glass of red wine. "What's got you so preoccupied lately? You barely come around anymore."

"I'm sorry, babe," I said quietly. "I've got… some things on my mind."

"What things?"

I looked at her. After Kimberley's reaction, I wasn't about to bring up the skin diver theory—Amy was a lot more down-to-earth than Kim, after all. But I had to give her a reason, a good one at that. "I'm taking shooting lessons," I said honestly.

"Shooting lessons? Why?"

"Because I wanted to learn how to shoot."

"Well, duh," she said, chuckling. "But didn't you already get your permit?"

"Yeah, I mean… I got a Glock, but I'm looking into rifles now."

She frowned. "Rifles…"

I took a gulp of my beer.

"Should I be worried?"

"No, why would you be?"

"I don't know. Just wondering. Why are you suddenly into rifles? What are you hoping to shoot?"

I swallowed. The cogs in my mind turned rapidly. "Well, I saw this survivalist show a while back, and this guy was hunting, right? He had to shoot his own dinner." I gestured at the half-eaten steak on my plate. "It looked kinda cool."

She rolled her eyes. "Guys and their coolness. As long as it's loud and fast, you're happy, right?"

I smiled. "Pretty much. But I don't hear you complaining about my speed."

"That's because your car is pretty sick," she said, winking. "And it's got good suspension."

"You know that's right."

"But," she continued, "you'd better not start treating me like second place. I come before guns."

"Roger," I replied.

She raised her eyebrows.

Damn it, I thought. Lately, it felt like I was living a second life in a different world—one filled with skin divers, crates of beer, whizzing monitors, and loud gunshots… and Scott, with his tobacco stench and semi-permanent scowl. And now, those worlds were starting to collide.

"How about this?" I started. "There's a Farmer's Market near the center next weekend. I'll pick you up in the morning, treat you to the best coffee in town, and take you there."

Her face lit up. "I'd love that," she said.

I knew she would. It was me who didn't like those markets. But sometimes, you gotta compromise. I just hoped I'd be back in time for target practice. I doubted Scott would let me back on his property if I stood him up.

I picked Amy up on Saturday morning. She opened the door, wearing a cute green sweater, and I handed her a steaming cup of coffee from *Ricky's Roast*. Together, we walked toward a large, open parking lot near the center, where rows of tents and stalls were set up.

Her nostrils flared as she happily inhaled the scents of fresh produce, flowers and baked goods—I knew she was going to ask me for a cinnamon roll. Before we reached the bakery stall, she got distracted by a vendor selling fresh flowers. She examined the buckets filled with daisies, sunflowers and wildflowers, then struck up a conversation with the vendor. She picked out a small bouquet, flashing me a big smile—looks like I'd be carrying it around for the rest of the morning.

Over at the bakery shop, she eagerly eyed the cinnamon rolls, so I bought us a couple, along with some other pastries. She happily munched on them, and it made my chest tighten in a way I couldn't ignore.

She was a woman in her late 20s, but her wide-eyed excitement made her seem like a kid in a candy store, and I found that absolutely adorable.

The way she smiled could light up the entire damn city.

We wandered past a musician playing acoustic guitar and watched a few kids dance nearby. We passed some stalls selling handmade crafts—

pottery, candles, and knitted scarves—and local honey and jams. She spotted a jar of raspberry jam and insisted we should get it because it would be 'perfect for breakfast'. At that moment, my mind wandered to Kimberley—if she was going to keep the child, she and Thomas would become a family… having breakfast with raspberry jam on Sunday mornings.

Before leaving, we stopped at a small coffee stand. She instantly started talking with the barista, and we went home with two iced lattes and a bag of dark roasted beans.

It was 2:40 p.m. when we arrived at her house. I gave her a big hug and a long kiss. My hands lingered on her waist as I looked her in the eyes. I swallowed.

"Do you wanna date?" I asked, the words finally spilling out.

She blinked. "Weren't we dating already?"

My mouth hung open and I didn't know what to say.

She started laughing. "Seriously, James, how are you so dense? I mean…" She paused, her expression shifting. She looked at me intently, biting her lip. "You didn't… with anyone else, right? I mean, these past few months?"

I shook my head quickly. "Nah, I just… I never asked you. Properly, I mean."

She smiled before kissing me. "You didn't have to, silly. Wanna come in?"

I checked my phone. "Shit, I gotta go." I let go of her. "Target practice," I added.

"Try not to blow your foot off, 'kay?" She waved and went inside.

I quickly got into my car and sped over to Scott's, breaking the speed limit.

When I arrived, he was standing on his porch with his arms crossed.

I parked my baby behind his truck and rushed over to him. "Sorry I'm late," I said.

He squinted his eyes. "Be your first and last time," he stated in a gruff voice.

I emptied several clips and made some decent hits. Now, Scott was going to show me "how a man does it".

I watched from a distance, curious about his ability to shoot without the aid of a bipod or any other support.

He removed a cigarette from his pack and lit it casually while walking over to his shooting position. He took a long drag, then set the cigarette aside and grabbed the M1 Garand, assuming a solid stance. He placed his feet shoulder-width apart, slightly bending his knees.

I eyed his stance and decided to try the same thing next time I held the rifle.

He held the rifle with a firm grip, bracing it against his shoulder. He aimed at a target set up at 300 yards. His eyes were focused, his hands steady. He exhaled slowly and squeezed the trigger. The rifle kicked back but he managed the recoil with ease—which kinda impressed me.

There was a clear clanging sound.

"Not bad," he remarked, taking another drag from his cigarette. "Takes some practice to get it right, but it's all about control."

I nodded slowly. "I can see that. You make it look easy."

He smirked, his eyes still focused on the range. "Just years of practice and a lot of patience, kid. You'll get there with time."

He continued shooting, hitting targets consistently, even at 400 yards.

A little while later, he disassembled the rifle and started cleaning it. That was his way of saying the lesson was over.

I watched him clean the rifle with such focus, it was nearly meditative to look at.

Scott told me I had to buy my own rifle and ammo for the next lesson, so we met in front of the gun shop at around 10 am the next Saturday.

"Pack it up, Lester," Scott barked at the gun shop owner after handing him the M1 Garand he'd picked out for me in the shop. He wasn't going to pay for that, of course, but he was making sure I didn't "go home with another fucking pea shooter," as he put it. He also threw in a few cases of ammo—both for me and for himself—since I had "wasted plenty of his".

Meanwhile, I had wandered over to the handguns. Scott had made me feel kinda bad about my Glock and I thought of switching it out for something better.

"So, what gun are you lookin' at?" he asked as he walked over to me, like he was quizzing me.

"What about this one? Smith & Wesson," I read out loud. "M&P 9 millimeter."

"Hell, I thought you might've learned something by now. Thing's a starter pistol, not a damn weapon."

The gun shop owner retaliated, "It's got plenty of stopping power, Scott."

Scott sneered. "Against what, a squirrel? Probably won't even kill the thing, just piss it off." Then he pointed at another case. "Get yourself the Colt, kid. Now *that's* a gun that packs a punch. It'll knock down anything in its path and keep it there."

The owner nodded. "1911's a classic. Tried and true. A bit heavier, sure, but you won't be second-guessing it when you need it."

I picked up the gun and handled it, feeling its weight. "Feels solid."

Scott grinned. "That's because it is. You want a gun that's gonna do more than just look pretty. You want somethin' that says *back the fuck off* without havin' to pull the trigger. The .45 will do that every time. Trust me, I know. Got one just like it."

I nodded. "Alright, let's do it."

He slammed me on the back. "Now you're thinkin' like a man who wants to stay alive."

That was the first time he referred to me as a man.

I went home for lunch after I picked up a bottle of Knob Creek—I'd have to properly apologize to Riley at some point—and got to Scott's at 3 p.m. sharp, ready to shoot with my very own M1 Garand. It went pretty smoothly and Scott even let me practice at 400 yards.

Over the months, I felt like I had gotten to know Scott quite a bit. He was the kind of guy who always had something to complain about. Whether it was the weather, the government, a kid playing too close to his house or the state of the world. He was never shy about sharing his opinions, especially when it came to his distrust of the system. He could be incredibly exhausting in that way. He distrusted anyone who tried to tell him how to live his life and he'd often reminisce about the "good old days," when everything was so much simpler, at least in his mind. He was a cranky old bastard and he was stubborn to a fault, but he was also dependable, blatantly honest and surprisingly handy. I'd learned that time and time again.

Once you were in his super small circle, you were in it for life. Betty was one of those people, along with a friend he called T, and of course, his mom—when she was still alive. As for me, I wasn't sure where I stood yet, but it didn't really matter.

Autumn was starting to set in and temperatures dropped to around 40°F in the evenings. Hints of yellow, orange and red started to emerge from the foliage.

As I drove back home from my shift on a Thursday, I spotted Scott on his porch. I had saved up some comments on the website for him to look at, so I decided now was the time. I offered him a ride, telling him I'd drop him off back home after.

"I ain't no fuckin' princess, kid," he grumbled. "Besides, I ain't stepping foot inside that rice rocket of yours."

"It's more than just a rice rocket," I said, grinning. "She's a piece of art. And if you're lucky, maybe one day you'll get to see what she can really do."

He scoffed. "Well, I don't need some souped-up toy to feel like a man. I bet that thing's all show and no go."

"Ouch," I said, putting a hand to my heart. "You wound me, Scott. Tell you what, I'll race you. Your old rusty bucket against my Skyline. Winner buys the beer."

He laughed, genuinely amused. "Oh, you're on kid. But don't cry when you lose."

I raised my eyebrows. "Really? I thought you said speed's for teenagers and idiots. So which one are you, old man?"

"This is just teachin' you some fucking manners," he cackled.

"We'll see about that," I replied.

Needless to say, I'd be buying him beer.

Once in front of my monitor, Scott took a look at the reply written by SilentWitness:

I've never posted anything like this before, but I really need to get this off my chest. A few years back, my mother suddenly passed away. The doctors said it was natural causes, but I can't shake the feeling that something else was at play. Because the night before she died, I saw something… I was going to the bathroom and I saw some sort of shadow in front of her bedroom—or whatever it was. It moved like it was alive. I thought I was dreaming, but the next morning, my mother was dead. Has anyone else experienced something like this? I'm scared to even talk about it out loud.

"Damn, kid. Idiots always gotta make it about themselves," he grumbled. "This one's just fishing for sympathy. And why the fuck's he talking about shadows? It ain't a cat or a dog, right? This's got nothing to do with skin eaters."

"Could be," I said. "But they sound pretty shaken up. Might've seen something and just didn't understand what it was—I get that. Maybe he didn't get a clear look and thought it was a shadow, but it was actually something tangible. And his mother died… Maybe it's worth looking into."

"Nah, kid. This's just way too thin."

"Then what about this one?" I pointed at a newer comment by NightOwl:

I once saw a stray dog break through a window in my neighborhood. The way it moved was just… wrong. Almost like it wasn't really a dog. Not sure about the eyes though, it was too dark to see. Could this be what you described?

"Hmm. This one's something," he mumbled. "Though I doubt he could tell us anythin' useful." He grabbed the mouse from my hand and started scrolling, his eyes scanning the screen. "Racked up quite some tales," he remarked.

"Yeah, I mean, it's been up for a while. Although it's mostly skeptics and people talking about paranormal stuff that I don't think quite matches what we're looking for."

He cackled. "Yeah, these fuckers ain't leavin' ectoplasm."

I read along with Scott and saw posts mentioning Skinwalkers, psychomanteum and cryptid sightings.

"Look at this one," I said, bumping my finger against the screen.

He started reading out loud. "I've heard of things like this before, though never so brutal. The morphing eyes are key… These things, whatever they are, aren't natural. They can shift in ways that defy logic. What you saw wasn't just a dog—it was something much darker. Be careful, they seem to be drawn to fear."

Silence filled the room—so thick, even the monitor's low whirr couldn't break it.

"Well, thank you, CreepingShadow," I said silently.

"Can you ask where he's from?"

"Yeah." I replied to the comment, then looked up at Scott.

He intently eyed my screen. "So, what'd he say?"

I had to hold back my laughter. "Doesn't go that fast, old man. Depending on his time zo-"

"I know how the fuckin' world works, okay?" he bit at me.

"Not the digital one, you don't," I replied sharply.

"Just get me a fucking beer."

I grabbed him a cold one, and was about to re-enter my room when I heard him reading some comments out loud and reacting to them. I stood still and bit my tongue, trying not to laugh.

"*A cat killing a driver? Come on, man. Cats don't have the strength to kill a person like that… Maybe the guy had a heart att*—oh, fuck you, you fuckin' idiot, it says it's not a cat. Fuck's wrong with people these days? Can he not read?" He mumbled something inaudible. "*No offense, but have you considered seeing a therapist?* No, have you!? Fucking twat—'course you haven't, you need a fuckin' brain for that." He slammed the desk.

I walked into the room with tears streaming down my face, trying not to make a single sound.

Scott's head snapped back and he looked at me with wide, piercing his eyes—his face distorted. His hands twitched and curled up to a sort of gun-holding posture.

My smile vanished. "Scott?" I asked loudly.

He blinked, keeping silent for a moment. Then he barked, "Took you long enough."

I stood frozen in place. Was he pretending nothing had just happened? What the hell happened, anyway? Is that what PTSD looks like? I handed him the beer and suddenly wished I'd run out, so he'd have to go home.

He gulped down his beer and headed out shortly after without uttering another word.

I breathed a sigh of relief. I had gotten so accustomed to our banter and him opening up to me, that I nearly forgot the man who'd scared the living shit out of me several times already. He was still one and the same. I shook my head and read a few more comments in an attempt to clear my mind.

DoubtingThomas had replied:

These posts are starting to sound like urban legends. I'm having a hard time believing any of this happened. Where's the evidence? Any old newspaper clippings or something?

I considered posting about the jar of ashes soon—not that they'd take it as 'evidence', but the believers would believe me either way. And the skeptics, well… they were just noise, much like the user posting under the name SkepticGuy:

This forum is starting to sound like a conspiracy theory hub. What's next, Bigfoot with laser eyes? Seriously, this just doesn't hold up. It's probably just your mind playing tricks on you.

Logical_Liz said:

I've never heard of anything remotely like this. If something like this actually happened, it would be all over the news or whatever. I think there's a more reasonable explanation you're missing here.

I mean, she did have a point. Why wasn't it on the news? If my mom— even in her current state—was able to make a video of the bird, then how come there was nothing else out there? Maybe it was time to post the video as well.

I read a few other comments. Someone thought there may have been a gas leak. Someone else thought the skin divers came from another dimension. Another person claimed it was a government experiment gone wrong—I was sure Scott would have latched onto that one. And another person wondered whether the skin divers only took the form of dogs and cats or if they could be any animal.

Because of that, I decided to post my mom's video.

Here's the video I captured of a bird that I'm certain was a skin diver. Watch how it moves. Anyone seen anything similar? Please upload your evidence here.

Next, I uploaded some photos of the jar with ashes.

They can die! I managed to actually kill one with a bullet. I opened up the corpse, hoping to find some answers, but I found no bones or organs or anything. Just… ashes!? Has anyone else come across this, ever? What could it mean?

Just as I posted them, a notification showed a new reply. I immediately clicked on it, thinking someone had already reacted to the bird or the ashes, but it was under the cat post:

This is insane, but I'm hooked. Do you have any idea what happened to the person on the porch? Did they see anything? And what about the cat—did it just disappear after the crash? Where did it go? I need to know more about how this went down.

I stared at the screen. Fuck, I thought to myself. Fuck, fuck, fuck! I got up from my chair and started pacing around my house. What happened to that cat, indeed? Scott never really told me what happened—what he had seen or felt. He slipped into his coma and the cat… it came to my house. It showed up on my doorstep and it didn't seem to *be* a skin diver anymore. If the cat itself wasn't the skin diver, then where did the skin diver go that was inside that fucking cat?

My throat felt so dry I couldn't swallow. My heart beat so fast I was starting to get dizzy. I stumbled over to my couch and sank down.

What if the skin diver… was still inside Scott?

Chapter 11

I lay shivering under my blanket that night, unable to fall asleep. My mind raced with every conversation I'd had with Scott, every image of him burned into my retinas. I analyzed his strange behavior—his predatory stare, aiming between my eyes with his rifle, and that distorted grimace from before. I thought back to the cat sitting on my doorstep when he was in the hospital. How long had he been in a coma? Would the skin diver have persisted for so long? Wouldn't the doctors have noticed something strange? And what about the eyes?

Halfway through the night, drenched in sweat and still unable to rest, I began to spiral.

What if he *was* a skin diver—or at least taken over by one? Would I have to kill him? So far, he hadn't harmed anyone. Well, not yet, at least—…I think. Anxiety took me on a horrible, nauseating spin. I could barely breathe as I lay staring at my ceiling, heart pounding, palms sweaty, and legs heavy. My entire body felt both frozen, stuck in place, overheated. What if the skin diver had evolved? What if it could now blend in with the crowd?

I shot up, finally able to move, and turned on my PC. I read through the comments and reread the one by *TruthSeeker* over and over again. I hesitated for a moment, knowing Scott could check this website at any moment—if he even had an internet connection—and then posted a reply:

Hey TruthSeeker, the person on the porch survived, indeed. They were in a coma for months, but they're up and about now. I'm not sure what happened to the cat. I saw it enter the person's back, and I was sure it had killed them, but I didn't stay to find out. The cat showed up on my doorstep a while later, it even bit me, but it seemed like a normal cat again. This made me think that the dogs and cats are actually hosts to the skin divers, not skin divers themselves. What do you think could have happened? Any theories?

I bit the nail of my thumb and walked over to my living room. I wasn't going to get any shuteye like this anyway, so I might as well stay up.

Tomorrow's shift would just have to deal with my zombie-like me. I knew Chris had seen worse.

I turned on the TV, grabbed a beer from the fridge, and sank down on the couch. I could barely follow what was happening on the screen—my heart still racing and my palms sweaty—but it was enough of a distraction for me to drift off into slumber, even if just for a few moments.

At some point I figured I was tired enough to fall asleep and I went back to my bedroom. I was about to turn off my monitor when I saw that TruthSeeker had already posted a reply:

Damn, they're lucky to have survived, that's for sure. But if it is what you say it is, and the skin divers really hop bodies, there's a good chance that the survivor actually hosts one of them right now. It freaks me out to even think about it. Maybe… they need to start with small bodies before they move on to bigger ones. Yikes.

I felt sick to my stomach.

I hadn't slept, and my shift at Dover Wheels was particularly dreadful that day. Fortunately, this was my last shift before the weekend. But the closer I got to the end of the day, the more I thought about the shooting lessons tomorrow. What was I going to do?

Should I tell Scott about my suspicions? We had just started to bond… But I knew I couldn't keep hanging around him with this fear gnawing at me. What if the skin diver was just lying in wait?

The thought haunted me as I watched the clock tick down the final minutes of my shift. Every time I looked up from the Lexus I was working on, I saw his face in my mind, his intense eyes locking onto mine, as if he knew exactly what I was thinking.

My hands trembled while I tightened the last bolt and the wrench slipped from my grip. I cursed under my breath. I threw down my tools and headed for the locker room, feeling Crazy Eddie's eyes burn into my back.

The late afternoon sun blinded me as soon as I stepped outside, but it did little to lift the dark cloud hanging over me. I needed a plan, a solid one. But my mind was a tangled mess of fear and doubt.

I hopped into my car and let the engine roar—one of my small comforts. But even the thought of speeding down the highway, something that usually cleared my head, couldn't push away the dread settling deep inside my chest.

Driving home, my thoughts raced as fast as my Skyline. Should I go and confront Scott? Or try and gather more evidence before making any moves? The idea of being alone with him, armed with nothing but suspicions… I shivered.

I pulled up into my driveway and killed the engine without even parking in my garage. I just sat there, staring at the steering wheel. Tomorrow was coming, whether I was ready or not. And I had to make a choice. Had our bond become a trap? What if I'd been bonding with a skin diver all along? Was that even possible? And if I *were* to talk to him about my suspicions… how would he react? How would *I* react if someone said a skin diver could be lurking in me? Maybe one had already crept inside me as I slept. Maybe the cat hadn't jumped to Scott, but to me instead, through that bite.

I shook my head. Fuck. I was getting absolutely nowhere. My rational mind was decaying and it made it harder and harder to come up with a solution.

I breathed out slowly and went inside, immediately grabbing a beer from the fridge. I chugged it and grabbed another one before checking my website again.

There was a new reply from WatchfulEye:

Considering you've reported two car accidents involving these 'skin divers', that's definitely something worth digging into. I wonder if a car was involved in the other attack too—the one on the elderly couple, Burt and Katy?

I frowned at the screen. True, there were cars involved in two of the attacks, but the other two had nothing to do with vehicles. With the elderly couple… sure, my car had been there; I was driving by, after all— or at least attempting to. I sighed heavily, the memory of that night surfacing against my will. I didn't want to relive it. I could still feel the

cold sweat, the terror that had left me shaking, and the shit running
down my pants. I typed a quick reply:

*Could be, but there was no car involved in Burt and Katy's attack. Will you look
into it?*

The response came almost instantly:

I will.

The next day around 2 p.m., I was sitting on the little stairs in front of
my door. I hadn't slept at all, and it felt like I was clinging to the last of
my sanity. How the hell had it come to this? Even after all I'd been
through, I was supposed to be carefree and enjoying life—just cruising in
my Skyline, hanging out with my girl, fixing up sweet rides at Dover
Wheels. But somehow, I had slipped back into that excruciating rabbit
hole, where it was just me and my anxiety. This whole other world with
skin divers and Scott.

If I had a choice, wouldn't I choose the other world? The one with Amy
and blissful ignorance?

But either way, the threat was real, whether I wanted to face it or not.
Ignorance wouldn't save me from the sinister danger lurking beneath the
surface. And if I chose to look away, who else might pay the price?

Right now, I had a more immediate choice to make: stay home and
possibly wreck the bond Scott and I had—probably forever—or go to
his house, risking the terror of seeing his eyes morph and being torn to
pieces.

My phone rang. It was Andrew, whom I hadn't talked to in over two
weeks. "Hey, lil' bro," I said. "What's up?"

"Hey, James," he replied, sounding surprisingly chipper. "You're not
going to believe what Brooke and I did."

I grinned, leaning back against the stairs. "What's that?"

"We got a puppy!" he exclaimed.

Truth be told, I was a little taken aback. I thought he'd popped the
question by now and was calling to tell me she'd said yes.

"A little golden retriever", he continued. "She's adorable, man. We
named her Daisy."

I forced a smile—my mind immediately went to the skin divers. "That's great, Drew. Bet she's a handful already."

"Oh, totally. She's already chewed up one of Brooke's shoes," he laughed. "But seriously, you should come by and meet her. Brooke's dying to show her off."

My chest tightened. "Yeah, maybe I will," I said, trying to keep my tone normal. "How's our father doing?"

"He's alright. You know him. Pam and Nancy are here now."

"Oh, you're with him?"

"Yeah, Brooke wanted him to meet Daisy. He's actually pretty smitten with her. It's kinda hilarious."

"Glad to hear it," I replied, though I couldn't help but worry. A puppy… could it be? Or was I just losing it? The invisible threat, a lack of sleep and spending weeks on end in Scott's vicinity kinda had that effect, I guess. "I'll let you know when I can swing by. Work's been a bit crazy lately," I said. I was lying, but I felt like I had no other choice.

"Cool, man. Talk to you later?"

"Yeah, later." I hung up and stared at the phone in my hand. It was a quarter to three. Time to go. I took a deep breath. Maybe there was a way to expose the possible skin diver inside him, I suddenly realized. I didn't know how yet, but maybe I could test him.

I walked back inside, grabbed the camera and drove over to Scott's. When I arrived, I found him smoking on his porch.

"Hey," I said, trying to sound casual. "Got something to show you." I put the camera on the little table, right next to his Colt, and let the video play. "Tell me what you think."

He crossed his arms, leaned back in his chair and watched the video. His eyes squinted for a moment, but his expression was unreadable. It was his usual grumpy frown.

The screen was pretty dark and the details were hard to make out, especially on a small screen like that, but the sound was enough to make anyone uneasy. The frantic pecking, the bird slamming into the window, and the panicked breathing of my mom.

I watched him closely, hoping to gauge his reaction.

He exhaled sharply through his nose. "Damn video's too dark to see much, but that bird's definitely acting weird. Ain't seen much like it, though animals can act a lil' off right before disasters and shit." He turned to me. "Where'd you get this?"

"My mom recorded it," I replied, looking him dead in the eyes.

He frowned, his eyes narrowing.

"She said its eyes had morphed."

He grabbed the camera and replayed the video. His nose nearly touched the screen as he tried to make out the bird's eyes.

I heard my mother's panicked breathing and knew the video had ended. Scott watched it again, then put the camera back on the table. "I don't know, kid. It's really too fuckin' dark to tell. Couldn't she have used a fuckin' flashlight or whatever?"

I bit my lip. That would've definitely been useful, but with my mom's current state, I was just happy she made the video in the first place.

"Can't she make a new one?" he asked.

I shook my head. "She recently moved, away from that place with the bird. She's in a home in Boston now."

He grunted. "Well, we're gonna need more than this." He lit another cigarette.

"How are we going to get it?" I asked.

"Well, kid, I thought you'd never ask." He looked up at me, the tip of his cigarette burning bright orange as he took a deep drag. Smoke exhaled from his nose. "We know these fuckers can die, yeah?"

I nodded.

"And you've been taking shooting lessons from a real pro, right?"

I nodded again.

"Hell, you're even a little decent at it," he continued, making me feel a bit proud. "Though I wouldn't ever put my life in your hands, if I had a fuckin' say about it," he added in his gruff voice.

"So, what're you getting at?"

"Fuckin' hell, kid, is that head of yours just for show or what?"

"It *is* quite a show, isn't it?" I said with a smirk.

He shook his head, scowling. "Idiot."

"So, what you're saying is… we're going to *hunt* skin divers?" I asked, my face dead serious.

"Well, I ain't gonna sit around, waitin' to become a tasty snack for one of these fuckers. So yeah, kid, I'm sayin' we should hunt us some fuckin' skin divers."

I grinned. If there really was a skin diver inside Scott, he did a damn good job at hiding itself.

"We should make a plan first, though," he muttered, more to himself. "I mean, how often do we really run into one? But maybe… yeah, maybe there's something they're attracted to. Or places they frequent…"

"Yeah, it's not going to be easy," I replied. "First time, I waited fourteen years for another one to show up."

"Did you ask around yet?" he suddenly asked.

I frowned. "About what?"

He glared at me. "The ashes, you idiot. It's the only lead we have right now."

"No, not yet," I replied, shaking my head. "But I've posted about it on the website. We might find someone willing to take a look at it."

At that moment, I saw William's patrol car driving by in an awkwardly slow pace. I tried not to stare at it and focused my attention on Scott.

"Fuckin' cop," he grumbled, his gaze fixated on the car. "Come on, grab your gun."

My breath faltered. "W-what?"

He looked at me. "For practice, you idiot."

"Oh…"

He chuckled. "You get some strange ideas in that head of yours."

I forced a smile and followed him to the shooting range in the backyard. I practiced with both the Garand and my Colt. I noticed that I was getting better at it, especially with the handgun, and it somehow made my anxiety fade—just a little, though.

"Look," I said, putting down my rifle. "I gotta skip next week's practice."

Scott glared, saying nothing.

"I made plans to visit my brother," I continued. I hadn't set anything in stone yet, but it would buy me some time to think and make a plan. Sure, I still had no solid proof that the skin diver had taken over Scott, but I

also had no proof that it hadn't. I just had to stay on my toes. If there
was a skin diver inside him, it would reveal itself sooner or later. And if
it did… it would probably be too late, but still… I had to do something
to feel in control. Under normal circumstances, I would've gone to
Michael with my concerns, but I knew he wasn't fond of my 'delusions'.
"Well, your funeral," Scott grumbled.
I raised my eyebrows. "What do you mean?"
He shrugged and took aim at the 600-yard target with his Garand,
standing firm with no balancing aids, no nothing. He pulled the trigger
and the bullet seared through the air. A metallic clank echoed.
I swallowed hard.

I stayed over at Amy's that night and didn't check the website until late in
the afternoon on Sunday. While I spent Saturday evening at a football
game, enjoying beers, and strolled around a craft fair with Amy the next
day, a new reply had been posted that would change everything. There
was another witness.

When I got home, I walked straight to my bedroom to turn on my PC
and check the website. There were several new notifications. The website
was finally taking off, and it eased my feelings of dread and anxiety a
little.
Nowadays, there were fewer skeptics replying to posts and more people
who either believed me or shared their own theories. So far, there hadn't
been a conclusive post from someone who shared the experience itself.
Until now.
NightmareFuel had posted:

*I've actually seen something like this. I thought it was just a really bad, lucid
nightmare, but now I'm not so sure. My neighbors had a Pomeranian. It was full of
energy and was often outside; I'd even played with it several times. But one day, it was
acting strangely, just sitting on the lawn and staring straight ahead. It didn't respond
to its name or anything—just sat there like a statue for hours on end. I thought it
was odd but didn't think much of it.*

*When my neighbor (let's call him Mark) came home from work, he parked his
car in the driveway, got out, and started walking toward the door. I waved to him*

from my bedroom window—my desk is right in front of it, so we usually greeted each other that way. But then I saw the Pomeranian. Its neck was twisted all the way around, while its body remained frozen in that statue-like pose. It was staring directly at Mark, its eyes unnaturally huge. And then… it went for him! It was super fast and agile. It leaped toward him and suddenly, it vanished. Completely disappeared.

Mark went inside the house like nothing had happened, so I figured I must've seen it wrong. Maybe I'd fallen asleep while studying and had a strange nightmare, right? But about ten minutes later, an ambulance pulled up with sirens blaring. Apparently, Mark had collapsed as he stumbled over the doorstep. His head had cracked open on the hallway table, and there was blood everywhere. There was nothing the paramedics could do—he was gone. And so was the Pom… I never saw the dog again. I eventually asked Mark's wife about it, but she snapped at me, saying it must've run away or something. She really didn't want to talk about that day, so I didn't press the issue.

I tried to tell my mom what I had seen, but she looked at me as if I'd gone crazy, saying it must've been a nightmare. I never mentioned it to anyone again, but it's never sat right with me.

I stumbled upon your website the other week and hesitated to post this, but I feel like we experienced something very similar. I called it a 'body diver' back then. 'Skin diver' sounds fitting.

I stared at the post in disbelief, my heart skipping a beat. This was real— there was someone else out there who had experienced the same thing. I exhaled deeply and posted a reply:

Hey, NightmareFuel. Thank you so much for sharing your experience. It sounds awfully similar, and I believe we're dealing with the same creature. You're not crazy. You didn't have a nightmare. It was real. Mind if I ask where you live? We need to figure out whether this is a local, national or global issue.

I spent the next hour glued to my laptop, re-reading NightmareFuel's account, running through the possible implications, and hoping for a swift reply. I desperately wanted to show the post to Scott, but something held me back.

Chapter 12

I checked the website every day that week, but was met with
disappointment every day as there were no new replies.
On Friday evening, I drove down to Philly to visit my little brother,
where I'd be crashing for two nights. I arrived around 2 a.m., and
Andrew and I shared a few beers before going to bed.
The next morning, I met the golden retriever puppy, Daisy. She was
pretty cute and full of energy, with a naughty side to her—she'd chewed
up Andrew's slippers overnight. And I truly tried to enjoy the moment
because she clearly made my little brother happy, but I felt this constant
nagging in the back of my head. *What if?*
The four of us—Andrew, Brooke, Daisy and I—went for a stroll in
Fairmount Park and later grabbed a bite to eat on South Street. In the
evening, Andrew and I went out for drinks while Brooke stayed home
with the pup. It was all pretty relaxed and fun, even though my mind
kept drifting back to the website. Back to Scott.
The next day, we went to the zoo and I drove back home right after,
grabbing a bite to eat underway. I called Amy when I was still in the car,
making plans for Tuesday.

As I neared my house, I knew something was off—I could feel it in my
gut. Scott's blue Chevy was parked outside. I pulled into the driveway
and saw him sitting on the steps in front of my door. I approached him.
He looked more serious than I'd ever seen him.
"Hey, Scott, what's going on?" I asked, trying to keep my voice steady.
"I saw the new story," he replied, his tone clipped and terse. "You're not
the only one keeping an eye on that *site*, you know. I've been watching it
too."
The knot in my stomach twisted. "Ah, that's great. I was just about to-"
"Cut the crap," he interrupted, holding up a crumpled piece of paper. "I
already made contact with this Gary guy. He's agreed to meet, and I've
set up a location."

"You've already met him?" I asked, unable to hide my frustration; it felt like Scott had sidestepped me.

"Not yet. But we've been in touch. He seems credible. Agreed to meet us with more information."

I nodded slowly. "Where are we meeting him?"

He handed me the paper. "There's a rundown diner on the edge of town. We'll meet him there at eight. I'm bringing the ashes."

"The ashes?" I repeated.

"That's what I said," he retorted. "We need to bring them for whatever this Gary guy has to tell us. If there's anything to learn, it's going to be from him."

I took the paper and glanced at the address scribbled on it, which I could barely read in the dim light coming from my porch light, then glanced at the clock on my phone. It was half past seven. "Okay. Let's go, I guess."

He glared at me. "You guess? Fuck is wrong with you, kid!? You've been acting like a complete idiot lately. Withholding information, evidence… Skipping practice. Now this half-assed attitude of yours. You out or what?"

I breathed slowly, trying to steady my heartbeat.

His eyes narrowed. "This about that fucker on the cat post?"

"Which fucker?" I asked, feigning ignorance.

His eyes narrowed further and his brow furrowed deeper. "Don't fucking lie to me, you son of a bitch. Don't you ever fucking do that again, you hear me!?" The vein on his forehead swelled up, looking like it was about to burst.

I flinched.

"Now, get the fuck in my truck." He stomped over to his Chevy and turned on the engine. The rumble echoed in the quiet night.

"Isn't it safer if we take two separate cars?" I asked through the passenger window, trying to sound nonchalant. "I mean, what if this Gary guy isn't who he says he is?" I knew I was playing into Scott's paranoia, which was kinda mean, but I *really* didn't want to get in a car with him.

He just glared at me.

I sighed. "Well, don't say I didn't warn you if anything goes wrong." I got in the truck and he maneuvered out of my driveway, nearly scraping my Skyline's side mirror in the process.

We drove in silence and the tension between us was palpable. The streets of our town seemed unusually deserted, and the headlights of his Chevy cut through the darkness like twin searchlights.

When we arrived at the parking area around the old diner, the place looked even more rundown than I had anticipated on that silent, tensed ride. The neon sign flickered every now and then, casting an eerie glow on the cracked pavement. Scott parked the car in a far corner and pulled out his Colt, checking it with a practiced motion. He grabbed the jar of ashes from the back seat and shoved it into my hands. "Guard this," he grumbled, still clearly frustrated, before getting out of the car and checking the perimeter.

It was five minutes to eight.

I tried to steady my nerves as we waited for the other witness to show up. My mind raced with questions. I wondered what Scott and Gary had talked about, and was annoyed that I hadn't gotten the chance to read their interactions before meeting this guy—although, knowing Scott, they probably communicated through other means beside the public forum. And how long had Scott waited on my porch, anyway? I never told him what ti-

A sudden knock at the window beside me made me jump.

"Get out, kid. We're going inside."

I slipped the jar of ashes in the pocket of my jacket and followed Scott into the diner. The bell above the door jingled as we entered. The place was nearly abandoned—just two other customers sat scattered around. We took a seat in the booth furthest away from the door. Scott kept his eyes locked on the entrance. I ordered us both some coffee from the waitress, who gave us a strange look before heading back to the counter.

"So, how'd you make contact with this guy?" I asked.

"Told him to call a number," he responded curtly.

"*Your* number?"

He glared at me. "Of course not, you idiot. A burner's."

"Alright then," I said, raising my eyebrows. "How was I supposed to know? You suddenly drag me all the way here, keeping me in the dark."

"Sucks, huh, being sidelined?" he grunted. His eyes fixated on mine.

"I've just been busy," I defended myself.

"Nah, kid, you've been scared," he said in a soft tone. He stared in front of himself. "No shame in that."

The waitress came over with our coffee, and we waited in silence.

At exactly eight, a man walked in. He looked to be in his late forties. He was tall, with a slender face and weary eyes. He had the kind of demeanor that suggested he'd seen his share of troubles—or perhaps had fallen to the bottom of the bottle a few too many times.

That must be him, I thought.

The man spotted us and approached our table with caution. "James, Scott?" he asked, glancing around nervously.

"That's us," Scott said. "You've got something for us?"

The man nodded, sliding into the booth across from us. "I'm not sure how much I can help, but I know what I saw, and I've been keeping tabs on the same things you have," he said, his voice barely above a whisper.

The waitress walked up to us and took Gary's order—a diet coke. Scott grumbled softly under his breath and I knew him long enough to know he was cursing at Gary for his choice of drink.

"I'm Gary," he said, extending his hand to me.

"James." I shook his hand, noting the firmness of his grip.

He extended his hand to Scott, but Scott refused to shake it, his eyes cold and unyielding.

"Skip the niceties," Scott said in a gruff voice. "Tell him what you told me." He nodded in my direction, and I felt a pang of frustration at being left out of the loop.

Gary glanced at me and then back at Scott. "Alright," he said, his voice trembling slightly.

He fell silent when the waitress came back over and put down the diet coke in front of him. He nodded, waiting for her to go back to the counter before speaking. "Well… I've been researching this phenomenon for a while, actually. I also had a horrible run-in with one of them, y'know, and I barely survived." He shuddered.

"Yeah, the Pomeranian, right?" I asked.

He shook his head. "No, that was the first one."

I frowned.

"This one was after I moved. I went to this nice new neighborhood. Fancy lawns and big houses, y'know. Thought I'd have a fresh start there. But I felt like…" he glanced around nervously, "it had followed me, somehow."

"The Pomeranian?" I repeated myself. "You said in your post that you never saw it again."

"Well, as I told Scott, I was careful with providing certain information, because… y'know."

I looked at Scott questioningly.

"Never know who you can trust," he clarified in his gruff tone, his eyes locking onto mine.

"Exactly," Gary continued. "So, yeah, I guess I'll tell you about the Pomeranian one first. I did see that one again, on a playground. I had been looking for it for days, carrying around these smelly sausages." He swallowed visibly. "It looked entirely normal, like you'd expect from a dog, y'know. I tried feeding it some sausages and it gulped it right up— like, nothing unusual, right? And, I don't know, I figured I should bring it home; study it up close." He glanced around. "So, I took it to our shed, because I couldn't let my mom see it, y'know."

I frowned.

"She didn't like me bringing strays into the home," he said, as if that was an explanation.

"But it wasn't a stray," I said. "It was your neighbor's."

"Well, yeah, but… y'know." His eyes shifted.

I wanted to ask what the hell he was talking about, but instead, I asked, "How long ago was this?"

"About ten years ago," he replied.

I heaved a sigh. He must've been in his late thirties when he had his first run-in with a skin diver— still living with his mom.

"So, I took it into the shed, right?" he continued. "And I knew I had to open it up to try and get some answers. So, I took my knife and just did it, y'know."

I felt a hot ball rising up from my gut. "You what?"
Scott kicked my shin.
"I just did what had to be done," Gary said.
"We get it," Scott said. "Just get the fuck on with it."
I kept silent.
Gary turned his head, whispering even more silently. "And when I did… there was nothing. Like, no organs, no bones, no blood… Just this fine, black ash." He hesitated. "You guys posted about those ashes, right? Of the dog you killed?"
Scott and I exchanged a glance—he had his poker face on, but I could tell he was as uneasy as I was.
"Yeah, that's right," I said slowly. "But you already knew that."
"Yeah, well… those *ashes*… they're not what they seem. They're something… different."
A chill ran down my spine.
Scott clenched his jaw, staring at Gary. "Different how?"
"The ashes—they're like a residue, but not just of the animal they were in. They're the remnants of whatever the hell these skin divers are." He sighed heavily. "And they're dangerous," he added.
"What do you mean?" Scott asked. His eyes narrowed.
"Well… you breathe that stuff in, and it can mess with your head, y'know. Make you see things, hear things that aren't really there. I think it's how these things operate. They get inside the animals, but when they're killed, they leave behind this… this toxin or whatever it is."
I swallowed. "You're saying these ashes are like a weapon?"
"Not exactly," he replied. "More like a defense mechanism. It doesn't hurt everyone, but if you're exposed to it long enough, it starts to affect you. Hallucinations, paranoia, even physical symptoms like nausea and dizziness."
Scott's jaw tightened. "And you think that's what we've got here?"
"I'd bet on it," Gary said. "That's why I wanted to meet you guys. You really need to be careful with those ashes. Don't breathe it in, don't touch it more than you have to. And whatever you do, don't let it get into the wrong hands." His voice died away.

I stared at the cup of coffee in front of me. I could almost feel the jar of ashes burn a hole through my jacket. We'd been breathing it in right after Scott cut into that poodle, and he'd touched it with his bare hands. And then there's the jar under my bed… does the glass even keep that stuff contained? Is this why I've been feeling so unnerved lately?

"How do you know all this?" I finally managed.

Gary looked at me for a moment. "Did you bring them?" he asked cautiously, dodging my question. "The ashes?"

Scott nodded slowly.

"Can I see them?"

Scott stared at him for a while. Then, he turned to me and nodded.

I looked around, pulled out the jar and put it down right in front of me. Gary's hands stretched out over the table, but Scott grabbed both his wrists in one swift motion. "Use your eyes," he grunted.

"Is it the same?" I asked.

Gary leaned forward and squinted, intently staring at the jar. "Y-yeah, I think it is. It looks the same, but… how long have you had this?"

I exchanged a look with Scott and shrugged. "I don't know, about two months, maybe."

His expression quickly changed from curious to shock to agitated.

"That's bad," he whispered.

"What do you mean?"

"Well, I kept the pot, y'know, with the ashes. Just like you guys. And I was trying to find someone who could test it, both the ashes and the dog."

"The dog?" I asked.

"Yeah, I kept its carcass on ice, y'know. Just in case."

"What the—?"

"Good thinking," Scott quickly interrupted me. "So, you test it?"

He shook his head. "No, it… it disappeared before I could."

I frowned. "What do you mean?"

"It was just gone, y'know. All of it. The ashes, the dog."

"Someone steal it?" Scott asked.

Again, he shook his head. "No. The jar was still there—squeaky clean, in fact. And the lid was locked tight, y'know. But the ashes inside… they evaporated or something." He heaved a heavy sigh. "And the body just disappeared from the freezer."

"You sure your mom didn't clear it out?" I asked skeptically.

"She wouldn't. Trust me," he replied with a blank stare that sent shivers down my spine.

"What about the other time?" Scott changed the subject.

Gary blinked slowly. "Yeah, that time… I ran into another body diver, err, skin diver, as you call it, nearly three years ago. It was a big dog. Like, a really big one, y'know. It came at me out of nowhere…" He squinted. "It bit into me, right here," he whispered, rolling up his left sleeve and revealing a nasty-looking scar on his forearm—it looked nothing like the tiny puncture scar on my hand, courtesy of that cat.

I stared at it. "It bit you?"

He nodded, rolling his sleeve back down. "Just like that cat bit you, right? It tried to take me, but I had my knife on me and I was just a little bit quicker, y'know."

Scott clenched his fists.

"And this time, I'd found someone who could examine it—Dr. Linwood. So, I cut the dog open and again, there was only this black ash." He grimaced. "Like some sick joke. I filled up five bottles, 'cause I had plenty, y'know." His voice died away.

"So, what happened? Did you get it tested?" I asked.

"It disappeared again," he said, with that same blank stare from before. "Quickly, this time, like three days later. That's why I'm surprised…" He leaned forward, staring at the jar.

Scott and I looked at each other.

"There's someone I know," Gary said quickly, "who works in a lab. They can run tests on it—discreetly, y'know. Maybe figure out what the hell we're dealing with. I can give them the ashes. We just have to be quick, y'know. We can't have them fall into the wrong hands." He stretched his hand out over the table in an attempt to grab the jar.

Scott grabbed the jar before he could reach it, and tucked it in my pocket. Then he glanced at Gary. His eyes narrowed as he studied him. "And how do we know *you're* not the wrong hands? We ain't got no fuckin' clue who you really are and what you're about."

Gary's face went pale. "I-"

"Save it," Scott cut him off. "We're not handing over the ashes to anyone without knowing exactly who we're dealing with. You're not running off with them, and we're not just taking your word for it. We'll let your guy take a look, sure, but we'll be there every fuckin' step of the way, you better believe it. If you're on the level, then you won't mind us watching closely."

Gary looked between Scott and me, his face a mix of frustration and concern. "Fine," he said in a tight voice. "I understand your hesitation. I'll set up the appointment with my contact, and you can come along. Just… be careful, y'know. This thing is bigger-" His voice died away once more.

Scott nodded, his expression hardening. "That's the plan. And if we find out you're hiding something from us, or if you're fuckin' playing us, we gonna make sure you regret it. Got that?"

Gary swallowed visibly. "Y-yeah, I got it."

"Bet you do. Now, let's get movin'."

As we left the diner, I kept a tight grip on the jar of ashes. I scanned the surroundings vigorously, and I noticed Scott do the same. Somehow, the darkness of the street felt heavier than it had before.

I had wished for more witnesses. I had wished for this thing to be bigger than me, just so that I wouldn't feel so damn alone anymore. But now that it was, I felt fucking uneasy. And there was not enough booze in the world to make that feeling go away that night.

We drove back to my place in tense silence. Scott's eyes remained fixed on the road and his knuckles had turned white from gripping the steering wheel. The jar of ashes sat between us—a tangible reminder of the danger we were dealing with; that is, if Gary was telling the truth.

As we pulled into the driveway, Scott finally broke the silence. "We'll need to keep a close eye on that fucker. I don't trust him, and I sure as hell don't trust what he says about this shit." He gestured at the jar. "But he might be our best shot at figuring out what the fuck's really going on."

I nodded. My shoulders felt heavy. My throat felt too dry to talk, and my mind was foggy. Gary certainly was one off-putting guy and I didn't like him one bit. He didn't seem like the kind of person I'd just have to warm up to—no, he was a fuckin' freak. Dragging home 'strays' and cutting them open, because… *y'know.* I sighed wearily.

"Need me to take yours?" Scott suddenly asked.

I gave him a puzzled look.

"The ashes, kid."

"Ah, no, it's alright."

"Okay, then… Protect it well, but don't go dying over it. Got it? And sleep with one eye open." He glanced in the rearview mirror, but all that could be seen around us was pitch-black darkness. "Not just tonight," he added.

"Yeah." I opened the passenger's door and was about to hop out.

"Kid."

I turned to look at him.

"If you're really scared about… that." His eyes shifted. "Just shoot me. You know how to."

"W-what do you mean?"

He heaved a heavy sigh. "If there really is one of those fuckers inside me… kill me, okay? At the first fuckin' sign. Don't go hesitating like a lil' wimp."

I swallowed.

"Now get out," he grunted.

I got out of his truck and walked up to my front door. In the reflection of the door, I watched him back out of the driveway, but he didn't drive off until I was inside. I locked the door, double-checked the windows, then stumbled from the fridge toward the couch.

I stared in front of me, trying to comprehend everything that had happened. I was getting closer to discovering the truth about the skin divers, but every step forward only seemed to lead to more questions. Toxic ashes? Paranoia and hallucinations? Was my anxiety lately a byproduct from that fucking poodle? And what about Scott? Did it explain his strange behavior?

A lump formed in my throat as I recalled the words he just said to me. "Kill me," I whispered, repeating his words. He said it with such conviction, such… I shook my head. He knew why I was pulling away.

He had read TruthSeeker's post and my reply to it. Say what you will about Scott, but he could see straight through people.

I gulped down three beers in a row, trying to obtain my regular buzz. I turned on the TV and mindlessly watched monster truck do stunts on an elaborate parkour. I drank a fourth and a fifth beer and noticed the clock striking 1 a.m. Somewhere during my seventh beer, I fell asleep on the couch, the TV still mumbling.

The next morning, there was a loud knock on my door. I jumped up and started to look around, but immediately grabbed my head and groaned. I stumbled toward the door. My fingers fumbled with the lock and I opened the door—the storm door shielding me from whoever was outside.

It was Scott.

"What the—?" I moaned.

"Yeah, mornin' to you too, kid. Come on, let's go."

"Wha—? Go where?"

"The contact," he grumbled. "The lab guy Gary told us about."

I rubbed my eyes and ran a hand through my disheveled hair. "What time is it?"

"Almost seven."

"Yeah, well, I'm getting up in an hour, and then I'm going to work."

He glared at me. "Fine, I'll go by myself." He turned around, growling.

Shit, I thought. "Wait," I said loudly. "Fucking hell, Scott. Just… wait, okay? Let me pop in an aspirin and get some coffee."

He looked back at me. "Well, alright, princess. Your chariot awaits."

Despite my pounding headache, I couldn't help but chuckle. I took a couple of aspirins, a bottle of water from the fridge, and made a pot of coffee. "You want some?" I yelled.

"Whatever," he responded, gruffly.

I grabbed two mugs, poured the coffee in and went outside, locking the doors behind me.

Scott was already sitting in his truck.

"Nuh-uh," I said, shaking my head. "Nope. If you're waking me up *this* early and you're bein' a little bitch about it, you're getting in *my* car."

He frowned, his hand tapping the steering wheel.

"Come on, Scott. If you wanna go somewhere, do it steady," I repeated his own words to him. "But if you can go fast as well, pick that." I opened my garage and put the mugs in the cup holders of my Skyline. I turned the key in the ignition and let the engine roar to life.

Scott's truck started moving, and for a moment I thought he was gonna drive out on his own and I'd had to follow him—sipping two cups of coffee. But he parked the truck to the side to make way, got out with the jar of ashes, and begrudgingly hopped into my car.

"Stupid idiot," he groaned. "This Tupperware on wheels attracts way too much attention."

"That's the point, old man."

He shook his head and stared outside.

"So, where are we going?"

He turned to me and grinned. "If only you knew, huh?"

"Too early," I snapped.

"You're one lazy fuck," he shot back at me, grabbing a crumpled piece of paper from his pocket and handing it to me.

I unfolded the paper, looked at the address, and put it in my Garmin Nuvi. "It's a three hour drive," I said with a loud sigh.

"Got a problem with that? My truck's right there."

I shook my head and took a sip of the steaming hot coffee. "Nope. Just saying. This… what's his name, Dr. Linwood, better be worth the drive. Plus, it'd take even longer with your rust bucket. Now buckle the fuck up."

At around half past eight, we made a quick pit stop in which I called my boss to tell him I wasn't coming in because I was feeling under the weather. I also moved my dinner plans with Amy to tomorrow, since I didn't know what time I'd be back. Scott used the break to smoke three cigarettes in a row, because I didn't let him smoke in my car.

We arrived near the lab just before 10 a.m. thanks to my baby's speed. The building was pretty unassuming, nestled in a quiet part of town. We exchanged a look, a silent agreement to stay on alert. He checked his Colt and tucked the jar in his pocket before I parked my car down the street. There was plenty of space on the lab's parking lot, but we weren't taking any chances. Who knew what lurked inside?

We approached the building and were first greeted by security. It took five full minutes and a lot of swearing on Scott's side for them to finally let us pass—probably because of the phone call they received. We entered the building and were then greeted by Gary.

"You made it," he said.

"Why? You surprised?" Scott sneered.

"N-no, just…"

"Ignore him," I said, wanting to get this over with. "Where to?"

"This way." Gary gestured down the hallway, and Scott started stomping down it. Gary then looked at me and smiled faintly. "Hadn't had his morning coffee yet, I take it?"

I glared at him. No amount of coffee could fix Scott, but I wasn't going to say that to this creep.

We rounded a corner, passed a couple of hallways and then entered a well-lit room. The space was immaculately clean, with gleaming white tile floors and walls lined with sleek, stainless steel cabinets. There was a large window, but the blinds were partially drawn, so only slivers of daylight filtered through. The overhead fluorescent lights cast an eerie glow on the long, polished steel table in the center of the room.

I looked at the various pieces of sophisticated equipment, neatly arranged on the table. I recognized a few tools from my science classes at school. There was a gas chromatograph, and a microscope—far more advanced than the ones we used to use. A centrifuge sat in the corner, waiting to spin down samples at a moment's notice. Monitors flickered with graphs I couldn't make sense of, and at the far corner of the room, a small fume hood released a faint scent of chemicals.

Dr. Linwood, the lab analyst Gary had mentioned, stood at the workstation and appeared to be a woman in her late forties with shoulder-length chestnut hair, streaked with hints of gray. I felt awkward for assuming the doc would've been a man and exchanged a glance with Scott, who seemed equally taken aback.

When the door closed behind us, the woman turned around and looked at us. "Scott, I assume," she said with a calm voice, stepping toward us. "And you must be James. Gary's told me a bit about your situation." Scott quietly eyed Gary, while I nodded. "We need answers," I said, as Scott grabbed the jar of ashes from his pocket and held it out with caution.

Dr. Linwood took the jar and held it up to the light. The blackish powder inside shifted a little, almost unnoticed, but the weight of what it represented hung heavy in the air. "Isn't that curious," she said, almost like a whisper. "I'll run the analysis right away." She turned her back to us, putting the jar on the center table. She slipped on a pair of gloves, carefully opened the jar, and placed some ashes in a small, clear dish before she began preparing the equipment.

Scott and I looked on as she worked. He had his arms crossed tightly over his chest, not uttering a single word. His eyes were fixated on her the entire time as she methodically prepared the sample. Every now and then, his eyes squinted and his brow furrowed.

"We'll know more soon enough," she said quietly, more to herself than to us, as she placed the sample into the gas chromatograph. The machine started working and a soft whirring sound filled the room.

"How long will it take?" I asked.

She glanced over her shoulder. "For something standard, just under a few hours. But given what Gary's told me and what I see here… it might take a bit longer." She turned back to the machine. "This is an unusual sample, to say the least, and I may need to run several tests to get the full picture."

Scott grunted, clearly displeased with the idea of waiting. "How much longer?" he pressed.

She hesitated for a moment. "If you're looking for a detailed analysis, you're looking at a full day, maybe more. But I can give you an initial read on the composition today. In three to five hours, hopefully. You'll want to stick around, though. If this is as strange as you think, there might be some follow-up questions."

"Oh, we're not going anywhere," Scott responded.

I nodded. "We'll wait."

She gestured toward a small break area in the corner, closest to the door. "There's coffee in the corner if you need it. But I don't have any magazines for you." She chuckled.

Scott shrugged awkwardly and moved over to one of the plastic chairs. He sat down, leaned back and looked around the lab.

I sat down in one of the other chairs, unsuccessfully trying to get comfortable, and fidgeted with my phone. I pulled up my website and scrolled through old messages on the forum. I quietly wondered how we had gotten to this point—sitting in a strange lab, with people we didn't know, running tests on toxic ashes, pulled from the inside of a skinned poodle.

Gary made some coffee and sat down with us, staring at his own phone with such intense focus, that it looked like he was drowning in the screen. He seemed too awkward to say a single word.

After a few minutes, I broke the silence. "You think we're onto something?"

Scott looked up and met my eyes. "Don't know, but we gotta see this through."

Gary nodded as well.

"Just remember, kid, this is just the beginning. Whatever we find out, it's only gonna lead to more questions. You can be sure of that."

I heaved a heavy sigh. "I know. But at least we're not alone in this anymore."

Gary smiled faintly, "Yeah, you can trust us."

Scott eyed him for a while, muttering.

The hours dragged on while we waited.

Dr. Linwood occasionally passed by, glancing at the screen attached to the gas chromatograph with an unreadable expression. She told us we could go outside, take a stroll around town—even recommended a local diner—but Scott was having none of it. He refused to budge from his seat—even though he clearly needed to use the bathroom—staring intently at her workstation.

Finally, after what felt like a damn eternity, Dr. Linwood approached us, holding a printout in her hand. She frowned slightly. "Preliminary results are in," she said in a low voice, "and you're going to want to see this for yourself."

We got up and followed her to the center table, with Gary shadowing us. She laid out the printout, tracing the graph's peaks and valleys with her finger.

"The composition is… unusual, to say the least," she began. "The ash particles are uniform, more so than any organic material I've seen before. Under the microscope, there are no cellular structures, no bone fragments—nothing that would indicate this came from a regular organic source."

Scott leaned in, his face inches away from the paper. "So, what does it mean?" he asked in a gruff voice.

She pointed to a specific section of the printout. "The elemental analysis shows a mix of carbon, calcium, phosphorus, and sulfur in unusual ratios. We also found compounds that don't match anything in our database—particularly a strange phosphorus-sulfur compound that I've never seen before."

Scott's brow furrowed. "So…?"

She shook her head slowly. "I can't give you a definitive answer yet. The presence of these compounds suggests that whatever this came from underwent a process we don't fully understand. There are traces of organic material, but it's minimal and doesn't seem to behave like any biological tissue I'm familiar with. The fact that I couldn't extract any DNA… it complicates things further." Her eyes glimmered. "It's as if this ash has been through something extreme, something that completely denatured any biological material."

"Denatured?" I asked.

"It means it altered its natural structure, losing its original form."

A chill ran down my spine. The vague results and the uncertainty in her voice pointed to something far beyond our understanding.

"What do we do now?" I asked.

She folded her arms and looked at us with a stern expression. "I need more time to run additional tests, but even then, I'm not sure I'll have concrete answers for you, to be blatantly honest. This sample is highly anomalous—unlike anything I've seen before." A faint smile crept over her face, "It's going to take specialized equipment and possibly a collaboration with other labs to get closer to the truth."

Scott's jaw clenched as he stared at her with his fierce grey eyes before turning to Gary. "You said it'd be discreet," he barked.

Gary immediately put up his hands in a defensive gesture. "She is! You can trust her."

"I assure you," Dr. Linwood said in a low voice, "I'll handle this as discreetly as humanly possible."

Scott glanced at her, scowling.

"I'll try and keep it in this lab as much as possible. And you can trust that I handpick the people I work with. They're good ones."

Gary nodded. "Yes, yes. I trust you."

Scott glared at him, then looked back at her.

"Just… give me some time to run additional tests," she pleaded.

"How much more time?" he asked with a hardened voice.

She bit her lip and hesitated before answering. "Give me until tomorrow afternoon. By then, I should have a more complete analysis. Please, trust me on this. I'll handle everything with the utmost care."

Scott's jaw clenched even more and he gave me a sharp look.

"Alright," I said quickly. "We'll be back tomorrow."

"Certainly." She bowed slightly and gestured toward the door.

We left the lab with Gary on our heels and walked through the corridor, leaving the ashes with Dr. Linwood. I knew Scott wasn't happy about that, but I felt some relief having a back-up jar at home—though *relieved* wasn't the right word. Content, maybe. Still, with the danger these ashes posed, I would have preferred if Scott held onto them.

"So, what do you think?" Gary asked me. "We've got something tangible, don't we?"

"I don't know, Gary. But yeah, hopefully," I replied.

"She's really good, y'know. Very trustworthy—believe me. If she'd have a second name, it would be Discreet, y'know," he rambled.

Scott didn't say a word.

We left the building and walked past the parking lot.

"I'm over here," Gary said, motioning to a red Honda in the corner.

I glanced at his license plate and noticed Scott do the same.

"Y'know, if you had any more of those ashes…" he began, "she could work twice as fast."

"There's plenty of ashes in that jar," I remarked.

"Sure, sure, just saying," he replied with a crooked smile.

"Too bad we don't," I retorted. "Drive safe."

"You too," he said, waving his hand. He got inside his car and we heard the engine purr as we quietly left the parking lot and started walking down the street at a leisurely pace. His Honda drove past us and Scott eyed it until it was well out of sight.

"Jittery creep," I remarked.

"Good thinking, kid."

"Yeah, well… you're kinda rubbing off on me," I replied with a genuine smile. "But it's probably a good thing he introduced us to Dr. Linwood."

"Only if we walk out of here without a fuckin' knife in our backs," he said in a harsh tone. "They kept throwing around 'trust' as if they were girl scouts handing out chocolate chip fuckin' cookies."

I suppressed the urge to chuckle. "Yeah, trust's gotta be earned."

He eyed me for a moment, and said nothing.

We walked back to my baby in silence. He clutched his concealed Colt before we got in.

I let the engine roar to life, then turned to look at him. "This isn't gonna be simple, is it?"

He glanced at me with a grim expression. "Nothing ever is, kid. But there ain't no turnin' back."

I nodded, frowning.

"Just one more thing," he said slowly.

"Hm?"

"We're taking my truck tomorrow."

"Speed's making you nauseous?" I asked with a grin.

He shook his head, his eyes scanning our surroundings. "We need to stay low, kid."

I looked at him questioningly. "Did you sense something or what?"

He didn't answer.

The next day, we pulled up near an old cinema in town with Scott's truck and got out. We cautiously walked toward the lab and again had some trouble getting past security.

Dr. Linwood herself came to fetch us. "Ah, you're here," she said as we walked over to us. "Let them through, Connor." She nodded at the guard. "Come this way, please."

She led us back to her lab without saying a word. Once inside, she started talking. "I've run some additional tests, and the results are… troubling."

Scott and I exchanged a look.

"How troubling?" I asked.

She gestured for us to come closer, then pointed to one of the monitors, displaying complex data charts and chemical breakdowns. "I focused on the unknown compounds found in the ashes. After several advanced tests, I found that these phosphorus-sulfur compounds aren't just chemically unusual—they're reactive under certain conditions."

I didn't quite understand what she was saying, but I asked anyway, "Reactive, how?"

"I introduced a small amount of the ash to a controlled environment that simulated the conditions of a human respiratory system—moisture, heat, slight acidity." She paused, her eyes shimmering. "The ashes emitted a vapor when exposed to these conditions. This vapor, I suspect, could be the source of the hallucinations and paranoia you've mentioned."

Scott's eyes narrowed. "So, breathin' it in…" he began.

"Would be dangerous," she confirmed. "This isn't just ash; it's like a carrier for… something more insidious—though I have yet do identify what exactly. For now, it's safe to say prolonged exposure could lead to severe physiological and possibly neurological effects."

"So it's like Gary said," I replied. "It can cause hallucinations and paranoia."

"Well, I'm not too sure about the exact effects, but he would know," she said.

Scott looked around. "Where's that bastard anyway?"

She shrugged. "I thought he would arrive along with you guys."

Scott and I exchanged glances, and I felt a shiver run down my spine. Something wasn't right.

"Anyway," she continued. "It seems like some sort of defense mechanism and I believe it's designed to protect itself by disorienting or disabling those who come into contact with it." Her lips curled up. "Those… skin divers and what they leave behind—it's like some last-ditch effort to keep people from figuring out what they really are. It's ingenious, really," she said enthusiastically.

I frowned.

"S-sorry, I get carried away at times," she said quickly. "I blame my curious nature."

Scott eyed her. "So, now what?" he grumbled.

"Well…" she began, "you should probably try to find out more about these skin divers, and you should do it quickly. If you ask me, this substance is too dangerous to leave unexplored. I'll keep working on the sample you left with me, but you need to be very, very careful. If someone were to weaponize this-"

"It could be catastrophic," he finished for her, his voice grim.

She nodded.

"How catastrophic are we talking about?" I asked.

He turned to me. "You ever imagine the end of the fuckin' world?"

I felt the blood drain from my face as I nodded.

"Well, there you go," he muttered.

Chapter 13

We drove back, pretty much in silence the entire way. Before we left, I exchanged phone numbers with Dr. Linwood, whose first name was— and no, I'm not fucking kidding—Ashley. I felt a strange tingle in my stomach when she revealed that—it was like I'd come full circle with this skin diver thing.

There was a growing knot in my stomach as we wondered about Gary's whereabouts and why he hadn't been there when the additional information on the ashes was revealed. Scott couldn't get a hold of him either, and it seemed like there were really only two scenarios: Gary got fucked, or Gary fucked us. And we were about to find out.

We pulled onto my driveway, and I immediately jumped out of the truck, bolting toward the door, terrified at the sight of my house.

My storm door smashed off its hinges, and someone had tried to break through the front door. I tried the knob, but it was still locked. I ran around the house, with Scott on my heels, and my heart sank as soon I saw my kitchen window. It was shattered.

"Fuck," I said loudly.

"Where'd you stash the ash?" he asked, his voice tense.

"Underneath my bed," I shouted as I ran back to the front door, unlocked it, and sprinted to my bedroom. Out of the corner of my eye, I could see the mess in my living room: drawers pulled from their cabinets, doors wide open, stuff thrown to the floor, lamps knocked over, and even my couch flipped upside down.

I fell to my knees and groped around under the bed. My hands brushed against my rifle and a box of ammo, shoving them aside. I grabbed a flashlight and shined it into the dark space under my bed, only to confirm what I feared: the jar of ashes was gone.

I rose to one knee and looked at Scott, slowly shaking my head.

"Fuckin' twatfucking son of a bitch," he muttered. "I'm goin' to kill that motherfucker." He stormed out. "Think you can mess with us!?" he yelled, running toward his truck. He jumped in, kicked the engine into gear and sped away.

I felt sick to my stomach while I started putting my things back in their place. My mind was hazy and my body felt numb. Had it really been Gary? How did he know where I lived? Did he follow us?

I cursed myself for insisting on driving my Skyline the day before. How could I not have noticed? How could *we* not have noticed? Worse yet, why did he even take the ashes in the first place? What was his plan? I had no idea about his intentions—I truly hoped Scott did, since he was the one who set up the meeting with the guy. If those ashes really are a weapon… I looked around and prayed he hadn't spread them around my place. I'd have to kill him twice over.

Once my house was reasonably tidy, I put a board against the broken window.

I was half a mind to grab my rifle and follow Scott, trying to track Gary down and punish him, but Scott was probably long gone. Was he really going to kill him? Deep down, I already knew the answer. This was Scott, after all.

I spent the rest of the night in a state of uneasy vigilance. Every creak of the house set my nerves on edge. The mess from the break-in was mostly tidied up, but no amount of cleaning could erase the sense of violation. My home had been my last refuge, pretty much, and now even that felt tainted. The boarded-up window was a constant reminder that someone had been inside—someone who might return.

I didn't sleep much. Instead, I lay on the couch with my rifle within reach, the flickering TV providing just enough noise to drown out my racing thoughts. I'd already chugged down enough beer to numb most of it, and I didn't want to drink any more, because I needed to be alert.

By morning, the adrenaline had worn off, leaving me exhausted and jittery. I called into work, telling them I wouldn't be in today either. Chris didn't pry. I felt a little guilty toward him, but I also felt like I had way more important matters to deal with—the possible end of the fuckin' world, for example.

After pacing the house for a while, I decided to give Dr. Linwood a call
—ignoring the several missed calls from Amy. I needed to do something,
anything, to feel like I had some control over the situation.

She picked up on the second ring. "James? What's going on?"

"Dr. Linwood… Ashley," I said, my voice sounding more uncertain than
I intended. "I just wanted to give you a heads-up. There's been a…" I
sighed. "My place got broken into last night."

She was silent for a moment. "Okay… Shouldn't you be on the phone
with the police then?"

"This ain't a police matter," I replied swiftly.

"Ah… Got it. Was anything… taken?"

"The ashes," I answered, my stomach twisting as I said it out loud.
"Gary's missing, and we think he might've been the one who took them.
I have no fucking clue what his intentions are, but it can't be anything
good."

She swore under her breath. "I'll make sure he is blocked from accessing
the lab. If he tries anything over here, we'll know."

"Thanks," I muttered. "I just… I'm not sure what I should do."

"Hmmm. Is Scott with you right now?"

"No. He… he's looking for Gary."

She exhaled sharply. "Well, let him handle it. You stay home, James.
Don't go looking for trouble. I'll keep working on the ashes, see if I can
find a way to neutralize whatever's in them. We'll need that, even if it's
just for precaution."

I nodded—even though she couldn't see that. "Alright. Just be careful,
okay? If Gary's really gone rogue, he might try something desperate."
And probably something worse than breaking into someone's home, I
thought to myself.

"You too," she replied. "And James… you're not alone in this. We'll
figure it out."

I hung up, feeling slightly more grounded, but the fear was still there,
gnawing at the edges of my thoughts. The idea of staying home, of
doing nothing, felt unbearable. But what choice did I have? Scott was out
there somewhere, hunting down a man who might've betrayed us, and all
I could do was wait. And if Scott did find him, he'd likely turn up at my

place after. He didn't have my phone number—yeah, we seriously hadn't exchanged those yet—so he wouldn't be able to find me if I stayed over at Amy's, for example. The thought of staying over at Amy's was really tempting, though.

I spent the day moving between tasks, trying to keep busy. I patched up the window as best as I could with the supplies I had at home. I checked and rechecked the locks on the doors, as my mind kept playing tricks on me—imagining footsteps on the porch or shadows creeping past the window.

I stashed my smashed storm door—which was now completely useless —and resisted the urge to drive down to the city to buy a new one. The risk of running into one of my colleagues on an errand, added to the fact that Scott could show up at any minute, kept me shut inside my house.

When all my tasks were completed, I looked around for more things to do. I wandered into my bedroom and stared at my monitor. I sat down and logged onto the Skin Divers website. I hadn't posted anything new in days, and the messages were piling up.

Under normal circumstances, I'd be responding to all of the non-skeptical comments, sharing what little information I had with others who were just as desperate for answers. I would've definitely posted the findings of the lab analysis on the ashes. But now, every new message felt like a potential threat. Gary could be lurking here, watching, waiting —hungry for every bit of information. I couldn't risk it.

I scrolled through the comments, mostly skimming past them, until one caught my eye. It was from WatchfulEye, a user who'd posted before— about the involvement of cars—the one I'd assumed was just another paranoid guy looking into unrelated things. But something about his words now seemed different, more pointed.

I'm not at liberty to disclose too much, but I've been tracking a series of recent missing persons cases that have been raising red flags. On the surface, the victims don't appear to have anything in common, but there's something… off about the way they disappeared. No signs of forced entry, no apparent struggle, no solid leads, they just… vanished. There have also been unofficial reports of strange sightings around the times of these disappearances. One detail that stands out is a mention of ash

I reread the comment and something started to click. This WatchfulEye guy… his words sounded a lot like those of a cop. If there really was a cop on this forum, that had to mean something. It could be both a blessing and a curse—on one hand, having someone on the force who believed us could be a huge help; on the other hand, it could open up a whole new set of problems. And we already had enough problems on our hands with the break-in. Gary had stabbed us in the back and was now on the loose with a potentially life-threatening substance, planning God knows what. As the day passed, I became more and more convinced that Gary had been the culprit. I mean, who else could it have been? Nobody else knew about the ashes, except the people on the forum, and they didn't even know who I was, let alone where I lived. I briefly considered someone from the lab, but that didn't make sense either—they already had a sample. The only other person who knew was with me all day. And it wouldn't make sense for Scott to have someone break into my home to steal the ashes.

By nightfall, nobody had come to my door. No Scott, and fortunately, no Gary either. I went to bed, still feeling uneasy, and decided to go to work the next day, if only to keep my mind off things for a bit.

In the morning, I got a call from Amy and picked up hesitantly.

"Hey," she said in a flat tone.

"Hey," I said, trying to sound cheerful. "I'm really sorry about yesterday."

"Yeah…" she replied.

"Something came up," I explained. "And I totally forgot to call you. I'm really sorry."

She breathed softly, but didn't say a word.

"Let me make it up to you," I pleaded. "I'll take you out to a really nice restaurant soon and buy you anything you like afterwards. Would you like that?"

"..."

"Please say something, Ames."

She sighed. "Fine. But don't let this happen again. And don't think you can just buy me off with gifts. I am not content with that," she replied in a stately voice.

"I won't," I said.

"So, when?"

"I'll text you, alright?" I replied. My eyes shifted. I first had to deal with this Gary-situation.

"Fine. Don't wait too long," she said and hung up.

I stared at the screen and sighed.

I heard the sound of an engine rumbling up my driveway. The deep growl of the truck was unmistakable—it was Scott. I opened the door just as he was stepping out of the truck. The way he moved told me everything I needed to know.

He looked at me, slowly shaking his head. "Lil' fucker slipped away."

A cold wave of disappointment washed over me. "He escaped?"

"Nah, kid. Couldn't even find the fucker," he muttered. "Tracked him as far as I could, but the bastard's good at covering his tracks." He came walking up the steps, and I let hem inside. "We're dealing with more than just some idiot who got lucky," he growled. "That fucker's got help or something. No way he could've pulled this off on his own." He dropped onto the couch, rubbing his temples. "Any word from Lin?" he asked, glancing at the board that covered the kitchen window.

"Nothing new yet. But I informed her on what happened, just to be safe," I said, sitting down across from him. "She said she'd block access to the lab and if he tries anything, we'll know."

"Good," he grumbled.

"I've been lying low," I continued. "Figured it's best to stay off the radar until we know what Gary's up to."

He nodded, his eyes narrowing as he stared at the table between us. "We need to be ready."

There was a long silence.

He leaned back, his hand resting on his gun. "We're gonna get him," he said, more to himself than to me. "One way or another, we gon' get that son of a bitch."

I nodded slowly. "How did he know?"

"Know what?"

"The ashes, that we had more of them."

He shrugged. "The lid, probably."

I looked at him. "The lid?"

"Yeah, mine had a brass one."

I frowned, still confused.

He snorted. "You know, sometimes I think you might actually be smart, and then you pull this kinda crap."

It finally clicked. "The photo on the website," I said under my breath.

He nodded.

"Fuck…" I got up and ran my hands through my hair in frustration. "Beer?" I asked.

"Gonna need somethin' stronger to wash away this filthy taste," he responded, smacking his lips.

I rummaged through my kitchen cabinets. Somewhere amidst the tidying up, I'd spotted a bottle of Knob Creek I'd bought for Riley as an apology—which I still hadn't given him. I grabbed it and handed it to Scott. "It's the only thing I've got."

He took it with a slight nod. "It'll do." He uncapped it and took a deep swig straight from the bottle, his face tightening as the liquor burned down his throat. "Needed that," he muttered.

I grabbed myself a beer and sat back down.

"He knows where you live," he remarked in a blunt tone.

I nodded.

His eyes flicked to the corner of the room. "If you want… I've got a Murphy bed."

I looked at him, my eyebrows raising. "A Murphy bed?"

"It's nothin' fancy, but it's a place to crash if you need it." He gave me a thoughtful look.

I weighed his offer carefully. Scott's questions often felt like navigating a minefield—I could never be sure which answer might set him off. While

his offer was a form of support I did appreciate, the idea of staying with him unsettled me, especially given the current circumstances. I still didn't know where the skin diver from the cat had gone, and I couldn't shake the thought of sleeping side by side with that thing. Plus, if I had to leave my home, I figured I'd be better off at Amy's.
"Thanks," I said after a long silence. "But I've been ignoring my girlfriend for way too long. I think I'll crash at her place for now."
He frowned, staring in front of him. "Be careful, kid," he said as he got up off the coach. "Can't protect everyone." He left without saying another word, taking the bottle of bourbon with him.

I lay in my own bed that night, holding the rifle to my chest, replaying all the events of the past few days in my head. I wondered about the skin diver that supposedly infested a large dog. I pondered over the disappearing ashes. I recalled the crazy things that creep had said.
Who was he and what exactly were we dealing with?
I was half a mind to take the website down at this point, but it would erase everything *and* shut the door on any other witnesses and reports, like the one from WatchfulEye; Scott would probably read that one soon. I sighed and watched the clock strike 4 a.m.

The next morning—although it was closer to noon—the sun's rays filtered weakly through the blinds as I lay in bed, staring blankly at the ceiling. The rifle I'd clutched now rested against my wall. My phone's screen was flashing with missed calls and messages. I rubbed my eyes and squinted at the notifications. Some were from Amy, the rest from work, but I didn't have the mental energy to deal with that just yet. I felt drained.
When I finally dragged myself out of bed and stumbled to the kitchen, the silence of the house felt oppressive. I had barely eaten or slept over the past few days, and I drank more beer than water. Now, the exhaustion and dehydration were taking their toll. I begrudgingly chugged down a few glasses of water and poured myself a cup of coffee. When I sank down on the couch, there was a loud knock on the door.

I jolted up. My eyes scanned my surroundings and I reached for my Colt, tucking it in my back pocket. I walked to the door and opened it cautiously—not knowing who to expect.

"You look like a zombie," William said as soon as he came into view. He awkwardly held a cigarette, as if he'd just taken up smoking. "No, you look even worse than a zombie." He grinned. "Did something happen?"

I rubbed my temple. If the dehydration hadn't already given me a headache, William would have. I shook my head. "Not really, why?"

"Interesting," he said. "I heard something about a break-in."

I reluctantly looked him in the eye. "I reported no such thing."

"I know," he replied. "You didn't. Which seems rather strange to me… why would your neighbor report a break-in, but not you?"

I forced myself to shrug. "I didn't feel the need."

He eyed me intently. "Did they take anything?"

My heart skipped a beat. "Not that I'm aware of," I said in a sharp tone.

"Are you sure?"

My throat tightened, and I kept silent.

"Nothing of value?" he continued, looking past me into the living room. "Nothing at all?"

I shook my head. "Is that all? I have a massive headache."

"A headache?" he asked in a skeptical tone. "Is that why you're staying home from work?"

My heart dropped. "Yeah," I said, narrowing my eyes. "But how do you know that?"

He casually tucked his hands in his pockets. "I ran into your boss yesterday. We had an interesting talk. Wanna know what we discussed?"

"Not if it doesn't involve me," I said dismissively.

"It definitely involves you," he replied. "I heard you've been skipping out on work these past few days…" He stopped talking, studying my face.

"Yeah, I'm sick," I said curtly. "Do you always go around asking about sick employees?"

He smiled. "Not usually. But it does pique my interest when I see their car speed down the highway."

I swallowed.

"Wanna tell me why you were cruising down toward Springfield?"

"Springfield?" I repeated, trying to hide my surprise.

He nodded slowly.

"Medicine," I said, forcing myself to look into his eyes.

"Must be some special kind of medicine for you to drive all the way down there."

"It is."

He smiled again. "Does getting medicine require Scott Johnson to escort you?"

My jaw clenched. "What's it to you?" I snapped.

"Careful now, James," he said, still with that fucking smile plastered on his face. "You wouldn't want to slip up now, would you?"

"Slip up about what?"

He stared at me, his eyes wide. "Lying," he replied.

"I'm not lying."

"Oh, but you are. I *know* you are. And you have quite the history of lying, don't you?"

My hands balled into fists as I gritted my teeth. "I don't know what you're on about, but if there's nothing more, I'd like to go back to bed now."

"Oh, sure," he said. "You go lie in your bed." He turned around and walked off the stairs. "Be safe, James," he said, without looking back. "You never know what lurks in the shadows."

I slammed the door shut.

My phone rang and I expected it to be either Chris or Amy, but it was Michael. "Hey, bro," I said.

"James," Michael said in a severe, yet reluctant voice.

I kept silent for a moment. "What's up?"

He heaved a heavy sigh. "It's Dad. He…," he swallowed audibly, "passed away."

My gut twisted. "What? How?"

"It was his heart. The pacemaker… it failed. The doctors said it just… gave out. They couldn't do a fucking thing." He tried to keep his voice calm and steady, but I heard a clear tremor.

The room around me started spinning. "Jesus… I… when? When did this happen?"

"Earlier today," he replied. "Around midday. Andrew and Brooke were with him. They were out back with Daisy when it happened. Dad was just sitting on the porch, and… suddenly, he was just… gone." His voice broke.

My mind flashed to the puppy, and how fragile my father had looked when I last saw him. Something started gnawing at my thoughts and I tried with all my might to push it aside. "Are they okay? Andrew and Brooke, I mean?"

"Well, they're shaken up, obviously. But yeah, they're… okay-ish." He sighed.

I took a deep breath and tried to steady my voice. "What can I do?"

"I've already started making the arrangements. Contacted the funeral home, they'll take care of most of it. Wake will be in a couple of days. I thought we should have it at his house."

"Yes, that's…," I said quietly, without finishing my sentence.

"You just need to be there, help with a few things," he continued, "maybe pick up some flowers. Can you do that?"

"Of course, I'll handle that."

"And be there for Andrew, I think it's… I don't know. Given his history and all."

"Yeah, I'll be there," I said.

"Thanks, Jamie."

"Should I pick you up on my way over?"

"I'm already at the house. When are you driving down?"

"I don't know," I replied. "I can leave right now, if that's…" I wanted to say 'if that's what you want', but the last time I said something like that, it didn't go well, so I bit my tongue.

"It'll be dark soon. Probably best to catch some sleep and drive over tomorrow."

I doubted I'd catch any sleep, even though I was exhausted, but I agreed nonetheless. "I'll head over first thing in the morning."

"Okay, man, see you tomorrow. Hang tight."

"You too, bro, hang tight," I replied. My voice cracked.

He hung up, and I sat there in silence, staring out in front of me. My stomach started churning, my gut twisting, my heart pounding, and my pulse quickening.

I wanted to grab a beer to numb myself, but I couldn't get myself off the couch. I felt the urge to gag and the need to sleep, but neither would come and bring me relief. There was just that huge lump in my throat, burning and grazing. My body was so hot, I could nearly see steam coming off of my skin.

I couldn't move for hours.

Chapter 14

The next few days were a haze. I drove down to Philly and hugged my brothers, first thing. I picked up flowers for the wake and joined Michael to meet with the funeral director. I tried keeping Andrew occupied, in an attempt to keep his head clear—although I could sense that he was slipping. I had a long conversation with Brooke about him, and I secretly kept a close watch on Daisy, the golden retriever pup.
The funeral was held in a small, traditional chapel, and the weather was appropriately gloomy with overcast skies and a slight chill in the air. My half-sisters, Nancy and Pam, sat on the front row with us, and his ex-wife, Nicole, one row behind. She was sobbing her eyes out.
I wanted to shed tears, and I truly expected them to come, but I felt hollow and numb, and no tears would come. Even through the cremation and the reception, I didn't shed a single tear. Neither did Michael—but when all our family and friends had left, and a thick silence filled the air, he finally broke down. It was only then that my tears started flowing. I couldn't even remember the last time I saw my big brother cry.

Michael was my father's executor and he took care of the legalities. I wasn't too interested in any of that, so I mostly focused my attention on keeping Andrew straight—making sure he stayed off the stuff. On top of dealing with our grief, we were getting more and more worried about his behavior and state of mind, until Brooke asked me if he could stay with me for a while. Maybe a different environment would do him good, she suggested.
I agreed, but I did clarify that I wouldn't be able to watch him all day, since I'd have to go back to work. She said it was the same for her and that he just really needed a change of scenery, away from our father's home and its surroundings. Away from Philly. She also asked me to take Daisy with us.
I agreed reluctantly.

A week later, I drove home with Andrew next to me and Daisy on the back seat. Brooke had put down a towel for her, which I appreciated—Daisy's nails were pretty sharp after all. I looked at her every now and then, still wondering. A malfunctioning pacemaker… Could it be? When I got home, I gave Chris a call and informed him of my father's passing. He gave me two weeks off—five days paid and the rest as unused vacation days.

Over the next few days, my house turned into a cramped doghouse. Andrew slept in my bed, with Daisy curled up beside him, and I ended up on the couch, clutching my rifle. Andrew didn't get it—not really. I told him about the break-in, but to him, it just seemed like I was overreacting. Dog hair was everywhere, toys scattered around, and no matter how often I cracked the windows, the house always smelled like dog food.

Andrew started vacuuming obsessively, every day without fail. The hum of the vacuum became part of the background noise, along with the constant clicking of Daisy's nails against the floor and the squeaking of her toys.

When I got home from work, he was usually in the kitchen, trying out new recipes—something he'd picked up from Brooke. She called every day, making sure he was pulling through, and that was the most I heard from him in a day. We barely talked. The house was quieter than it should have been, with only Daisy's noises and the murmur of the TV cutting through the silence.

One night, after coming back from work, I noticed his eyes were red-rimmed. He quickly looked away when I glanced at him. He was barely holding it together.

I hadn't heard him cry, except once, muffled behind the sound of the shower. I pretended I didn't notice, but it gnawed at me.

Daisy was the focus of his attention. He'd spend hours playing with her, brushing her fur and taking her on long walks. But there was a tension in him, a barely contained energy that I could feel every time I walked into the room—it started to suffocate me.

It was a Saturday afternoon, after I'd reluctantly gone over to Scott's for some more target practice, when it happened. I just came back, and saw Daisy running around the house. Her paws were caked with mud. As soon as I opened the door, she dashed in ahead of me, streaking through the living room and leaving a dark, messy trail.

"DAISY, NO!" Andrew's voice shot through the house, startling both her and me. He jumped up from the couch, his face flushed with anger, and before I could react, he grabbed one of her toys and threw it across the room with a force that made Daisy yelp and cower in the corner.

"What the hell, Drew?" I snapped, more out of shock than anything else. He stood there, eyes wild and chest heaving.

The room was dead silent, except for Daisy's nervous whimper as she glanced between us.

His hands started to shake and he stared at the mess on the floor like it was a trail of blood. "I'm sorry," he muttered. His voice cracked. He didn't look at me, just turned away, as his shoulders slumped. "I didn't mean to…"

I took a deep breath, trying to find the right words. "It's just mud, dude. She didn't mean any harm."

He nodded silently and sank down on the couch, burying his face in his hands.

This wasn't just about Daisy. It was everything—our father, the funeral, the strain of keeping it together, and, probably most difficult of all, trying to stay clean.

"Drew…" I started, but I didn't know how to finish. What could I say what would make any of this easier?

He finally looked up at me with glassy eyes. "I'm trying, James," he whispered, and for a moment, I saw the kid he used to be—the one who looked up to me, like I looked up to Michael, before everything went to shit in our house, after the first skin diver attack.

I sighed wearily. It felt like it was all their fault. Maybe it was. "I know," I said to him. "I know you are." I sat down with him and watched Daisy slowly approaching him, whining softly, and nudging his leg with her nose.

He reached down to pet her with trembling fingers.

For a split second, her eyes seemed to grow.

I blinked and stared at her, frozen—her eyes looked normal. Was it my imagination? Was it the stress? Or was she really one of them, and was she the reason our father was now dead?

We sat there for a long time, neither of us saying a word. I stared up at the ceiling and wondered how long we could keep going like this before something else broke. Maybe Andrew did need a change of scenery and he probably needed more support than I was able to offer.

I also didn't trust Daisy and I expected her to turn into one of those things at any moment. It filled me with dread and anxiety. That, combined with the frustration, worry and helplessness I felt over Andrew, and the pit in my stomach that had been there since the funeral, steered me into making a terrible decision that night.

I waited for Andrew to go to bed before I called Michael, talking as quietly as I could.

"Michael," I began, right after he picked up at the second ring. The lump in my throat had already started to swell. "I don't know…" I took a deep breath. "I don't know what to do with Andrew. He's not… he's not doing well. You know that. And I don't think I can help him, not like this. Can he stay with you?"

There was a pause on the other end, a heavy silence that I wasn't sure how to interpret.

"James, it's late," he finally said, sounding exhausted. "Can this wait until morning?"

"No, it can't. I'm losing him, Michael. I'm really losing him this time. He can't stay here any longer." My voice cracked, and I could feel the tears prickling the corners of my eyes. "And I'm scared. Scared that… that something's going to happen, and I won't be able to stop it."

"Something's going to happen? What are you talking about? Is he using again?"

"No, it's not that…"

"What is it then?"

"It's just… something's going to go wrong. I can feel it."

"What do you expect me to do, James? I'm already dealing with
everything—Dad's estate, setting his affairs, managing the paperwork—
do you have any idea how much work this is?"
"I know," I said quietly, "and I'm sorry, but this is different, Michael. It's
not just about Drew. I don't trust Daisy. I don't… I've got a bad feeling."
"Daisy?" he asked bewildered. "What about Daisy?"
"She's… she was there when Dad died, right? And I keep thinking about
the skin divers, about what happened with Mom and Ashley. What if-"
"For fuck's sake, James, not this again!" he interrupted, his voice
suddenly furious. "I don't have the time or patience to deal with your
fucking paranoia right now. There *are* no skin divers! There never were.
That was some messed-up story you made up because you were
traumatized, and you have got to let it go!"
"But Michael-"
"No, James," he cut me off, harsher this time. "I'm dealing with enough
as it is. Do you think I *want* to be sorting through Dad's affairs alone? Do
you think I don't have my own shit to handle? And now you're telling me
to take Andrew in, like that's just something I can do on a whim!?"
"He's our fucking brother," I shot back, desperation creeping into my
voice. "He needs it, Michael. He needs you."
"And I need you to get your head on straight!" Michael snapped. "I'm
sorry you're having a rough time. We all are. But I can't take on more
right now. I just can't. There's shit going on at work, and Stacy, she's…"
He sighed like an angry bull. "And I definitely can't handle you spiraling
over some ridiculous fantasy about skin divers and conspiracies. You've
got to stop this, James. For all of our sakes."
His words stung, but I couldn't stop now. "Bro, I'm not making this up. I
swear to you, something's not right. Scott's been acting off too, and
Gary—this witness we met—he broke into my house and stole the ashes
we had. Because we killed one, Michael. We *killed* one of them. I put it
on my website, and there's so many people leaving com-"
"Jesus Christ, James!" Michael's voice was full of exasperation now. "You
need help. *Real* help. Not whatever rabbit hole you're going down online.
You need to get a grip on reality before you drag us all down with you."

I felt the weight of his words settle in my chest, heavy and suffocating. He didn't believe me. He didn't believe a word I said and he probably never once did—even when I told him about the bird video. I suddenly felt like a crazy person on a rant, and that made me all the more frustrated. "Michael, please," I pleaded with a small voice. "I just… I just don't know what to do."

There was another long silence on the other end of the line. When Michael finally spoke again, his tone was softer, but still firm. "James, listen to me. You need to take care of yourself first. You're no good to Andrew if you're falling apart. You know what can…" His voice faded away. "This feels like 2007 all over again, and I can't handle this right now. Please, just… try to get some rest. We'll talk tomorrow."

"But Andrew-"

"We'll talk tomorrow," he repeated, more insistent this time. "Get some sleep, James." He hung up before I could say anything else.

I sat there for a long time, staring at the phone in my hand. His words echoed in my mind.

Then, the silence was broken by a soft ticking on the floor.

I turned my head and looked at the golden retriever pup, standing in front of my bedroom door. The door was cracked open just a bit, but she had squeezed through, and now, she was staring at me. She didn't move at all. No tail wagging, no nose sniffing, no paws scratching.

My pulse quickened. "What?" I asked out loud—secretly hoping it would wake up Andrew.

She didn't respond. She just kept on staring at me.

A chill ran down my spine and my hand made its way to my rifle. "Not today," I said silently. "If you're in there, you creeping little fuck, I'm going to drag you out. I won't let you take me." My jaw clenched as I stared back into her eyes and cocked my Garand. "Just try it," I whispered.

She slowly sat down, still staring at me, and the corners of her mouth pulled up wide—showing a strange, twisted grin on her face.

Her eyes started out of their sockets.

I aimed the gun at her, feeling my heart pound like a sledgehammer.

She sprung up and bolted toward me.

But before she could reach me, I pulled the trigger.

Michael picked Andrew up the next day without even sparing me a
glance. Andrew left quietly and would never speak to me again. I bore
that, knowing I had kept him safe—even though he'd spend the rest of
his life believing that his brother shot his puppy—his only solace—in a
paranoid haze, just weeks after our father died.
Amy broke up with me after hearing what happened, although I
expected her to leave either way. I hadn't exactly been thoughtful of her
lately.
A month later, I got fired from my job due to repeated absences, stupid
mistakes and missed deadlines.
And that's how 2010 became the year I lost everything.

Everything seemed pointless now.
I felt numb.
I felt numb all through winter, which was cold as hell this year, and all
through spring and summer—which just to be my favorite seasons. I felt
numb after hearing the news of Amy's engagement. And I felt numb
when my calls to Michael and Andrew went unanswered.
I started drinking more and more, even though my money was running
out. I had to sell my Skyline to pay the mortgage and struggled to find
another job in the area. Plenty of people knew about the incident; this
was the second dog that had turned up dead right in front of me—and I
pulled the trigger on this one—in just a few months.
I heard whispers in the shadows, rumors about me being a serial killer, or
at least one in the making, and no one seemed to want to talk to me.
Which was all the same to me, honestly, because I had no interest in
socializing anymore. I even completely dropped Thomas and Riley, not
that they tried to reach out to me anyway.
The only people who seemed to be on my side were Scott and Crazy
Eddie, who'd drop by every now and then to check on me. The house
always smelled of tobacco when Eddie visited—his smoking habits were
worse than Scott's.

I didn't see Scott much; he was still hunting down a guy that didn't want to be found, and there was no news from Dr. Linwood. Everything around me seemed to have gone quiet, except for the website. It had taken on a life of its own, but I didn't even want to look at it anymore. I thought about moving. It had done me good the first time around, but only for a while, since it had also brought me to this point. The skin divers seemed to be everywhere, and there was no escaping them.
At least I had one ally here, and allies were hard to come by. Besides, my spiraling depression would have turned every place into a shithole.

Chapter 15

In October 2011, I was working the night shift at a warehouse downtown—the last one of the week. My tasks were simple: sorting, packing and loading goods, making sure that the right packages were in the right place. It was a mindless kind of job, but it paid the bills.
As I drove back home in my Toyota Corolla—a model I could easily fix myself and was cheap enough to maintain—I looked at the autumn foliage and felt a strange gnawing in my stomach. A year had passed already and the days bled together in a monotonous cycle of night shifts and solitude.
There were no answers to my questions and the whole skin diver thing started to feel like a story that had happened to someone else. They were a distant memory, though a constant, nagging one.
Just as I pulled up the driveway, my phone buzzed. I grabbed it from its holder and looked at it. There was a message from Scott.
For the first time in months, I felt a jolt of something other than numbness.
We needed to talk.

The drive to Scott's place felt surprisingly long, perhaps because I hadn't been there in ages. All the while, my mind was racing. I wondered what he had to say. Maybe it was news about the skin divers or another lead on the ashes. Maybe he had talked to Dr. Linwood and found out something interesting, finally.
But as I pulled up to his house and saw the front door slightly ajar, my heart dropped.
I pushed through the door and was hit by the stale smell of sweat, blood and fear.
Scott was hunching over the couch, and I could see a figure lying there, covered in a blanket. He turned to me and his face showed a mix of relief and worry. "Kid," he said, standing up as I walked in. "It's Gary."

For a moment, I couldn't process what he was saying. Gary? I looked at the man on the couch. It was him, alright—though he wasn't the same man who'd vanished roughly a year ago.

I moved closer and my stomach twisted at the sight. Gary was a shell of himself. His face was gaunt, bruised and swollen. His eyes were wild, darting around the room like he expected something—or someone—to burst in at any moment. His hands trembled as he clutched the blanket to his chest.

There was dried blood on his hands. All of his fingernails were missing.

"Did you do this to him?" I asked under my breath.

Scott scowled. "The fuck, kid," he said quietly. "I found him like this."

I felt strangely relieved and knelt down beside Gary, trying to get a read on him. His breathing was shallow, his skin clammy. He looked like he hadn't eaten or slept in days. Weeks, even. But the worst part was his eyes. There was a terror in them. A deep, primal fear that I'd never seen in anyone before, even with all of my experiences. It made my skin crawl just looking at him.

"Gary," I said in a gentle voice, unsure if he could even hear me. "It's James." I paused and tried to find the right words. "You're safe now. Can you tell us what happened?"

For a moment, there was nothing. Just the sound of his ragged breathing. Then, slowly, he turned his head to look at me. When he spoke, his voice was hoarse, barely more than a whisper, like it hurt to even form the words. "He… he took me," he managed, his eyes flicking toward the door. "I didn't know… he came out of nowhere… one minute, I was in my car, and then… everything went black."

Scott and I exchanged a glance.

"He wanted info," he continued, his voice shaking. "About the ashes… about the skin divers. I told him I… I didn't know anything." He broke off, his thin frame shuddering, clutching the blanket tighter. "He didn't believe me. He… he kept asking. Over and over, and he…" He trailed off. His eyes glazed over as he relived whatever horrors he'd been subjected to.

I didn't push him to continue; I wasn't sure I wanted to hear the details.

But after a moment, he spoke again, his voice even quieter. "He hurt me," he said, his eyes filling with tears. "I don't even know for how long. Weeks… months… it all blurred together. I thought I was going to die. I *wanted* to die. But then, he just… left me. Dumped me somewhere in the woods. I had no idea where I was. It was cold, *so* cold. I had to crawl my way out and… and…" He broke down, sobbing violently, and I felt a lump in my throat as I watched him. This man was broken to the point that he didn't even speak the way he used to anymore.

I suddenly missed his catchphrase, *y'know.*

"Found him near the woods," Scott started, "Covered in dirt, blood and shit." He looked at me with a grim expression. "I knew right there and then." He looked back at Gary. "No wonder I couldn't find him."

"Did you see his face?" I asked Gary carefully. "Of the man who did this to you?"

He slowly shook his head. "I was blindfolded."

"You never saw or noticed *anything*?"

Gary's eyes flicked toward the door before he shook his head.

I bit my lip.

"You can't think of a single thing? There must be something," Scott pressed.

He kept shaking his head. "I don't remember."

Scott sighed. "Well… I can think of a way to jog your memory. But it's not gonna be pretty. What do you think, Gary?"

He swallowed visibly, but remained silent.

"What about you, kid?"

I hesitated. I didn't want to traumatize Gary even further, but we did need answers. "What do you have in mind?"

Without saying a word, Scott disappeared into the room next to the kitchen. He came back out shortly after, and walked over, clutching something in his fist.

As soon as he opened his fist, revealing what was inside, Gary started shrieking.

It was a blindfold.

"I'm sorry, dude, but it's pretty much a surefire way to get some answers," he said.

I half-expected him to forcefully put the blindfold on, but he just waited patiently.

"You want us to find whoever did this to you?" Scott urged in a soothing voice. "Want us to get revenge of that fucker?"

Gary nodded slightly.

"Then you have to help us."

Finally, Gary bowed his head and allowed Scott to put the blindfold on him. His hands trembled, his breathing was heavy, and tears streamed down his face. His nailless fingers grasped the fabric, and he began to murmur.

"M-maybe… one time, yes. The blindfold… it came off when he was…" he gasped for air, "punching me in the face." He squinted, trying to recall the looks of his captor. "He was tall." He tore off the blindfold—his eyes were glazed over. "He had a square jaw. And his eyes…" He stopped talking.

I turned to Scott. "Where did you find him? Somewhere near?"

He nodded. "I looked everywhere for that ba-" he glanced at Gary, "for him. Driven miles and miles, even so far as Springfield, only to find him near Pudding fuckin' Hill."

"Pudding Hill?" I asked in surprise. "Are you kidding?"

"I'm never kiddin', kid," he replied gruffly.

"But that's close. I mean, really, really close."

"It is." He eyed me. "That's why I asked you here. The motherfucker who's done this has been close all along."

I frowned.

"You ever talk to anyone else 'bout the ashes or the skin eaters?"

I started to shake my head, but then stopped. There were a few people I had told, but none of them believed me and none of them seemed even slightly capable of harming another human, let alone torture one.

"Who?" he pressed.

"My brother," I answered. "And my mother."

"Hm. Your brother grey?"

I shook my head. "No, and it's not him, trust me."

He eyed me for a while, then turned his attention to Gary. "What about the ashes? What'd you do with them?"

Gary looked up at him. "W-what do you mean?"

"You stole 'em, right? Broke into the kid's home and took it."

He blinked and lowered his head. "I… I didn't mean to. I just…" he whimpered, "I needed them."

I sighed. "What for?"

He stared at his knees and shrugged half-heartedly. "It's no use. He took it."

"Fuck," I responded. "Did he know what it was?"

"I… I don't know. He didn't seem to know… at first."

"So you told him," Scott said, his tone gruff.

Gary let his head hang and softly started sobbing. "I d-didn't know much," he cried. "Just what Dr. Linwood told us."

Scott and I exchanged a glance.

"Now what?" I asked softly.

Scott stared down at Gary, then turned to me. "Gotta get him in better shape and keep him safe," he grumbled. "And get Lin on the phone. If he spilled the beans, she's in danger."

"When did you last speak to her?" I asked.

His eyebrows raised and then turned into a frown. "At the lab," he said. "Why?"

"Because I've never heard from her again." My heart dropped as I said it.

His frown deepened. "Could've said something, kid, I mean… shit." He shook his head in disbelief. "Don't think that's valuable information? Not worth my time, or what? Or is it because you still don't trust me."

I hesitated to answer.

"Whatever," he grumbled, as he walked over to his phone. "Here's to hopin' she ain't kicked the bucket." He grabbed his phone and dialed her number. He hesitated before pressing 'call'.

Gary had fallen silent, his eyes fixed on the floor.

I wanted to comfort him and tell him he was going to be okay, but the words stuck in my throat—I didn't believe them myself.

Scott put the phone on speaker and it rang once, twice, then a third time. Just when I thought it would go to voicemail, there was a sound on the other end.

"Hello?" Ashley Linwood's voice was soft, almost tentative.

"Lin, it's Scott," he said in his usual gruff voice. "We need to talk."
There was a pause, then her voice came back, more guarded now. "Scott?
What's going on?"
He glanced at us. "We've got a situation. Gary turned up."
"Gary?" Her voice wavered with disbelief. "But how… where has he
been?"
"He's in bad shape," Scott continued in a flat tone. "He was taken.
Tortured for months. Fucker who did this wanted information—about
the ashes, the skin divers."
The line went silent for a moment.
"Scott, I… I don't know what to say," she finally replied.
"He blabbed and you could be in danger," he continued. "We need your
help. You're the only one who knows enough 'bout this to give us an
edge. You find anything? Like a neutralizer, or some shit?"
"No," she replied curtly. "The ashes vanished."
"What?"
"They're gone. Disappeared into thin air, overnight."
Gary looked up and Scott and I exchanged glances.
"And I think it's better this way," she added, more quietly now. "They're
dangerous."
"Whoever did this is dangerous," I cut in, unable to stay quiet. "A lot
more dangerous."
"James? Is that you?"
"Yeah, it's me."
There was a sharp intake of breath on the other end, and when she
spoke again, her voice was trembling. "I think you should forget about all
of this. I warned you before."
"We can't," I said, trying to keep my despair from seeping through. "He's
out there, Ashley. He's out there and he's not just coming after the ashes.
He's coming after anyone who knows about them—maybe even you." I
turned to Gary. "You told him about her, didn't you?" I pressed.
Gary cowered.
"Damn right he did," Scott grumbled. "Fucker."

There was a deep silence. "I know," Ashley said, silent like a mouse. "That's why… that's why I've been keeping my head down. I haven't been in the lab for months. I even had to move to another city…"

My eyes widened as I looked at Scott. "W-why? Did you see him? Did he come for you?"

Another silence.

Scott's grip on the phone tightened and his knuckled turned even whiter. "Lin, we can't just wait around for this fucker. We need to know who he is and what he wants."

"I don't know who they are," she said with a shaky voice. "But I know their type. They latch onto something and they don't let go, even when it's long gone. If they're still looking for the ashes, then…" She went silent.

"They?" Scott asked.

Another long, deep silence.

"So what do we do?" I asked, trying to keep my voice steady. "Just wait for him—or them—to come after us?"

"Protect yourselves," she replied. "And protect Gary. These men are dangerous, you've seen what they're capable of." She paused for a while. "Don't go looking for them, Scott."

There was something about the way she said that.

"And don't call me again."

The call disconnected.

Scott and I looked at each other in disbelief.

"She's in danger," he said slowly.

"So are we…"

He frowned. "Unless this ba-," he glanced at Gary, "unless he spilled, those fuckers wouldn't have a clue where to look for us. Besides, we don't even have the ashes anymore."

I swallowed, visibly enough for him to glare at me.

"Do we?" he pressed.

"I might have some…" I started, softly. "It hasn't disappeared. Not yet."

Gary squealed, his eyes trembling in their sockets as he looked up at me.

"Kid…" Scott grumbled. "You go hunting alone?"

I shook my head. "Killed my brother's puppy," I said in a flat tone. "At least, that's how he sees it."

"Damn."

I looked at Gary. "What about him? Should he stay here?"

"Here is as safe as it gets," Scott replied, glancing at his cabinet full of guns. "But he can't stay long, so we'll need to catch those fuckers as soon as possible."

"So, how do you wanna handle this?"

"We start by canvassing the area. Since they dropped his ass off at Pudding fuckin' Hill, they might live nearby—or at least one of them does. So, we'll start by looking around the spot where I found him." He nodded at Gary. "There anythin' else you can tell us about those bastards? Anything that might help us locate them?"

"I thought it was only one man." His face turned pale. "I… I don't know." He swallowed hard, his gaze drifting to the blindfold, now lying on the floor. "Yes… yes, I remember. Of course, I remember. How could I forget?" His eyes glazed over. "There was this smell. The stench of his cigarette breath. Every time he came close, I couldn't breathe. The stink of Marlboros—I'll never forget it. I could smell it on his firsts every time he hit me."

"Marlboros?" Scott repeated. "Alright, we'll keep an eye out for that. Might be key."

"And what about Lin?" I asked. "Shouldn't she take a look at the ashes? She said she would find a way to neutralize them."

He shook his head. "That was then, not now. Not while she's hiding. She's scared shitless and for good reason. We can't rely on her to handle this. We need to act."

I looked at him, quietly wondering.

"Grab him," Scott said.

We helped Gary onto his feet and got him settled in a spare room that Scott had filled with books, weapons and supplies. Newspaper clippings covered the walls, just like I had done at my place some time ago.

I glanced over them while Scott made Gary as comfortable as possible. There were articles on fatal car accidents, drug overdoses, disappearances, and some unusual hospital cases—all from New Hampshire and all within the past year, during my numbed-out period. Scott grabbed a flashlight and a couple of maps. "Don't just stand there, lookin' like an idiot," he grumbled at me.

I turned to him with a questioning look. "Why?" was the only word I managed to get out.

"'Cause we need to get a move on, kid."

"No, I mean…" I gestured at the clippings.

"Oh, that," he said before grabbing some cans of food and other essentials and stuffing them into a military backpack. "Well, while you were nodding off or whatever, I did all the heavy lifting. Hand me those bottles." He nodded at a tray of water bottles standing to my right, and I handed him the entire tray. "Anything that could be connected to the ashes and what they do…" he sighed as he hoisted the large bag onto his back, "I put up there. Now, let's go."

He walked toward the door, then turned around, looking at Gary. "Don't touch anything. And if there's somethin' wrong, use that." He pointed at the burner phone on the table beside Gary. "Our numbers are the only ones in there."

I followed him into the living room. "Shouldn't we take him to a hospital?" I asked quietly.

"Too dangerous," he replied sharply.

"But he could have internal blee-"

"Too dangerous," he repeated, looking at me with his piercing eyes. He grabbed a bag from his cabinet and shoved it in my hands. "Ammo," he said. "And some weapons." He headed toward the door. "We'll start with the forest and work our way out from there. If these fuckers've been operating close to home, there's a good chance they've got some kind of base nearby."

I waited on the porch, watching him meticulously lock his door.

"Nothin' in, nothin' out," he said quietly, marching toward his Chevy. He then stood still and glanced at the Toyota behind it. "The fuck?" He turned around. "Traded in your plastic toy for a piece of gum?"

If I was anything like my slightly younger self, I would've bantered with him, but the grimness of my reality was no longer something I could find humor in. I gave him a look, and said nothing.

"Sorry, kid," he grumbled before he tossed the backpack into the back seat of his rusty old truck.

The night was dark and cold as we drove to Pudding Hill, the truck's headlights cutting through the fog. Scott parked the car and we got out, scanning the area.

"Keep your eyes peeled," he instructed. "If he's been around here, he might have left something behind." He reached for his Colt. "Got yours?"

I nodded, tapping my pocket. We walked through the woods in the dark, guided by only the dim light of the moon and our flashlights. The sound of leaves crunching under our feet broke the stillness as I carefully followed Scott. He looked around, inspected broken branches and got down on one knee to inspect trampled grass.

"Isn't it easier to search in the light of day?" I asked.

"Easier, sure," he grumbled. "Easier for us to be found, as well." He picked up a cigarette butt and stared at it. His eyes narrowed as he looked at the red band near the filter. "Marlboro Red," he muttered. "Don't care much about his lungs." He tucked it in a little plastic bag. We continued our search. It was around 3 a.m. when we reached a clearing. I noticed something glinting on the ground when my flashlight glanced it. I knelt down and picked up a keychain. It was a brass pendant that was shaped like an ornate compass. It was a bit tarnished and worn with age. At the top, where the keyring attached, was a small, engraved plague that read: *To find your way, even when lost.*

"Look at this," I said, holding it up.

Scott squinted at the keychain. "Hm, interesting." He handed me a plastic bag. "Should've dragged that bastard out here, might've got some answers on the spot."

"The guy can barely walk," I muttered, sliding the keychain into the bag. He grunted in response, his eyes scanning the ground as we continued searching for a clue, any clue. We combed the area, but all we turned up

204

were crunched cans, empty bottles, rusted tools, and a mess of poison ivy.

"We should head back," Scott said after a while. "There's nothin' here. If he's got a base, it ain't in this forest. Maybe the bastard can tell us more about this compass."

On the drive back to Scott's, my mind raced. I tried to recall the keychain with the compass in my mind, but I was sure I'd never seen it before.

I thought of every person I'd ever seen smoke: Scott, myself, my brother Michael, Thomas, Riley, Kimberley, my boss Chris, Crazy Eddie…

Suddenly, it hit me. My eyes widened. I turned sharply to Scott.

He caught the movement from the corner of his eye. "What is it, kid?"

My voice caught in my throat. "I think… maybe there's someone…" I stumbled over the words, the realization sinking in. "There's one person who's been keeping tabs on me."

His frown deepened, his knuckles whitening as he gripped the wheel. "Who?"

I hesitated. His name felt heavy on my tongue. "William. William Abbott."

Chapter 16

Back at Scott's place, Gary was huddled on the couch, staring at us with an exhausted, fearful expression.

Scott glanced into the room where we had left him before we went to Pudding Hill, then grabbed a chair. He sat down and placed the plastic bags containing the keychain and the cigarette butt on the coffee table. "Found these in the woods," he said, nodding toward the items. "Recognize 'em?"

Gary's eyes locked onto the bags and he carefully reached for them. With trembling fingers, he opened the bag with the cigarette, and his nose wrinkled as if he could still smell the stench clinging to it. "Marlboro Red," he muttered, almost to himself. "Yes… this is it… this is his smell," he confirmed with a hoarse voice.

"What about the keychain?" I asked.

Gary put the bagged cigarette back on the table, breathing heavily, and looked at the little compass. He turned the thing over and over in his hands, and frowned.

"It was just lyin' there," Scott said. "Could belong to anyone. But maybe you've seen it before."

Gary slowly shook his head. "I don't remember this."

I swallowed hard, feeling the knot of tension in my stomach tighten. I sat down next to him on the couch and leaned in. "Gary, listen. I've been thinking… I might know who's responsible for… for what happened to you. There's someone who's been lurking around. Someone who's had eyes on me. On us. It's William. William Abbott."

His eyes shot up to meet mine. "William…" he whispered.

"Could it be him?" I pressed. "He's a," I paused, "a detective."

Gary's eyes clouded over with fear. He swallowed hard, his eyes darting between the keychain and the cigarette butt. "I… I don't know. It could be. But I don't know that… detective." He sighed wearily. "But the smell, that fucking smell…"

Scott's eyes never left Gary's face. "We'll find out tomorrow. We'll take a drive down to the station. See if we can lure the bastard out. Find out if he's our guy…"

Gary's face paled. "What if he sees me? What if he knows it's *me*?"

"We'll keep you hidden," he retorted. "You just gotta tell us if it's him or not. That's all." He then turned his gaze to me. "You should come too, but that fuckin' cop'll recognize you right away."

"I know," I said, my mind spinning. "Maybe that's a good thing." But even as I said it, a cold knot of dread settled in my stomach, right on top of the knot that'd been there since the drive back. Nothing about this felt right.

The more I thought about it, the more the pieces started to fall into place. I felt a wave of frustration and self-reproach for not realizing it sooner. He'd been suspicious of me all along, and I'd felt the same about him, but I never connected these two dots. I never imagined that a detective—someone who was supposed to uphold the law, and someone who'd known me since I was 10 years old—could harm someone the way he'd harmed Gary.

Worse, I hadn't known he was aware of the skin divers.

The next morning, the cold autumn air was thick with a tension that clung to our skin like sweat. Scott drove with his usual stoic focus, eyes fixed on the road, while I sat in the passenger seat, trying to ignore the knot in my stomach. Gary was huddled under a blanket in the back seat, his body trembling with each bump in the road.

We parked a little distance from the police station, choosing a spot that gave us a clear view of the entrance but kept us somewhat concealed. The plan was simple: wait for William to step outside for his smoke break and have Gary confirm his identity.

"You sure about this, Scott?" I asked, my voice barely above a whisper, as I nodded toward the propped up blanket—Gary's eyes just barely squinted through an opening.

"Ain't no other way to know for sure," he replied. "We just sit tight and wait."

Minutes passed, each one stretching longer than the last.

The door of the police station swung open and I shifted in my seat. Tammy stepped out.

I leaned back and watched her as she made her way to the coffee shop down the road. I thought of the day I met her, when I had to come in to give my statement. My raging hormones had clouded my mind, but that time was long gone. I missed it.

Tammy walked back with three coffees and a large box of donuts. There were at least three people inside, I concluded, exchanging a glance with Scott.

More time passed and I was starting to feel uneasy. What if William was up and about? What if he didn't even work at this station anymore? I mean, he'd moved before and-

My racing mind was interrupted by the door opening again.

Finally, William stepped out. He moved with a deliberate ease—the kind of confidence that comes from someone who feels fucking untouchable —pulling a pack of Marlboro Reds from this pocket and tapping out a cigarette. He lit it with a flick of his lighter.

I felt my heart pound in my chest as I glanced back at Gary, who was peeking out from under the blanket. His eyes were wide and his pupils were dilated, but he didn't say a word. He just watched as William took a deep drag of his cigarette, exhaling a cloud of smoke into the chill morning air.

William's eyes scanned the street lazily, then narrowed as they landed on Scott's truck.

"Fuck," I said under my breath. "Did he see us?"

William flicked the cigarette, knocking off some ash, and started walking toward us.

My breath caught in my throat as I watched him approach.

Scott's grip tightened on the steering wheel. "Stay calm," he muttered.

William stopped a few feet from the truck and leaned down to peer through the window. His eyes lingered on me for a moment before he walked up to the passenger side. He tapped on the glass, gesturing for me to roll the window down.

I rolled it down just a crack and saw his gaze drift to the back seat, where Gary was trying his best to remain unseen under his shield of blankets.

A smile, cold and calculated, tugged at the corner of his mouth.

"Morning," he said smoothly. "What brings you boys out here?"

"Just passin' through," Scott replied, his tone gruff.

William nodded, but his eyes were still locked on the back seat. "Looking for someone?" he asked in a low voice.

"No one in particular," Scott answered. "Just drivin' around."

"Funny," he remarked. "You're not driving, though. Just parked."

"So?" Scott shot back. "I can park here."

William's smile didn't falter. He took a long drag from his cigarette, then exhaled the smoke right through the crack in the window. His gaze lingered for a moment longer, as if he was savoring the tension in the air. Then, without another word, he straightened up and walked back toward the station, the cigarette smoldering between his fingers.

As soon as he was out of sight, I turned to Gary. "Well?"

His face was as pale as a ghost, his eyes wide and filled with confusion and fear. Tears welled up as he shook his head. "It's… it's not him," he whispered with a trembling voice.

I felt a cold wave of shock wash over me. The certainty I'd felt just moments ago crumbled to dust.

Scott's jaw clenched, and without a word, he pulled the truck away from the station. His eyes were hard as steel as we drove through the streets of Dover.

"Now what?" I asked hesitantly.

The tires screeched and Scott maneuvered the Chevy onto a nearly empty parking lot. He put the car in neutral and stared at me. "I don't trust him. Not one bit."

Gary shivered under his blanket. "But I… I told you everything!" he squealed.

"Not you, you idiot," he barked at him. "That fuckin' cop." He looked me dead in the eyes. "He knows something. He definitely knows something. I could tell." His nostrils flared and he turned to Gary. "That smell," he grumbled, "you recognized it, didn't you? It was Marlboro Red."

Gary just nodded, then pulled the blanket over his face.

"I think it's like this: you smelled *him*," Scott continued, "and you *saw* the other."

I raised my eyebrows. "You really think so?"

He nodded. "That fucker's guilty as they come—I've seen enough bastards like him to know. He's one half of our Devil Duo; now we just need to find the other half. And if Mr. Tall with a square jaw's out there, he's bound to show up near him."

"We should keep an eye on him, then."

"No shit, kid. Still playin' Sherlock, huh?"

I rolled my eyes and turned toward the window, slightly smirking.

"Stay sharp, though," he added in a lower voice. "Can't be too sure that fucker ain't still sittin' on a stash of those ashes."

"What do you mean?" I asked. "Ashley said it disappeared."

"Yeah, well, you got your hands on some. And I'm bettin' that fucker's a way better shot than you. Might've gone huntin' for a skin eater himself."

I sighed, imagining the worst case scenario.

"So, where does he live?" he asked.

I turned my head. "How the fuck should I know? I ain't buddies with him. Never even liked the guy."

He snorted. "Well, what good are you then?" He glanced at his rearview mirror. "Guess we'll be tailin' him, then."

We drove back home, swapping out Scott's truck for my Corolla to remain discreet. Gary begged us to drop him off at Scott's place, but Scott refused.

"We need you there," he said in his gruff voice. "His partner might show up."

Gary whimpered.

Around half past four we drove back down to the police station. This time, we kept a lot more distance. I could pinpoint William's patrol car pretty easily, having seen it plenty of times—it was always the one that was thoroughly washed, and I knew his license plate by heart.

We waited patiently for William to come outside.

When he did, I started the car without turning the headlights on.

We watched his car pull off the lot and drive down Orchard Road, then followed him down Central Ave, keeping about four to five cars between us at all times. We passed the municipal building, one of the bars I used to frequent with Thomas and Riley, and a church. I had a very familiar feeling as we continued to drive down Central Ave, passing Summer Street. I glanced at Amy's house and swallowed.

As we neared a fork in the road, I half-expected him to turn onto Stark Avenue, but he went right.

We kept on following him, and traffic was starting to thin out, making it harder for us to stay four or five cars behind him without losing sight of him. He turned onto Back River Road and we passed some impressive looking houses. I expected him to turn onto one of these driveways at any moment, but he just kept on driving.

The area became more and more woodsy and the sun was setting.

I looked in the rearview mirror to check on Gary, hoping he might recognize something, but he was cowering under his blanket. I looked back to the road and sighed. "Do you think he's on to us?" I asked Scott. "Maybe he's giving us the runaround, just driving randomly."

Scott didn't answer.

Finally, William slowed down and pulled onto a driveway.

"Drive past," Scott grumbled. "Park down the street, 'round the corner."

I followed his advice, took a left and parked next to the curb, behind a large white truck.

"We now know where he lives. It's getting dark, so it's prime time to scope out the perimeter." He turned to Gary. "You wait here. And don't think of bailin'. Try anythin' funny and I'll find you, drag you back here, and hand you to that fucker myself. Got it?"

Gary shrunk down and nodded.

"Good. Let's get a move on." He got out and I followed his lead, walking farther down the street.

"You shouldn't be so hard on him," I berated him. "Guy's pissing his pants as it is."

He gave me a look. "Some folks need a lil' motivation, kid. Just to be sure. 'Sides, that bastard broke into your house, remember?"

"I think he's long paid for that," I retorted, as we walked onto Shady Lane—what a fitting name.

He shrugged. "He knows about the ashes, too." He paused. "I just keep wondering what he wanted to do with 'em. Nothing good, if you ask me." He looked past the fences of two backyards. "Cut through here," he grumbled.

Cloaked by the dark, we sneaked between the fences, past the backyards, toward some trees.

"This way," he whispered.

I followed him carefully, trying not to alarm any dog chilling outside.

"That's the one," he said, staying low and pointing at a large house with two sheds—one small, one large.

We crept a little closer.

A light on the second floor turned on, and I froze.

"What do we do now?" I asked in a low voice.

"Watch him," he replied curtly.

I waited for him to say more, but he held his tongue.

And so, we watched. We saw the light in another room turn on—which Scott assumed was the bathroom—and off again a little while later. Scott peered over the fence and gestured for me to do the same.

I could see William in his kitchen, standing behind the kitchen island, staring at a carton in his hands. It looked like a package of pasta. I grew increasingly uneasy as he went about his routine—cooking, eating his meal slowly, then sitting down in front of the TV. All the while, Scott didn't say a word. He just stared at him, wide-eyed, breathing silently.

At last, he turned around. "Let's get back."

We slipped past the houses and made our way back to my car. Before we got in, Scott lifted the blanket to confirm it was really Gary hiding in the back seat.

"My place," he grunted, folding his arms and leaning back.

As soon as we pulled into his driveway, Scott jumped out of the car and marched up to the porch. He unlocked the door with practiced ease, quickly working through several locks, and went inside. I helped Gary get out of the car, and we followed him.

Gary stumbled over to the couch and sank into it, while I watched Scott spread out a large piece of paper on the table. He began sketching a map, and as I moved closer, I recognized what he was drawing: William's house and a portion of the surrounding area. It wasn't fully detailed, of course, but Scott hard marked out quite a bit—some room layouts, the backyard, the sizes of the sheds, and the neighboring yards.

"We'll watch him for the next few days, check out his routine," Scott said.

I glanced at him. "I can't. I've got to go to work. Can't afford not to."

He looked at me, then back at the map. "Fine. I'll do it. But when it comes down to it-"

"I'll be there," I finished his sentence.

He nodded. "Let's see who this fucker hangs out with and where he goes. Maybe even find out what the hell he's really up to. That fucker thinks he's got the upper hand, so we need somethin' to flip the script. He must be hiding *something* in that castle of his." He looked at me. "But first, we need to be prepared. We go in smart, we go in ready. I've got enough firepower in here to take down a goddamn army."

"We're going to break into his house?" I asked, frowning.

"What did you think we'd do?" he grumbled.

"I don't know. He… he's a detective."

"That's why we gotta wait for the right moment, kid." He looked back at the map. "I'll stick to him like a fucking shadow and watch his every move." He walked into the room full of supplies and came back out with something in his hand. He shoved the object into my palm. "Keep this on you at all times," he said.

I looked at the burner phone and nodded.

The next few days went by in a haze. Scott and I called once a day when I got back from my night shift, and he filled me in on any new details.

"Won't he recognize your truck?" I asked during our second phone call.

"Nah, got a car from Betty."

"Betty?" I repeated, recalling the elderly lady who'd shooed away the neighbors after Scott shot the poodle—no questions asked. "That's nice of her."

"Yeah, well, she owed me a favor," he grumbled. There was a softness in his voice he wasn't able to cover up with his gruff tone.

By mid-October, the sun set at around 5 p.m., so the streets were shrouded in a veil of darkness as I pulled up on Shady Lane that Friday. Scott was already there, sitting in a 1998 Buick LeSabre. It wasn't the type of car I'd expected from a sweet old lady like Betty, which intrigued me. I parked right behind Scott and killed the engine, but neither of us moved to get out. I waited for a while, then watched as he left the car. He had his military bag on his back and quickly walked down the street. My heart pounded in my throat as I checked my Colt. I followed about five minutes behind him, just like we'd planned. I kept my footsteps light and slipped between the houses, heading for William's backyard. As I approached William's house, I spotted Scott crouched behind a large oak tree, his eyes locked on the back door. He glanced back at me, then signaled with a quick hand gesture, *Wait*.
I paused, taking cover behind a bush. The house was dark, no lights on inside. It was hard to tell if William was home or if he was out on a late patrol—according to Scott, he should be out on patrol right now. His plan was to break in and find something, anything, that could tie him to Gary, the skin divers or us. He had a backup plan, too, in case William caught us. I just hoped it wouldn't get to that.
A few more minutes passed. Scott remained perfectly still, like a predator waiting for the right moment to strike. Finally, he moved. He crept closer to the house, sticking to the shadows. I followed behind him, breathing shallowly.
We reached the side of the house. He checked the windows in silence, then turned to me and nodded.
William wasn't home. This was our chance.
He pulled a small tool from his bag and worked on the back door. It took him less than a minute to pop the lock. *I should get him to teach me how to do that*, I thought, as we slipped inside.
The house was silent and smelled faintly of something chemical, like cleaning supplies.

We moved through the house, as quiet as mice. Scott used his red flashlight to scan the kitchen. It was unexpectedly neat. The living room was similarly spotless. No sign of personal clutter, just the bare essentials. I frowned as I looked around. This place felt more like a stage set, not a home.

Every creak of the floorboards sent my heart racing, but Scott remained calm, methodical. We were in enemy territory now, but I felt a bit at ease because of him. He had his head on straight and I could tell he'd done this many times before. I wondered where, when and why.

He motioned for me to take a look around, making his way to the stairs. I used my own red flashlight to rifle through the drawers, carefully putting everything back in its place. William seemed like the kind of person who'd notice if a lamp had been moved an inch, considering how neat he kept his home. I found nothing of interest and moved on to the stairs.

I crept up the stairs, each step creaking under my weight, and I wondered how Scott had gone upstairs so freaking quietly—the guy definitely weighed more than me. I looked around the hallway and entered the second door on the left, the only one that was open.

Scott was crouched by a safe, the door already cracked open. There were some files, a few bundles of cash and a small collection of what looked like USB drives. There was also a handgun and some other object.

He looked back at me and motioned for me to come closer. I took a good hard look at the item and recognized it immediately: it was the jar that had been under my bed. The one Gary had stolen.

"Fuck," I said silently.

Scott was about to reach for it when a sound from outside froze us both. Headlights—they swept across the front windows, cutting through the darkness like a knife. The rumble of a car engine filled the space.

I caught Scott's eye, and for the first time, I saw a flash of urgency in his usual calm.

"Move," he hissed.

We quickly closed the safe, making sure everything looked undisturbed, and slipped out of the room.

The sound of a car door slamming shut echoed through the house.

We had seconds, maybe less.

Scott led the way, moving faster now, but still quiet. We reached the bottom of the stairs just as the front door rattled with the sound of keys. We slipped into the living room as the door creaked open. The light in the hallway turned on as we tiptoed through the living room, past the bookcase on the left, and into the kitchen. The living room light turned on and footsteps echoed dangerously close after us. William was walking toward the kitchen.

We're not going to make it.

My collar got yanked and I sank to the floor, behind the kitchen island. The kitchen light flicked on and William entered. He opened the fridge, the sound slicing through the pressing silence. Something metal clinked on the island, followed by a hissing click—the sound of a beer being cracked opened.

Silence returned.

I pressed my back to the kitchen island, praying I was out of sight, and glanced at Scott. He sat like a statue, his thousand-yard stare fixed on the windows before us. I followed his gaze and saw what he was watching: our reflections.

William stood still, looking down at the can of beer. Suddenly, he turned and walked out of the kitchen with heavy footsteps.

Scott immediately started moving, silent as a mouse, and I followed closely behind. We reached the back door, left cracked open, and slipped out. I let Scott close it—he did so without making a single sound. I swear, that guy worked magic.

We took cover in the backyard, our hearts pounding, and glanced at the kitchen window. The kitchen was still empty. We exchanged a look and rushed back to our cars, taking cover under the trees.

Without saying another word, we got in and drove off, taking Shadow Drive to avoid the road in front of William's house.

About twelve minutes later, we were back at Scott's and gathered in the living room. Gary was looking a little better than roughly two weeks ago. Most of the bruises had faded and his lip was healed. His eye socket still looked deformed, though.

"Did you find anything?" he asked with a shrill voice.

Scott nodded. "Enough to tie him to you."

Gary shuddered.

"Did you take anything?" I asked.

He shook his head. "If we took anything now, he'd be on our trail for sure."

I bit my lip and looked at Gary. I thought of the moment in the kitchen, when we were watching our own reflections and that of William, my head blaring with anxiety. "Did he notice us?"

"Probably," Scott replied dryly, not seeming too alarmed. "Fucker's a detective, after all." He snorted. "Keeps a clean house, that's for sure, but that safe…"

"I wonder what's inside," I said. "Those files, those USBs…"

"Wish we'd had more time, but I did skim the files," he replied. "You're not going to like it, kid."

"Why?"

"Lot of printouts from the website, stills from the bird video, photos of the ashes, missing persons cases… and a whole lot of documents," he paused, "on you."

Gary gasped before I could even respond.

"Me?" I asked, my eyes wide.

"Yeah, kid, looks like he's been trackin' you for quite a while. Got documents on me, too. Even pulled my fuckin' hospital records from back then," he grumbled.

"Did you read any of it—of what he had on me?"

"Skimmed it."

"And?"

He slowly shook his head.

I waited for him to elaborate, but he just stared at the floor, jaw tight. I could feel Gary's eyes darting between us, desperate for more information but too afraid to ask.

Finally, Scott spoke, his voice low and grave. "He knows too much, kid. Stuff that even you probably forgot about. It's all there—where you've been, who you've talked to, hell, he's even got notes on your habits, your routines. It's like he's been building a case on you for years."

My body froze. "W-why?"

He shook his head again. "Don't know yet. But whatever it is, it ain't good. We need to be very fuckin' careful, watch our every move."

Gary swallowed hard, his voice trembling as he spoke. "What are we going to do?"

"We're going to stay a step ahead of him," Scott said. "We need to figure out what he's after before he makes his next move. And if it comes down to it..."

He didn't finish the sentence, but we all knew what he meant. If it came down to it, we'd have to take care of William before he took care of us. My knees buckled and I sank into the couch.

"Drink?" Scott asked.

I nodded. "Something strong."

He set down three glasses and poured a generous amount of Scotch into each, without bothering to ask if we wanted it neat or on the rocks. This was no drink to savor.

I took a small sip, then a big gulp, feeling the liquor burn as it went down my throat.

Scott stared at me with a stern expression. "You should stay here t'night, kid."

I nodded, and in that moment realized I wasn't afraid of him anymore—there *couldn't* be a skin diver inside him.

I took the couch that night, while Gary huddled up in the supply room. Scott sat on a chair at the table, not too far from me, which looked pretty uncomfortable to sleep on.

My dream was clouded in darkness. I dreamt that William barged in while I slept in my own bed, jumping on top of me and coiling his hands around my throat. I could still feel the air being squeezed out of me as I jolted awake. My eyes darted around the room and locked onto Scott's—he was awake, holding his rifle in his hands.

He nodded, reassuring me that everything was alright.

I slept over at Scott's the next evening too, but I had to go back home for my night shift on Sunday. I tried to get some rest during the day, but my dreams were plagues by skin divers, William, and another faceless threat. I jolted awake, sweating, and tried to shake it off as I got ready for work.

The cold night air hit me like a slap in the face as I stepped outside. I let out a tired yawn and stumbled toward the garage. My hand reached for the door, but before I could lift it, someone grabbed me from behind. I struggled, flailing my arms, trying to tear myself away, but the grip tightened. A cloth, damp and sticky, was shoved over my mouth. I gasped, trying to inhale, but all I could draw in was a sickly, ether-like stench, overpowering everything. My heart pounded in my chest, my vision blurring, fading… and then, everything went black.

Chapter 17

I woke up groggy, my head pounding, and an ache in my neck that felt like fire. The air around me was damp and musty, and there was a faint echo of dripping water. I blinked a few times, trying to clear my vision. As the haze began to lift, I realized I was tied to a metal chair, my wrists handcuffed, and my waist and ankles bound tightly with thick rope.

A dim light swung overhead, casting erratic shadows across what looked like the inside of an old shed. The wooden walls were decayed, some planks cracked and splintered, and rain was trickling on the damaged roof.

In front of me, leaning casually against the wall, was William. He watched me with his arms crossed, a small smirk tugging at the corner of his mouth.

"Isn't this nice?" he said, sharply exhaling. "You know, you didn't have to come all the way to my house. I could've just picked you up." He gestured around the room. "See? First-class service."

"Where the hell am I?" I croaked out.

He pushed himself off the wall and took a step closer, his boots echoing in the quiet room. "Somewhere private," he said in a low, steady voice. "Someplace we can talk."

"Talk?" I muttered, struggling against the binds. "This is how you start a conversation?"

He shrugged. "Had to make sure you wouldn't run off before we had a little heart-to-heart." He stepped a little closer and eyed me up and down. "You've got a habit of slipping away, slithering like a filthy eel. You see, I don't take too kindly to people breaking into my home. I'm sure you know what it's like." He put his hand on his heart. "It's just… *horrifying* to have someone take away that safety." He smiled crookedly. "You could've just rung the doorbell and I would've made you both a nice cup of tea. But instead, you hid in the dark and scurried off like scared little mice." His nostrils flared. "Did you find what you were looking for?"

I tried to steady my breath and forced myself to look at him. "Yeah, I did. What the fuck did you do with the jar!?"

He hunched over, his face inches from mine. "All in due time, James, all in due time. I'm sure you have a lot of questions for me now, but let me assure you… I have a lot more questions for you first. And you're in no position to take the lead. So, you're going to give *me* answers. And you better make sure I like them. Or I'll turn you into a pulp, just like your little friend Gary. Got it?"

I clenched my jaw.

"Tell me you understand," he said in a stomach-churning sweet voice.

I nodded curtly.

"That's good. That's *great*." He straightened up and looked over my head. "Then, let's get started, shall we?" He clapped in his hands. "I can't believe it's been, what, almost twenty years already? That beautiful sunny day in The Keystones State. I was born there, you know. Just like my father and mother. I was sure I was gonna grow old there, too. But something happened…" He looked at me expectantly. "Come on, tell me."

I gulped. "What do you want to hear?"

"Tell me what happened that day, again."

"M-my mom hit a girl with her car."

"And then what?"

"The girl died."

"The girl died," he repeated. "Sure, she did. But didn't you say she was dead even before that? Something about… a dog? You see, I'm much more interested in that part, not the fabrication you've come up with over the years."

"It's in your fuckin' report," I shot back, wondering if he really knew about the skin divers or if he was still trying to fill in the blanks.

He laughed harshly. "Yeah, the report. It pretty much glossed over the important stuff, didn't it? A girl dead in the road, right in the heart of a quiet, suburban neighborhood. A tragedy no one could look away from, right? But what about before? Before all that, when nobody was watching? That's what I want to hear about."

I swallowed hard, my throat dry. My hands were clammy, trembling slightly. He was digging, clawing at memories I had long buried. "I-I don't remember," I stammered.

His grin widened and it sent a chill down my spine. "Don't lie to me. You were just a kid back then, sure. But you remember. You've *always* remembered. That's why we're here, isn't it?"

I clenched my fists. "What's this about?"

He leaned forward, and I could feel his breath roll over my face—it stank of Marlboro Red. "It wasn't the car that killed her, was it?" His voice was barely above a whisper, but it sliced through the air like a knife. "No, no… The car was just an accident. That girl… she was already dead when she hit it. And you know why, don't you?" He nodded slowly. "You told me right then and there, and I didn't believe you. That's on me, I guess, but here we are now. And I need you to tell me again. We're not going to leave this room until you say it. Every. Last. Word." His eyes narrowed.

I couldn't breathe. I was trapped, and he knew it.

"What did you see that day?" he asked, more forcefully this time. "What happened before the car hit her?"

A memory flashed, quick and sharp like lightning. The little blue dress with white flowers on the seams. The bouncing ball. The blue Ford Escort. My baby brother in the back seat. The small Jack Russell, creeping in on Ashley. Its eyes. Its fucking eyes… And then, her little body, lying limp on the road.

I blinked, trying to shake the image from my mind. But it wouldn't go away. It had never gone away. "I… I saw a dog," I admitted.

"Yes," he coaxed, his voice dripping with anticipation. "And what did the dog do?"

"It… it attacked her," I said, the words tumbling out of my mouth before I could stop them. It was as if they had wanted to spill since 1992, but I'd built a dam to hold them in, and now, nearly twenty years later, it had finally broken. "I don't know why, but it—it just lunged at her, and it disappeared into her. I didn't understand what was happening. One moment, she was standing on the curb, playing with her ball, the next moment, her body flew onto the street. She just propelled sideways, as if she was thrown at it like a fuckin' ball. It didn't seem real…"

"And then your mother hit her with the car," he finished for me, his eyes gleaming with satisfaction.

I nodded slowly. I'd always wanted someone to believe me. Scott did. Gary did. Even Dr. Linwood did. But what I really wanted was for my father to have believed me—or the officer from back then… William. That wish felt especially cruel now.

"The dog…" he started, "is the part no one ever talks about. No one ever talks about the fucking dog."

I shuddered. "Why does it matter?"

He showed an eerie, stomach-turning smile. "You know why, James. I mean, damn… You know it wasn't just a dog. It was something else. Something you've spent twenty years trying to forget. But it just wouldn't let you, would it? It came back for you."

"F-for me?"

He nodded slowly. "Again and again…" His eyes glazed over. "You see, I found it pretty strange that you fled the scene of an accident, claiming you didn't have a phone, and simply didn't think of ringing a neighbor's door." He slowly started walking circles around me, and I tried to follow him with my gaze. "Yet, when I asked you about the driver swerving, you were pretty adamant that it had been a cat. Not a dog. A cat." His face showed a grim frown.

"So?"

"Well, it took me some time to connect the dots. But you made it really fucking simple for me when you put up that website."

"What website?" I asked, making one last attempt to feign ignorance.

This time, he didn't smile. "Don't act coy with me, boy. I knew it was you. Heck, you couldn't have made it any more obvious. Sure, you changed Ashley's age, although only slightly. But the year it happened, the car backing out, the eyes of the dog… it was all in my report. And that post about the cat!? Don't make me laugh." He stopped walking and looked me dead in the eye. "It's got Scott Aldridge written all over it, coma and all. You're not as smart as you think you are, James, trust me."

He hunched over, his face inches from mine, his breath warm against my skin. "Now, tell me about the other one."

My heart pounded in my throat as I hesitated.

"Come on, tell me about the elderly couple that was killed by… *a skin diver*." He exhaled fiercely through his nose.

My pulse quickened as his words sank in. He knew exactly where to dig. He tilted his head, his voice dropping to a low, menacing whisper. "I can wait all day, James. Trust me, I've got nothing but time. But I think it'll be more fun for you if you just start talking now."

I shifted in my seat, the cold metal of the chair digging into my back as I stared at the floor. The image of that night flickered back into my mind. I should've driven past that fucking house, never even looking at it. "I… I was just out for a drive," I started, "when something caught my eye. There were a man and a woman, sitting at the kitchen table, and there was a Cocker Spaniel in the background. But," I paused, "it didn't look like a dog. It was like that Jack Russell all over again. Its eyes were… they were huge and deformed, like those of a giant bee. And it was… it was staring at them."

William narrowed his eyes. "What did you do?"

"I… I thought I could warn them. So, I-"

"Why didn't you honk your horn?"

"What?"

"Why didn't you just honk your horn if you wanted to alert them?"

"Because… I didn't want to alert *it*."

"The skin diver?" he pressed.

I nodded. "I'd seen what it was capable of and I was scared. I thought, no… I *knew* it would harm them."

"You knew it would harm them," he repeated.

"I saw it leap at the man and it disappeared into him, just like the Jack Russell had with Ashley. I knew what was coming next, so I went inside." He scratched his chin, staring at me with wild eyes.

"I wanted to save the lady. I just wasn't sure how. I didn't have a gun or anything, so my… my best bet was to drag her outside. But she hadn't noticed the skin diver, or her husband shaking in his seat. She called me an intruder and threatened to call the police."

"So you killed her?"

"What? No!" I exclaimed. "The skin diver did! It leaped into her and I tried…" I gasped for air, "I tried to pull it out of here, but it latched on like, like a-" I stumbled over my words, trying to explain what had happened. "It's in the post. You read it, didn't you?"

"I read it," he confirmed, in a heavy voice. "I read it over and over and over. Because that broken window never sat right with me, you know. My colleagues wrote it off as coincidental. Maybe she—what'd you call her, Katy—broke the window in her panic. Or maybe it was already broken, even before they died. Strange, isn't it?" He narrowed his eyes. "No signs of forced entry or theft. No trauma on their bodies. They sure were quick to close that case." He sighed wearily. "Tell me, James, do you know their *real* names?"

I swallowed, hesitated, and slowly nodded.

"Tell me."

"They were… William and Dorothy Abbott."

He nodded. "William Abbott. Dorothy Abbott. Is it finally starting to make sense now, James?"

I looked at him, and it slowly dawned on me. A hard, cold lump formed in my throat, my face went pale, and my eyes quivered. "You're… their son," I muttered, the hairs on my arms standing on end.

His face twisted, contorting with years of pent-up anger. "Well, don't you deserve a fucking medal for figuring that out? Took you long enough, didn't it? What, you thought it was just some damn coincidence? Two William Abbotts from The Keystone States? Are you fucking *stupid?*"

My heart thrashed in my chest, my breathing shallow. "I-" was all I could manage.

"You killed them," he said, his face distorting into a horrible grimace. "You killed my folks. The people who gave me life, protected me, cared for me."

I shook my head wildly. "N-no, it was a skin diver!" I protested.

"Well, you led it there. It was after *you*. My parents were just in the way, like that driver in the convertible. My mother, my father… they're dead because of you. And you didn't even have the decency to stay and try to save them, did you? You fled the scene, just like you did three years ago, after that car crashed into Aldridge's porch. You didn't even call a fucking paramedic. They could've survived, but you took that chance away from them."

I kept shaking my head. "You're wrong! They were dead as soo-"

His fist hit me hard in the face and I could smell the stench of cigarettes as he did it.

"You don't know that," he barked at me. "And we never will, will we!? Because you ran away like a fucking coward and you left them there to die! I spent years trying to figure out what happened. *Years*, James. My parents's blood is on *your* hands. I know, because I lifted the prints myself, when all those useless fuckers were trying to ignore all the shit in the literal fucking sense." He glared at me."They didn't match anyone at first. Not in any database, not in any police report. It was like you didn't even exist. I couldn't track you down. I couldn't find you. I had nothing!" His nostrils flared as he yelled. "My colleagues told me to let it go. 'Move on,' they said. 'You're too close to this, Abbott. It's a closed case, Abbott.' But I couldn't. I couldn't let it go. I was like a dog with a bone, they said, but they're my *parents*!"

He slammed his fist against the wall, the wood groaning under the force. "Those fuckers sent me to Dover, hoping I'd cool off, get my mind on other things… told me to dig into missing person cases." He crept closer to me. "But I took their files with me because I needed answers."

I could see the torment in his eyes now. It wasn't just rage; it was deeper than that. It was the frustration of a son who'd been left in the dark, chasing shadows that never led anywhere. He had poured over this for years, while I'd been running, hiding, trying to make sense of it all myself.

"I went over every little detail, every piece of evidence," he continued, his voice shaking. "I knew something was off the moment they closed the case, but I couldn't prove it. And then you showed up with your little website and it was all right there. You gave yourself away, finally. But it wasn't enough, was it? Because no one else saw what I saw. There wasn't any fucking evidence, just your stupid little post." He let out a bitter laugh. "They thought I was losing it. Hell, maybe I was. But you and I both know the truth now, don't we?"

"You're… WatchfulEye," I grunted.

He smiled. "Well, aren't you clever."

"I didn't want any of this," I muttered.

"You didn't want it?" he snapped, his eyes blazing. "Do you think *I* wanted it? Do you think I wanted to bury my parents? To spend years chasing a ghost? To get demoted and sent here, to this shithole!? You're not the only one who lost something, James." His fists clenched. "I couldn't catch you. I couldn't even find you. You were nothing more than a set of prints that led nowhere." He paused, his voice thick with emotion. "Do you know what that feels like? To lose your family and have no one to hold responsible? To know deep down that something's wrong, but the world just moves on without you."

I wanted to nod, more than anything, because I did know what that's like. But I was afraid it would only piss him off more, so I bit my cheek and sat frozen.

He gritted his teeth. "But you… you got to walk away. Hell, you even followed me here, just to rub it in my face. Driving around in that fucking car of yours, banging chicks left and right, complaining about your sick mommy. And then, your father died. Finally, some justice!"

"Fuck you," I shot back.

His fist connected with my face again, harder this time, and a sharp crack echoed in my head. I felt something dislodge—a tooth, front and center —and blood filled my mouth almost instantly. The metallic taste made me gag, but before I could spit it out, the jagged piece of bone lodged in the back of my throat.

I choked, my hands instinctively reaching for my neck, but they were still cuffed behind my back. The room seemed to spin as I gasped for breath, my throat tightening painfully around the shard of my own tooth. Panic clawed at me, but I fought to stay conscious, focusing on the sounds around me.

He loomed over me, his anger giving way to a dark, hollow weariness. "Do you see now? Do you get why I couldn't just let it go?" His voice was quieter now, almost broken.

I struggled, my vision blurring as I fought to make a sound, but the choking sensation was overpowering.

"I followed your little investigation, your theories about those skin divers, every step of the way. It was easy, really—keeping tabs on you and your friends… Then I caught your little friend breaking into your house." He grinned viciously. "I'd wanted to take you, more than anything, because you always seemed to be one step ahead of me, always able to slither away between the cracks, like a cockroach." He shook his head slowly. "But luckily, your little friend was very chatty."

My vision flashed with black and I could hear his words faintly in the distance.

"And here we are now. There's no more hiding, James. My parents didn't matter enough for the system to care. But I cared, I still do. And I'm going to make sure you pay for what you did. And I'm going to use your own fucking theory against you."

His face was a mask of cold rage as he watched me struggle for breath. With a final, decisive move, he smacked me hard on the back.

The force dislodged the jagged tooth from my throat, sending it skittering across the floor. I gasped, coughing violently. My head felt heavy and a blaring pain welled up inside.

Before I could recover, his fist crashed into my face again and again, each blow more punishing than the last.

Pain exploded from my shattered eye socket. I could feel the blood streaming down my face, sticky and wet, mingling with the raw agony of each blow. He hammered his fists in quick succession, targeting my ribs and liver. I clung to consciousness, struggling against the pain and the haze that was creeping over me.

His heavy breathing was deafening—each exhale coming in short, ragged bursts. With one last, searing punch to my already battered side, he stepped back, eyeing his handiwork with a hint of satisfaction.

The faint sound of footsteps echoed through the shed.

Help, I tried to say, but no words came out.

The footsteps approached me from behind.

Please, Scott, let it be you. Save me.

William's gaze shifted to the new arrival. "Come on, bring it here," he said, his voice laced with dark anticipation.

A hand entered my blurred vision, holding a jar—the one containing Daisy's ashes.

William's expression twisted into a cruel grin as he grabbed the jar and unscrewed the lid. "You did me a favor with these," he said, his voice smooth and unsettling. "The other ashes just vanished, disappeared into thin air before I got to use them on you. It was a damn shame." He held the jar up, examining the contents with a sparkle in his eyes. "The effects are just way too fun," he continued in a childlike voice.

Without warning, he grabbed my jaw, forced open my mouth and poured the ashes down my throat. I tried to struggle, desperately attempting spit it out, but the stream was relentless. The gritty, fine particles scraped along my throat and filled my mouth.

I gagged. My body shook. Pain ripped through me like a bullet with every slight movement.

Panic surged as the ashes began to take hold.

The room around me started to warp and shift, the walls bending and swirling in ways that defied logic. I felt a wave of nausea roll over me and dizziness threatened to pull me under. Grotesque, nightmarish images danced in front of my eyes, blending with the pulsating pain throbbing through my battered body.

William watched with a detached interest. There was no smile, no satisfaction on his face.

As the hallucinations grew more intense, my sense of reality began to fracture. The room seemed to dissolve into a chaotic blend of shadows and twisted forms.

My breathing grew ragged, and I could barely tell where the pain ended and where the hallucinations began.

His cold voice cut through the madness. "This is what you wanted, isn't it? You wanted to chase ghosts. To leave people like me in the dark. Well, now you're going to live with the ghosts you've created, James. Every moment of paint. Every second of fear. It's all for you. And there's no escape."

The words echoed in my mind, distorted and jumbled. Cats and dogs came barging through the walls and falling from the sky. They ran around me in circles. Their eyes were big and black, devoid of life and soul.

My fingers trembled, my shallow breathing sputtered, my vision narrowed. My head spun. Anxiety took over my entire body, pushing away every other feeling. It was nothing like the panic attacks I'd had before, nothing like the anxiety I'd experienced—those all faded in comparison. Sweat dripped down my forehead, mixing with the blood that was starting to dry.

The agony went on for… so long. *So long.*

Every time I started to regain a bit of composure, a bit of sanity, he'd force my head back and pour some more ashes down my throat, instigating the entire thing all over again.

I lost all sense of time and place.

Salvation seemed far off.

Hours became days, and days became weeks.

I heard footsteps echoing through the warehouse, faint at first but growing louder. I tried to look around me, my blurry vision cluttered with the images of skin divers. "No," I whimpered softly as the footsteps approached me. I shrank down, trying to make myself invisible on the chair—which was impossible. "Not again," I begged as I felt a warm breath roll down my neck, spiking my pulse.

"Kid," a gruff voice said. "It's me. I'm here."

I gasped, trying to focus through the haze. "Scott?" I asked with a hoarse voice.

His hands were gentle but firm as he worked to release me from the restraints.

I tried to speak, but my voice came out as a weak rasp. My limbs were numb and my head swam with the effects of the ashes.

"Don't talk. Save your breath."

Scott's movements were a blur while he helped me to my feet. I could barely walk. Each step sent waves of pain through my battered body— both my shins were shattered from William's repeated kicking.

I winced and moaned as Scott helped me out of the shed. The world
outside was a disorienting blur with trees and bright skies.
There was a hum from a car, but I could barely hear it through my
shattered eardrums.
He helped me inside, gently lying me down on the back seat. "I'm getting
you out of here, kid. Hang tight."
The car started moving and hell began all over again. Every bump in the
road felt like a blunt knife stabbing into my body. I didn't want to cry—
because that, too, hurt—but I couldn't stop myself. I gasped for air,
groaning and moaning the entire way.
The road was long. Way too fucking long.

When the car finally came to a halt, I heaved a shaky sigh of relief.
Scott opened the door and helped me out of the car. My legs gave out,
and he had to carry me in his arms, right up the door of a cabin.
The door swung open and Gary's face appeared.
"You've got him!" he exclaimed.
"Get the first aid kit," Scott replied in a commanding but soft tone. He
carried me inside and laid me down on a bed. "You're safe now," he said,
his voice calm and soothing. "William won't find us here. I'm going to
take care of you, alright? Just hold on."
I tried to nod, but my head felt too heavy and was pounding like a
sledgehammer.
Scott first handed me a glass of water and a handful of painkillers—mild
ones, sadly, which barely took the edge off. He started cleaning my
wounds, pouring alcohol over them and rubbing them with a cloth,
which fucking hurt. Then he bandaged some of the wounds, leaving the
others to 'dry to the air', his hands moving gently but urgently.
Next, he mixed some fluids and medications to help with the nausea and
dizziness—I couldn't even tell him about that, but it's as if he knew, as if
he could see straight into my head, through the haze of pain.
Gary brought another glass of water and helped me take a few careful
sips.
While Scott splinted my shins, he started telling me what had happened.
He explained how he had received an anonymous tip from some guy—

he saw who it was, but didn't recognize him—and I was relieved to know that someone had helped him find me. He mentioned that William had been going about his life as if nothing had happened, trying to maintain his normal routine while I was kept hidden.

"Had to move all my gear and weapons to a new location," he explained. "We can't risk takin' you to a hospital right now. That motherfucker'll find us there, no doubt. Hospitals keep records, you know. Too many eyes, too many questions…" He paused, glancing at me with a grim expression. "And if that fucker's got any way to track you, he'll sniff us out fast. Ain't worth the risk. You need first aid, not a trail he can follow." He squinted. "This place is safe, for now."

I nodded weakly. I really didn't want to go to a hospital—I felt a lot safer here. With Scott. I exchanged a glance with Gary and felt like I understood more about him now. "How long?" I asked in a raspy voice.

"Gonna take a while to heal, kid," Scott replied.

I slowly shook my head.

Gary knew what I was trying to ask and he answered with a heavy voice, "Forty-nine days".

Forty-nine days. The number hit me like a blow to the chest, and I stared at Gary, trying to process what he'd just said. Seven weeks… Nearly two months…

Scott's hands didn't stop moving as he continued to adjust the bandages and the splints. He glanced up at me. "You've been through hell, kid. I'm not gonna sugarcoat it, you're gonna feel like shit for a while. But we're here. You're safe. You'll get through this."

I wanted to believe him, but the weight of the last few weeks pressed down on me like a lead blanket. The images of William's face, the torment I'd endured, the relentless hallucinations—all of it clung to my mind, making it hard to see anything beyond the misery I was trapped in. I opened my mouth to say something, but my throat was still dry and raw from the ashes, my voice barely a whisper. I couldn't remember if I was fed or given something to drink during my torture, but it must've happened, or I would've already died. At some point, I must've slept, too —though it felt impossible to recall.

"Why… didn't… he just… kill me?"

Scott frowned. "Fucker wanted you to suffer," he said, cautiously. "It's personal. But… do you know why?"

I swallowed and nodded carefully. I wanted to explain, but the words got caught in my throat.

"Later," he said. "When you're feelin' better."

"And… the tip?" I finally managed.

"I'll track him down," he replied. His tone shifted to a low growl, simmering with fury. "And I'm gonna kill that sorry excuse for a human being. I fuckin' swear to God, he'll wish he never laid a hand on you. But we'll deal with that later. Right now, you need to heal. Try 'n get some rest." He gently placed his hand on my crown, as if to pet me.

I looked at him, weakly trying to smile. "GOD…" I repeated, letting the word hang in the air, "I'll… pray to… you then."

His eyebrows shifted, surprise flashing across his face before he broke into full, sincere laughter. "Haven't lost your sense of humor, I see. That's good, kid."

As I let the darkness of sleep wash over me, the last thing I saw was Scott's face—resolute, determined, protective. Even through the haze of painkillers, I could feel the promise in his presence—he wasn't going to let anything else happen to me. And for the first time in weeks, I felt a glimmer of hope.

The pain in my legs had gotten worse, and Scott knew it. He'd done all he could—first aid, splints, pain meds—but it wasn't enough. Each day, the agony seemed to grow, and I could see it in his face. He was weighing his options while thousands of imaginary little daggers kept raining down on my legs, making me groan and whine through gritted teeth. Gary paced around the cabin with a worried look on his face, as the ghosts of his own trauma came back to haunt him.

We couldn't stay like this much longer. My shins felt like they were on fire and every slight movement sent waves of excruciating pain through my body.

Scott stood by the window, staring out at nothing in particular. Suddenly, he turned toward me. "Kid," he began, "we gotta get you to a hospital."

I shook my head weakly. "No hospital, Scott. You said-"

"I know what I said." His voice cut through my protest. His hands flexed at his sides. "But you're gettin' worse, and I can't fix this. Not here. Not with what I've got. We're running out of pain meds, too."
I winced as a new wave of pain shot through me and I bit back a groan. He came to my side and put a hand on my shoulder. "I got someone," he continued, almost reluctantly. "Old army doc. Guy patched me up more times than I care to count. But-" He hesitated, his eyes flickering with something I hadn't seen in him before. "I don't trust him. Not one damn bit. But we're runnin' outta options, kid. I… I don't know what else to do."
I blinked. I'd never seen Scott so vulnerable before. "You sure?" I rasped. His gaze dropped to the floor for a second. The tension in his shoulders tightened. When he met my eyes again, a flicker of something deeper— regret, maybe—crossed his face. "I ain't got much choice, kid. Not this time." He shook his head. "Look, this guy… He's good at what he does. But he's a piece of shit…" His voice trailed off, his hands curled into fists.
He was quiet for a long moment before he spoke again. "I lost people. In the service. Guys I was supposed to bring home. And this doc… he…" He swallowed. "But you need help, James. And I can't risk takin' you to a regular hospital."
The rawness in his voice made me realize how much this was costing him. Hell, he even called me by my name, for the first time since we met. This was serious. "Okay," I whispered.
He nodded once. "I'll make the call."

The drive felt like it stretched forever. Gary had stayed back at the cabin to watch our supplies, so it was just me and Scott. His silence was heavy. He gripped the steering wheel tighter than necessary, his knuckles pale under the strain, as he cautiously turned a corner.
The doc's place was tucked away on the outskirts of a small town about an hour from the cabin. It was a small, out-of-the-way clinic that seemed capable enough to stay off the radar. Scott parked the car behind the building, out of view.
"We're there," he muttered, cutting the engine.

I let out a breath I didn't realize I'd been holding. He got out and quickly moved around the car to help me. Every step I took, even with him half-carrying me, sent fresh jolts of pain through my legs, making me whimper like an abused dog.

The door to the clinic opened before we even reached it. A man stood there—gray hair, eyes sharp but cold. He didn't say a word, just stepped aside to let us in.

"Morris," Scott greeted him, his voice tight.

"Still alive, huh?" Morris replied dryly, eyeing Scott before his gaze flickered to me. "Get him inside." He led us into a small room and motioned for Scott to set me down on a narrow cot. He started cutting away the makeshift splints Scott had applied, and poked and prodded my legs.

"Both shins broken," he said in a flat tone. "He'll need surgery. I can fix it, but the recovery's gonna hurt like a son of a bitch. It'll take time."

I clenched my teeth as he continued his examination. The man barely looked at me.

Scott stood a few feet away with his arms crossed and his jaw set. His eyes never left Morris. "This gonna hold?" he asked in a sharp tone.

"It'll hold," Morris replied, glancing at Scott, then back at my legs. "I've done worse."

Scott didn't respond to that, but his eyes narrowed. "Got the meds?" he asked, his voice barely concealing his contempt.

Morris grunted. "I've got what he needs. But after this, you need to leave. I don't do charity, and I sure as hell don't want to deal with whatever mess you've got yourselves in."

Scott tensed, but said nothing.

The next few hours were a blur of anesthesia and metal tools.

When I finally woke up, the pain was still there, but it was different.

Scott was sitting by the cot, staring at the floor.

Morris was gone.

"How… bad?" I croaked.

He looked up, his face softer than I'd expected. "It's bad," he admitted, "but you'll live."

"Thanks," I mumbled.

He didn't say anything for a long moment, and when he did, he spoke softly, "I told you, kid. I ain't lettin' anything happen to you."

It took a few more weeks for my eye socket to heal. My shins were the real ordeal. Morris had to insert metal plates to stabilize the fractures, and I was stuck in casts for a while. Every movement sent shockwaves through my legs, making walking impossible for the first few weeks. I had to start physical therapy pretty early on, which was excruciating. But little by little, the pain eased, and my body was beginning to heal.

Chapter 18

Once I could walk around, I jumped right back into target practice. Scott had set up a shooting range around the cabin and had even taught Gary how to shoot, equipping him with a spare handgun.

"Where are we, anyway?" I asked, handling Scott's rifle. My own was still at home—assuming William hadn't broken in and taken it.

"Monadnock," Scott muttered.

"How'd you find this cabin?"

"It's mine."

I grinned. "Should've guessed. It looks pretty remote."

"It is. Enough to stay under the radar, at least. Unless that fucker's got a helicopter." He glanced up at the sky. "But I've got a nice surprise for him if he does." A vile smile stretched across his face.

"Do I wanna know?" I asked.

He gave me a look and chuckled. "Just aim for the 600, kid."

I adjusted the scope on the Garand and took aim at the metal board in the far distance. My second bullet hit its target. I took a deep breath and got up, meeting Scott's eyes.

"Can we kill him?" I asked.

He bit his lip. "We can, sure," he said slowly, "if that's what you really want, I'll make sure he eats bullets."

"*I* want to kill him."

He looked at me with a grim expression on his face. He was silent for a while before he thoughtfully continued, "There are other ways."

"Like what?"

"We could catch him red-handed. Put him on tape, like your mom did with that bird. Then let his own people turn on him, let the system deal with him. Give him a taste of his own damn medicine."

I shook my head. "We'd need a mountain of evidence to put a detective behind bars. Knowing him, he'll find a way to weasel out of it—and then he'll come for me. And I'd bet my life on this: he'll get away with killing me. Because there's no proof he tortured Gary or me, is there?"

He shook his head.

"I need to end him," I insisted. "There's no other way. He's obsessed—
he really believes that I'm the one responsible for this parent's deaths.
Not the skin divers. Me." I looked at Scott with wild eyes. "I can't go
back to my life—not my own house, not to my family, *nowhere*. If I move
across the country, he'll find me. Heck, even if I change my identity, he'll
track me down somehow He's a ticking time bomb and you know it.
None of us are safe with that fucker out there."

"You're right about that, kid. But there's gonna be fallout. Serious fallout.
Can't exactly break into his home, shoot him in the face, and walk away
clean. And taking a life…" He trailed off.

I swallowed. I had never even thought about taking someone's life before
I was abducted and tortured for weeks on end. But this was a matter of
survival.

Scott sighed. "Just… let me do what I do best. Walk away from this.
There's no need for you to get blood on your hands. Go buy another rice
rocket, marry a sweet girl and carry on with your life."

I looked at him. "Don't think I'll sit back and let you do all the work, old
man. This is personal—it has been since 1992. Don't get me wrong, I get
what you're trying to do, but I can't walk away from this. I've got to see it
through."

I looked up at the sky. Ever since Scott had rescued me from William's
torture shed, I'd been playing with ideas for getting revenge. One ideas in
particular kept coming back to me, and it was darkly poetic in its irony.

"What if we used the skin divers," I suggested.

His eyebrows shot up in surprise. "How?"

"Well, they kill people…"

"Duh."

"So we catch one and get it to kill William," I said in a sharp tone.

He looked at me for a long moment. "That… could work. But it'll be
dangerous. Needlessly dangerous, if you ask me." He gave me a skeptical
look.

I shrugged. "Well, we're looking at two choices: die by a skin diver or die
at the hands of a lunatic. Either way, I'd rather go out swinging."

He sighed, looking out at the range. "Fair enough."

"I don't know if we'll find any skin divers here, though," I said, looking around. "So far, I've only seen them close to people, like in the city."
"True," Gary agreed, walking over to us with a sniper rifle in hand. "They usually take the shape of pets."
"Meaning we'll need to get close to a city to catch one," I pressed.
Scott folded his arms and muttered, "Keene isn't far. Think we can just stuff one in a cage? We've no idea what they can do, other than the eyes and the ashes."
"Well, the way I see it, their eyes morphing is just a psychological effect from the ashes they spread, even before they attack."
"Assuming you're right," he started, "they could still off us within seconds."
"Yeah, well… we'll just have to be careful."
"You make it sound like a Sunday stroll, kid. This shit's serious."
I kept silent.
"I'm in," Gary declared.
"Alright then," Scott said. "So let's hunt us some fuckin' skin divers. For real, this time," he added, giving me a look.
I grinned.

It was a short ride to Keene.
It was still dark when we parked Betty's Buick at the curb somewhere on Washington Street. Scott turned off the engine and looked at us.
"Alright, here's the plan," he said in a low voice. "We split up, cover as much ground as we can. Look for any strays—cats, dogs, whatever we can find. Hell, they don't even need to be strays." He glanced at me when he said that. "We need to find one of 'em before noon, if we want this to work."
Gary's face was pale, but he nodded firmly.
"Got it," I confirmed. "We'll meet back here in a few hours. Stay safe."
A cool morning breeze greeted us as we got out of the car. We set off in different directions, each carrying a small handheld radio, some restraints and concealed weapons.

I took to George Street and made my way down to Beaver Street, while
Scott scoped out the public library and Gary patrolled around Keene
State College.

The city woke up around us as hours passed.

My feet were starting to ache, so I fetched a drink and a quick bite before
I continued searching. I'd seen plenty of people walking their dogs and
had eyed several birds and cats in the neighborhood, but none of them
triggered my internal radar like Daisy had right before she turned.
Nothing suspicious showed up.

It was noon when we regrouped at the car.

"No luck?" Scott asked, lighting a cigarette.

I shook my head. "Nothing. Not even a single stray, from what I've
seen."

"Same here," Gary chimed in. "Should we try again tonight?"

Scott nodded, and we drove back to the cottage for some more target
practice.

I'd gotten pretty damn good, barely earning gruff remarks from Scott.
He did bark at Gary at times, but nowhere near as much as he used to.
He even called him by his name, instead of *bastard* or *idiot*.

That night we drove back to Keene at around 9 p.m., and, once again,
scoured the city with the same lack of success.

The next morning, we came back earlier, hoping to draw less attention to
ourselves in case we ran into a skin diver and needed to catch it—which
would hardly go unnoticed. But luck wasn't on our side. Not that
running into one of those fuckers would've been lucky… Damn, shifting
priorities really messes with your head.

The process became routine: drive, search, return empty-handed. It was
exhausting, both physically and mentally. Every day without finding one
made me more and more nervous. William knew I was gone from his
torture shed, and I knew that he was looking for me.

I just prayed he wouldn't come all the way to Keene.

The breakthrough came on a foggy summer morning, on Marlboro
Street—of all places.

The sun had barely risen and we'd split up for only five minutes when I passed an alley. Suddenly, my inner alarm went off. I stopped and looked inside.

A faint sound. Movement.

I saw garbage being pushed aside as a dog rifled through it. Holding my breath, I stepped back and quietly called Scott and Gary over the radio. The plan was to keep the possible skin diver in place while the others hurried over. We'd either tranquilize it or I'd use my taser before restraining it with a foldable heavy-duty net—courtesy of Scott's military days. We all wore bulletproof vests, hoping they could slow a skin diver down if it attacked.

That was the plan.

But plans have a way of falling apart.

As I waited for them to arrive, just a short distance away from the alley, the dog peeked its head out. It had noticed me the way I'd noticed it.

My breath hitched as I stared at the beast. It wasn't a Jack Russell or Cocker Spaniel. It wasn't a poodle either. It was a big fucking German Shepherd. And it looked strong and angry.

"Fuck," I said out loud, quickly pulling up my face mask.

Either I was too late, or the ashes had nothing to do with it. The dog's eyes started to morph—large, black, bee-like.

Shit, shit, shit.

I grabbed my Colt instead of the taser. We'd finally found a skin diver, but my priority was staying alive. My fingers trembled as I cocked the gun.

The Shepherd lowered its head. Its muscles tensed as it creeped toward me.

"Stay the fuck back," I blurted out in a shaky voice.

"What's that, dear?" a croaky voice startled me.

I spun around and nearly shot the old lady standing just a few feet away.

"Get back!" I hissed, trying to steady my aim. "It's not safe."

The skin diving dog lunged without a sound.

My eyes widened and I pulled the trigger, shooting the dog in the chest. It changed direction mid-air, colliding with the frail old lady. Her terrified scream cut through the alley as the beast tore into her with savage force.

I shot into its flank and grabbed it by the legs, trying to pull it out of her
—just like I had with Dorothy six years ago—but this dog was stronger.
Way stronger. Its legs slipped from my grasp, just as Scott arrived.

He shoved me aside, threw his net over the lady, and shot her with the
tranquilizer.

"What the fuck?" I exclaimed.

"Get the fuckin' car," he barked, tossing me his keys. "Now!"

I bolted. My calves spasmed, lungs cutting with each breath as I sprinted
toward the car. I passed barely noticed Gary as I flew past him, jumped
in, and floored it.

I was back within a minute, but the street was already swarming with
people. They'd heard the shots and screams and now they were looking
for the source. And if they were to find it… we'd be in for a world of
trouble.

The tires screeched as I pulled up near the alley. Gary caught up, popped
the trunk and helped Scott lift the old lady—netted and sedated—inside.
The trunk slammed shut and they dove into the car. Scott hadn't even
shut his door when I gunned it.

We passed several surprised faces before disappearing behind the cover
of the trees on Chapman Road.

I was cursing all the way to Gilsum Road.

"We had no choice, kid," Scott said after a while. "Had to think fast."

"We have a dead fucking body in the trunk," I snapped. "A dead body
that we took with us. How the fuck do we explain this to anyone!?"

"Just get us back," he grunted.

Gary squirmed in the back seat. "I think she's coming to," he said, his
voice trembling as he glanced over his shoulder. "She's moving."

"She's a fucking corpse, Gary," I barked. "Corpses don't move."

"But she is," he insisted. He turned around with a face as white as chalk
and met my eyes in the rearview mirror.

I saw what he meant, and pushed 90 on the straight stretch, frantically
cursing.

The skin diver inside the old lady was moving, and it was trying to get
out. If it got through the net—which was a likely possibility—it'd kill the
three of us in an instant.

"Hit it," Scott growled, tossing Gary the tranquilizer gun.

Gary's fingers trembled as he aimed it at the old lady. "Where!?"

"Anywhere, for fucks sake!" I yelled, barely slowing down for the curve. The car skidded, just as Gary shot the gun, and his head slammed into the window. The gun slipped from his hands, clattering to the floor. Scott grasped the ceiling handle to stay firmly in his seat and when we regained traction, he quickly grabbed the gun from the floor and fired a dart into the old lady's throat. She had been sitting upright—seemingly unbothered by the G-forces at work—but her body immediately slumped.

"Careful, kid," he hissed. "We wanna make it back in one piece."

I nodded and started driving a bit more controlled—I still cut the roughly seventeen-minute drive back to the cabin down to eight minutes. Not a moment too soon though, because the body of the lady started moving again.

"Damn thing won't stay down, Scott grumbled, eyeing the dart stuck in her as he carefully pulled her out of the trunk.

I helped him carry her squirming body around the back, where we'd set up a reinforced cage. I was lucky to have Scott, I realized, with all his remnants from his military days. He often had the right tools for the job. He even had connections that pretty much saved my life—yeah, I owed my life to the grumpy old dude on the porch.

"What about her?" I asked, watching Scott trying to stuff her body inside the cage. "We can't just *take* her."

"Got a better idea?" he grumbled. "'Cause I'm all ears, kid. If you've got a way to get that fucker out of her and into the cage, without gettin' any of us killed…"

I bit my lip. "They come out the back," I started, "from where they dove in." I changed her position and put her back firmly to the opening in the cage. "This should work," I said, sounding less determined than I'd wanted to.

Scott didn't say a word, but he helped keep her body in place as it started shaking. The skin on her back pulsated and the giant head of the German Shepherd started to emerge.

"Fuck!" Gary exclaimed in a mix of fear and disgust.

"It's a big one," Scott grumbled, putting more force on her body to keep
it in place. The dog-like skin diver growled and foamed at the mouth as it
climbed out of her—front legs first, then its back legs, and finally its tail.
"Now!" he yelled, yanking her body away as I slammed the cage door
shut.

The shepherd snapped at me, and its teeth sunk deep into my hand.
Scott smashed the back of his Colt against its head, and I wrenched my
hand free. Blood dripped down my arm, and I rushed inside to clean and
bandage it.

Scott stayed outside, with Gary quivering at his side, guarding the cage. It
was barely large enough to contain the snarling beast. They both pulled
up their face masks, hoping to protect themselves from the dangerous
ashes that the skin diver might be omitting.

When I came back out, the sun shone brightly above the cabin, casting
grotesque shadows and creating a stark contrast with our grim hunting
trophy. The old lady lay lifeless in the grass beside it.

"What now?" Gary asked, pacing nervously. "What we do with… her?"
I stared at her. She was someone's mother, someone's grandmother,
probably someone's wife. "We can't leave her like this," I said.

"Our prints are all over her," he replied in a serious tone, looking me
dead in the eye. "You wanna get that son of a bitch or you wanna play
the town's hero right now?"

My breath got caught in my throat as he said those words.

"I'll bring her back," Gary said in a soft voice.

I turned to him. "You sure? If you get caught…"

"No," Scott cut me off. "Nobody's taking back anyone. We ain't got the
time or space for this shit." He eyed the caged beast. "She's dead. There's
nothin' we can do about that. And we're stuck with somethin' fucking
deadly."

"But what if-" Gary started.

"No," he barked. "You wanna bury her, there's a shovel in the shed."
I cursed silently, then turned to Gary. "He's right. We can bury her, but
we need to be fast, because this thing," I glanced at the cage, "needs to
get to William, and far away from us."

Gary squinted. "Fine, we'll go, but the grave comes first." He walked
toward the shed.

Scott eyed me. "We've no idea if this cage will hold. If this fucker
breaks…"

I nodded slowly. "Could you keep watch?" I asked. "I'll go help him."

"Kid, we've got a three hour drive ahead of us."

"I know. But the faster we dig, the sooner we can get this over with." I
glanced at the skin diver.

It stared back at me.

"We can just ditch Gary," he remarked.

I shook my head. "Not after everything William's done to him."

"Whatever," Scott retorted. He grabbed his rifle from the cabin before
plopping down on a chair facing the skin diver.

He guarded the thing while I helped Gary dig a grave for the old lady,
who had been in the wrong place at the wrong time. We only had one
shovel, so it took quite a while, taking turns digging, and I started feeling
more anxious by the minute. I really wanted to get this over with—I
wanted that murder-happy skin diver gone forever, just like William.
After we properly buried the lady—she didn't have a wallet on her or
anything, so we didn't even know her name—we finally loaded up the
Buick: firearms and ammo, heavy-duty nets, a taser and the tranquilizer
gun with its last three darts, a first aid kit, a cord and a strong wire, a
small bag containing metal materials, some food and water, Scotts map
of William's house, and the cage containing the skin diver in the back.
It was quite a hassle getting the cage into the car. We used a few thick
blankets to carefully wrap it, so the dog couldn't bite us—I was reminded
of the white cat on my doorstep for a moment.

While we drove back to Dover, we all silently prayed for the cage to hold
and for William to be out on duty when we arrived.

We were in luck. When we drove past William's house, his driveway was
empty. We took a risk parking the car next to his house, but it would've
been a bigger risk to carry the skin diver around the block.

The sun shone strongly above our heads as Scott shimmied the back
door. Our shirts stuck to our backs as we carried the cage inside, as

carefully as possible. We put the cage in the living room, just around the corner from the front door, and yanked off the blankets. The dog immediately started snarling at us.

Now, it was time for part two of the plan.

We used a broom from William's backyard and the strong wire to keep the dog in place, as Scott attached a cord to the latch of the cage door. He routed it through some pulleys and eyelets, securing it to the wall as inconspicuously as possible. He tied the end of the cord to the inside handle of the front door. It was tricky with gloves on—we were all trying to keep the place clean of our prints, even wearing bags around our shoes.

Gary and I were still keeping the dog in place when Scott stuck his head around the corner. "We're gonna need to test it," he said with a grim expression.

"Opening the door?" I asked.

He nodded.

I looked down at the skin diver, which was struggling against the wire and the endless probing of the broom's handle. "Fuck… better give this our all," I said.

"I know." He looked at Gary. "You good?"

Gary nodded to confirm.

"Alright, here goes nothing," Scott barked, unlocking the cage. "Hold it tight." He walked back to the front door and pushed down the handle. The cord tugged, and the cage door flew open, hitting the ground with a clang.

"Shit," I muttered, keeping the skin diver in place with all my might. "He's gonna notice that."

Scott came back into the living room, quickly closing the cage door. "No doubt about it."

Gary and I sighed in relief and stretched our hands, which had been gripping the broom's handle like it was our lifeline. "He'll probably turn right back around," I continued. "He's too clever to just walk in after hearing a strange sound from inside."

Scott didn't respond but folded one of the blankets and placed it in front of the cage. "Let's give it another try."

Gary and I tensed up, poking the German Shepherd as hard as we could to keep it in the open cage. It growled and its body shook as it tried to break free from our grip.

This time, when the cage door opened, it barely made a sound. Scott checked it quickly. "Works like a charm," he grumbled. "Now, let's get the fuck outta here."

"Won't it open too easily?" I asked as we carried our stuff outside, closing the backdoor behind us. "What if it jumps at the cage door and it just opens, like that?"

"Well, at least it's inside his house," Scott grunted.

"Not for long," I shot back. "They jump through windows, remember?"

He kept silent as we huddled together behind some bushes.

It was nearly five o'clock, and William should be home within half an hour, assuming he still followed his usual routine. We waited in the blistering heat, sweating and puffing, and the minutes ticked by too damn slowly.

"What if he's still out on patrol?" I asked, growing agitated.

Scott didn't answer, his eyes fixed on the driveway and the kitchen window, just like last time.

"He'll be here," Gary said softly.

We exchanged a glance, and I knew I had to keep hoping. There's no point in asking questions you won't get an answer to until you do—you'll just waste time worrying about possibilities instead of focusing on the present.

And right then, as if my letting go triggered something, a car pulled into the driveway.

It was William's patrol car.

"Duck," Scott hissed, and we all ducked our heads to stay hidden behind the bushes. We heard the car door slam, soft footsteps, and then a key rattling in the front door. None of us could resist peeking over the bushes when we heard the door open.

Silence.

I held my breath, my heart pounding in my throat.

And then…

RAAAAAHHHH!

We had to move quickly. We slipped through the backdoor and ran straight into the living room. We needed to take the cage, and possibly the skin diver, with us, just like we had with the old lady—may she rest in peace.

I froze in my tracks, my eyes wide, staring at the body on the floor. The air left my lungs as if I'd been punched in the gut with a sledgehammer. Gary gasped, and Scott started cursing.

It wasn't William.

"No," I squealed, kneeling beside the body. "No…"

"Help me with this," Scott barked, pulling Gary toward the cage. They hovered the cage over the body.

"No!" I yelled.

"Kid…" Scott looked at me with intent.

I knew what had to be done, but it was tearing me apart. I watched in horror as they placed the cage to the back of the body, lying lifeless on the floor, waiting for the telltale shaking that would signal the skin diver was crawling out.

But nothing happened.

Tears streamed down my face as the minutes dragged on, and by then, my DNA was everywhere.

The skin diver still wouldn't come back out.

"No…" I sobbed.

"Shit," Scott muttered. He and Gary lifted the cage again. "We need to regroup… rethink… C'mon, kid. On your feet." He nudged me with his leg, then carried the empty cage out of William's house.

I slowly got to my feet, still crying, and followed them outside.

"That was him," Gary said.

"Mr. Tall with a square jaw, I take it," Scott replied.

Gary nodded.

Scott glanced at me, his face serious. "Get in."

"But… how?" I muttered, crawling into the car. "His car… His keys… Why?"

"They must've been workin' together," he replied. "He was the other guy that…" His voice trailed off. "He must've been the one who tipped me off about where to find you. It's a small comfort, but he might've saved your life."

I rested my head against the window, listening to the empty cage rattle in the back of the car as we drove to Scott's house.

The image of Riley's lifeless body was seared into my mind.

Chapter 19

We didn't go inside Scott's house, because it was too dangerous—
William might've set a trap or got eyes on the place. Instead, we went to
Betty's—our only ally in town.
She was upstairs, knitting, after making us a sandwich.
I was slumped on the couch with the sandwich and a shot of scotch in
front of me, both untouched.
"What about the skin diver?" Gary asked, pacing nervously around
Betty's living room.
"How the fuck should I know?" Scott grumbled from the armchair next
to me, meticulously cleaning his rifle. "Probably waited for us to leave,
then fucked off on its merry murdery way."
"It's going to kill so many people," Gary squealed, wringing his hands.
Nobody responded.
After all that planning and preparing… after everything we had to do…
we should've been celebrating our meager victory instead of pacing
around the room, mourning on the couch, or cleaning weapons like we
were ready for round two.
A body lay in William's house, and we were no closer to getting rid of
that fucking lunatic. Worse, we were deeper in shit than ever. William
would definitely connect the dots. He'd know we were back in town, and
none of us were safe.
I stared at the tiny glass of scotch. Part of me ached to drink it and keep
drinking until I drowned in the bottle. I wanted to numb my pain, silence
my mind the way I'd gotten used to. But a small part of me—one I
barely recognized—held me back. Maybe it was the need to stay sharp,
with William still out there. Or maybe it was self-punishment.
"We're not safe here," I finally said, breaking the silence.
Scott finished assembling his rifle. "Roger that."
"We need to get back to the cabin," I muttered.
He shot me a puzzled look. "What, now? Don't you wanna end this shit,
once and for all? We've got a shot to take that fucker down. Let's finish
it."

"How?" I demanded. "How the fuck are we going to kill him and get away with it?"

"Don't worry about that," he replied darkly. "We're not gettin' caught."

"Of course we'll get caught!" I snapped. "He's a fucking detective."

Scott's eyes narrowed as he leaned forward. "Kid… I said, don't worry about it—okay?"

We didn't hear the door open.

It wasn't until Scott jumped up beside me and aimed his rifle that I realized something was wrong. I looked up and there he was—William, standing in the doorway, his hands resting casually in his pockets.

He gave us a slow, deliberate smile. "Well, isn't this cozy?" His voice was low, almost amused. "You boys all settled in, playing house? I guess my house isn't the only place you broke into."

Scott's grip tightened on his rifle, but he didn't move.

My stomach twisted into knots as William's eyes flicked toward me.

He looked at Gary, who was huddled in the corner. "I see little Gary's still jumpy as ever," he continued, taking a step into the room like he owned the place. "I always knew you had a fragile heart, Gary. How's it holding up?"

Gary didn't respond, just stared at the floor, trembling. His nostrils flared as the faint Marlboro stench crept closer.

William smiled, cold and knowingly. "You know, I almost missed our little chats." His gaze shifted to Scott, then to me. "Almost."

"What the fuck do you want?" Scott growled, his voice tight with barely suppressed rage.

"Want?" William cocked his head, feigning confusion. "I thought I'd stop by. Just some old friends catching up, isn't it? No need for all the hostility."

Scott took a step forward, keeping his rifle aimed at William's chest. "You fuckin' tortured 'em for months. Think we're just gonna sit here and listen to your shit?"

"Torture?" William raised an eyebrow, clearly enjoying himself. "You make it sound so dramatic. I prefer to think of it as… sharing information." His eyes gleamed as he locked onto Gary, who visibly recoiled under his gaze. "Speaking of which… why don't we have a little chat, Gary? Just you and me. For old times' sake."

Gary's breath hitched, and he looked frantically at Scott and me.

"I promise I won't bite," William whispered mockingly as he grabbed Gary by the arm and yanked him upright. "I'll be gentle this time."

"Get your fuckin' paws off him!" Scott barked, cocking his gun and aiming it square at William's head.

William turned to him, flashing both a grin and his badge, which was clipped to his belt. "You really want to interfere with an official police investigation, Scott Aldridge?" he said, his tone dripping with mockery. "I could throw you in a cell for, let's say, a day or three. Although… I'd absolutely love that." He tightened his grip on Gary's arm. "You see, I'm just *dying* to have another chat with James. Somewhere quiet… peaceful."

My fingers trembled as I forced myself to meet his gaze. "Fuck you," I muttered, the words barely audible.

His grin widened. "You boys just sit tight. Do some yoga or whatever. I promise you'll get him back." His voice dropped an octave as he locked eyes with me. "Eventually," he added in a low whisper before dragging Gary toward the kitchen.

Scott and I exchanged a look, my heart hammering in my chest.

His grip tightened on the rifle. His jaw clenched so hard I could see the muscles straining beneath his skin. For a moment, I thought he might just pull the trigger, consequences be damned—nothing silent, nothing secret, just out in the open, for all eyes to see.

Then came a sound. A low, muffled groan from the kitchen.

Scott's eyes went wide. Without waiting for me to respond, he moved. Fast.

I followed, my body acting on instinct. We burst through the kitchen door just in time to see William slam Gary's head down on the countertop. Gary's eyes rolled back, his body going limp.

Scott pulled the trigger, and the shot rang out through the kitchen.

William dropped to the floor, next to Gary's body.

I froze, then looked at Scott. He'd shot William right in the face, point-blank.

We were fucked.

I reached for the rifle, but Scott swung it away from me. "Don't touch it, kid."

"But I…" My head spun. "I… I don't wanna…" I tried to get the words out, but the two bodies lying at my feet made me choke.

Scott grabbed my arm and pulled me into the living room. "Here's what you're gonna do. You're gonna leave through the back door, don't even look at 'em— Kid!" He yanked my arm, forcing me to meet his gaze. "Don't even look at 'em, just go out the back, and go home. Don't run, just walk like you're mindin' your own damn business. You got it?"

I stared in his fierce grey eyes, and shook my head. "No. I'm not leaving you."

His eyes softened for a moment. "You have to, kid," he said gently.

"But you're all… all I've got," I whimpered.

"It's for the best," he said and he let go of my arm. "It's gonna be alright, kid. You're young. You'll get over this." He gave me a quick, reassuring hug before pushing me toward the door. "Go. Now."

My body obeyed and, even though I really didn't want to, I turned around. I was ready to walk into the kitchen—avoiding the pool of blood, a mix of Gary's and William"s—but an arm stopped me.

"Where are you going, sugar?" Betty's voice rasped. She took in the scene in the kitchen for a moment.

"Betty…" Scott began, but she cut him off.

"I know," she replied curtly. "Sit down." She grabbed Scott's rifle from his hands and guided us onto the couch. We sat awkwardly side by side in front of a wall of cat paintings.

Her eyes were sharp as she glanced out the window. Sirens were blaring in the distance. "I've always like you, Scotty," she rasped, "but you're putting me in quite the pickle."

He looked up at her. "Please, Betty, just let James-"

"Here's what happened." She looked back at us, her face set with grim determination. "Gary was hiding out here, trying to avoid William. When William found him, he attacked. I had no choice but to shoot him to protect Gary and me… even though it was too late. That's what we're sticking to."

"But Be-" Scott started.

"Get out. Now," she said firmly, rushing us into the kitchen and out the
back door, still clutching Scott's rifle. As soon as we were outside, she
fired two more bullets into William's body.
I looked back in terror, then quickly followed Scott as the sirens grew
louder.
We left her backyard, slipped around the neighboring houses, and across
the street to his porch. He shoved me down into one of the chairs.
"Shouldn't we—?" I started.
He lit a cigarette, William's blood still glistening on his cheeks, and
nodded at the police cars, already zooming down the street. Their wails
echoed off the wall behind us.
My heart pounded as Scott and I exchanged a final, silent look.
We watched the cars pull up in front of Betty's house.
An officer banged on her door while several others took cover behind
their cars and moved around back. We watched her calmly open the
door, covered in blood, with the rifle still in her hands.
"What about the rifle?" I asked quietly.
"We'll think of something," Scott replied gruffly, the cigarette hanging
from his lips.

I lay awake that night, my mind racing with a million thoughts I couldn't
quite piece together. Every time I closed my eyes, I saw the scene replay:
Betty opening the door, the police storming in, and the bloodstains that
would never fully wash away.

The following days were a blur of legal jargon and somber meetings.
Betty had given her statement: Gary was hiding out, afraid for his life,
William had broken in and attacked, and she had shot him in self-
defense.
The rifle was a potential weak link. Scott had registered it many years
ago, and if the police dug too deep, it could blow everything wide open.
But Betty was sharp—she'd already come up with a story to cover it. She
told the police that Scott had lent her the rifle a few weeks earlier. She
said she hadn't felt safe and wanted something for home defense, even if
only temporary, as Gary took cover there.

254

It helped that Betty had never fired a gun before, which fit perfectly with her claim that she had to shoot in self-defense and wasn't comfortable with firearms. There were some questions about her shooting William three times, but she managed to persuade them with her frail old voice. "I had no idea how these things worked," she croaked during her confession. "All I knew was that I wanted to stay alive, for the few months I have left. My biggest qualm is not having been able to protect Gary. He was… like a son to me."

It was a tightrope walk, but with the evidence—and Betty's calm, if not convincing, demeanor—the story held. She must've been an actress at some point in her life because that performance deserved a fucking Emmy.

The police didn't dig too deep. Apparently, they had noticed William's increasingly erratic behavior in the office and out on the street.

All the while, I couldn't stop wondering about Riley's body, still lying lifelessly inside William's house. I waited for a report—the police searched his home after all—but not a single word was mentioned on the matter.

A few weeks later, I was biking through the city, having just begged Chris for my job back at Dover Wheels. He gave it to me, but not without a stern warning to never go MIA again. Crazy Eddie was more than happy to welcome me back.

City Hall came up beside me. I glanced at it.

There was a wedding, and a happy couple stood on the front steps. I stared at the bride and groom. The groom I didn't recognize, but the bride… it was Amy.

I felt a punch in my gut. Her eyes met mine for a moment, and I pedaled faster, disappearing around the corner. A few hundred meters further down the street, I came to a halt and breathed heavily. I placed a hand on my heart and groaned.

Part of me wanted to pack my shit and skip town, because the lingering memories were fucking painful.

Riley…

Kimberley and Thomas…

Amy…

But William was finally out of the picture, I'd just gotten my old job back, and most importantly: Scott lived here. At this very moment, he was at Ashley Linwood's house, probably shacking up.

I smiled faintly and looked up at the sky.

There was something about summers in Dover, I thought, making a pact with myself to earn enough cash to buy another cool car. Whether it was another Skyline or a 2010 Evo X.

With everything that had happened, I let myself forget about the skin divers. But only for a while. Because reality always has a way of catching up, and it came suddenly.

As I got back on my bike, I looked up in the direction I was heading. There he was, walking the streets like nothing had happened.

Riley.

I nearly got hit by a car as I swerved over to him, not thinking about anything else. "Riley!" I yelled, in complete disbelief.

He turned to me and smiled. "Sup, dude? Long time no see."

I looked him up and down. "H-how are you doing?" I asked.

"Alright, what about you?" he replied casually.

My gaze met his. Was he playing dumb, or…? "Fine," I said after a short pause. "Didn't something… happen?" I pressed.

"I don't remember," he answered. "All I know is that I woke up in the hospital. The doctors said I'd been in a coma."

"A coma?" I repeated, my mind shifting to Scott.

"Yeah, last thing I remember is," he paused, a puzzled look crossing his face, "…being on the beach with you and Thomas." He grinned. "And the women."

I looked him in the eyes for a long time, not knowing how to respond. Suddenly, he burst out laughing. "Nahh, I'm just yanking your chain, dude. Wouldn't that be too fucking convenient?"

The bike nearly slipped from my hands. "What do you mean?"

His grin widened. "We can stop playing pretend now, James."

My body froze. "I'm not following," I stammered.

"Look." He suddenly grabbed my face with both hands, holding it tightly.
"We both know what you're after. And I guess you did well, killing a
bunch of us. Hell, you even made us betray and kill each other."
I grabbed his hands, trying to pull free, but his grip was like iron. "Let
go, dude," I muttered.
He tightened his hold, bringing his face so close to mine that our noses
brushed. "We've got great plans for you, James. Just wait and see."
As he said those words, screams echoed in the distance.

www.ingramcontent.com/pod-product-compliance
Lightning Source LLC
Chambersburg PA
CBHW072213150726
48002CB00005B/1788